Misguided VOWS

USA TODAY BESTSELLING AUTHOR
T.L. SMITH
KIA CARRINGTON-RUSSELL

She told him it was just a book, but little did he know...
When she falls asleep, she dreams of me.
Sincerely, your book boyfriend...

the one she wishes she was fucking

COPYRIGHT @ T.L. SMITH & KIA CARRINGTON-RUSSELL 2024

All Rights Reserved

This book is a work of fiction. Any references to real events, real people, and real places are used fictitiously. Other names, characters, places, and incidents are products of the Author's imagination and any resemblance to persons, living or dead, actual events, organizations or places is entirely coincidental.

All rights are reserved. This book is intended for the purchaser of this book ONLY. No part of this book may be reproduced or transmitted in any form or by any means, graphic, electronic, or mechanical, including photocopying, recording, taping, or by any information storage retrieval system, without the express written permission of the Author. All songs, song titles and lyrics contained in this book are the property of the respective songwriters and copyright holders.

Warning

This book contains sexually explicit scenes and adult language and may be considered offensive to some readers. This book is intended for adults ONLY. Please store your books wisely, where they cannot be accessed by under-aged readers.

Blurb

We met because of a job.

We played because he made a bet.

We carried on because we couldn't stop.

Now we're in too deep, and the secrets of our pasts will catch up.

It's supposed to only be a fling, but it's started a fire.

One that we're both in denial about.

CHAPTER 1
Alina

"If you tell me one more time to move, *I* will move *you*." I point my finger in the man's face. Sure, he's a bouncer thrice my size and blocking me from getting into the club, and I may or may not have drunk too much, but that's precisely why I'm certain I can take him on.

But now I'm sobering up.

Because of this asshole.

"You go! Go and tell the owner who you're not letting in," I scream at him.

He crosses his arms over his puffed-out chest.

I want to kick him between the legs, hard.

But then the small voice of reason in the back of my mind reminds me that assaulting him might give me a night behind bars. I'm not really in agreement with that voice right now though.

But what else can I do? I stare at the badge clipped to his pants pocket that identifies him as security. It reads "Wilson."

More like "Asshole."

"Fucking hell," I mutter as I reach into my bag and begin pushing shit around to find the invite. I swear I threw it in here, though I may have thrown it away.

I've been in England for almost a year—beautiful London. And while I don't plan to stay permanently, I couldn't pass up the opportunities that came with moving here, and I've come to love living here—except for moments like this with assholes like Wilson.

I shoot him the evil eye as I messily search through my belongings.

I design layouts for clubs and make them... more unique, like the club that this asshole is currently barring me from. I'm the designer. And tonight is the opening night. I didn't plan to come, but the owner sent me an invite, and I had one too many glasses of wine after work and decided to actually show up. I tend to make it a thing to only visit the clubs I go to once or twice. I don't know why; I think maybe it helps keep my creative juices flowing to seamlessly move from one project straight to the next. I see something and think *I can make that better. What can I do differently here? How can I leave my mark?*

Next time, however, perhaps I should suggest to the owner to not hire such assholes as security.

I hiccup as I finally feel what I hope is the invitation. When I go to pull it out, someone bumps into me from behind and my phone falls from my other hand.

Is it fuck over Alina night or what?

When I look up, a man is standing casually with his hands in his pockets. The first thing I notice are the bluest eyes I have ever seen as he looks me over. He kicks up an arrogant smile, forming a single dimple, as I blatantly stare at him. And I remind myself that even when drunk it's not okay to so obviously drool over a man. They don't need those kinds of confidence boosters.

"Come in, sir," the bouncer welcomes him.

Are you fucking kidding me?

I see red. Mister blue eyes bends down, picks up my phone, and hands it to me while the arrogant smile never leaves his lips. I swipe it from him, seriously wanting to wipe that smug expression from his face.

"Most women would say thank you. But who am I to teach etiquette to a stranger?" he says with a thick British accent. My jaw drops and, for the first and probably only time in my life, I'm speechless. He casually shrugs as he goes to walk past the bouncer.

"You just let him in. What, does he, like, fuck the owner or something?" I'm fully aware I'm yelling now and everyone around us can hear me. But I'll be fucked if I'm just going to be pushed around like this.

Mr. Blue Eyes scrunches his nose, as if torn as to whether he should keep walking or not, but he stops long enough to shoot me a patronizing glare. No, it's not the stare that infuriates me, it's that fucking smile. "I'm no bouncer, but I imagine even if you did have an invitation, there's no way you're getting in. You're clearly intoxicated," he says in his thick accent.

"And you're clearly an asshole, but apparently they don't discriminate for that," I say as I flip him off.

It looks like he bites the inside of his cheek and steps out of the way as a woman comes through the front doors.

"Alina." Maria, the owner of the club bounces out, shocked, as she eyes the bouncer. Mr. Blue Eyes seems to have vanished into the club. "What are you doing out here?" she asks, and waves for me to come in. I point to her bouncer with a perfectly manicured nail and narrow my gaze.

"I've been telling this man I was invited, and he has persisted that I should remain outside and freeze."

"She's drunk," he accuses.

I roll my eyes, which makes Maria almost laugh. We started off working together but have become friends.

"She designed this place. Alina is always welcome." She offers her hand to me. I point my nose up in the air, suddenly feeling inches taller—and not just because of the heels—as I walk past him.

There, take that, asshole.

I notice the wallet sticking out of the back pocket of his pants before lifting my gaze back to Maria. I was going to fuck with this guy.

The moment I pass through the doors my mood shifts with the atmosphere. I'm so glad I wore a tight, black dress and left my auburn hair down in waves. I always pull it back when I'm working since it almost touches my lower back, but tonight, I wanted to feel the vibe of the club.

A smile touches my lips as I look around. Everyone is dancing, the music is loud, and the bar is full. Maria wanted to go with an old-school mafia vibe, so the space is dark with brown leather couches in the VIP areas. Greenery hangs from the ceiling, and paintings of old mobsters are hung on the exposed brick. Although not a smoker myself, I appreciate the cigar area with a separate whiskey bar.

All the couches are filled. It looks like a full house tonight.

When I see it all in action, I can't help but smile. It's one of my favorite designs so far.

"I love it," I confess. And no one is a harsher critic than myself, but considering money wasn't a barrier on this place, I could execute every intricate detail.

"Me too. You were worth every penny and more," she gushes as she grabs my arm and squeezes. I don't often become friends with my clients, but it was almost immediate with Maria, and right now, it feels like we just won big together.

Every time I finish a project, it reminds me of how I started, and I'm so glad I backed myself from the very start. I started out studying design but dropped out because, ironically, I couldn't afford the tuition at the time. I wanted to go back, but instead ended up kind of doing my own thing. I revamped my apartment back in Los Angeles, and my roommate at the time was posting updates on social media without me knowing. Thanks to her, it kind of blew up from there, and I progressively continued gaining wealthier clients and bigger contracts. I went from being a dropout to carrying around a designer purse and loving my life.

A photographer walks past us, and Maria bounces and pleads, "Come get a photo with me."

"You know I don't take photos, but smile, this is your moment," I encourage.

Although all of my projects and updates are on social media, I've never once showed my face. The work speaks for itself. At least that's what I tell clients but we all have our own demons to run away from. Mine might simply find me on social media––something I'd like to actively avoid.

She takes the photo, having no issue with being the center of attention. Once the photographer gives her the thumbs up, she grabs my wrist and basically begins dragging me again.

"Come on. Some of my family and friends are here, and I would love for you to meet them." She takes me back to the VIP area where three men and two women are casually sitting on the couch. Their conversation comes to a stop as we approach. It's dark so I follow Maria's gaze to the first person on the left.

"This is Alina Harper," Maria says excitedly.

"So you're the one we've heard all about," one of the women says with a smile.

I eye Maria, and she gushes. "What? You're a baddie and the mastermind behind all of this. It's fucking incredible!"

Heat scorches my cheeks, and I don't think it has

anything to do with the few drinks I had before coming here.

I've only been doing this for two years and it all still feels like a pinch-me moment.

"This is my best friend, Pocket." Maria waves to the little blonde woman who spoke before. She goes around the list of people, but I freeze when she points to Mr. Blue Eyes at the end. His blond hair is trimmed short, and he nods with a knowing smirk. With a drink in hand, he adjusts his suit jacket smugly. How had I not noticed him right away?

"Is your phone safe?" he asks, and I'm certain the asshole is mocking me. I clutch my phone tightly to my chest. *Fuck*. How embarrassing. He would've seen me screaming at the bouncer and everything. Please tell me he's just a douchebag boyfriend to one of these women, and no one important.

"You know Alina?" Maria asks, surprised.

"No, he just helped me when I dropped my phone outside," I'm quick to explain.

"I would call it saving the helpless, but okay," he retorts in his strong British accent.

"Will, play nice," Maria scolds before looking at me apologetically. "Sorry, Alina, our parents never could beat the smartass out of him," she jokes.

"He's your brother?" I ask and try not to die from embarrassment.

"Yes, he's actually how I afforded all of this... and you. Remember how I told you my brother gave me a loan to get started?" she says, smiling.

I swallow. Hard. I remember, I just didn't think her brother was around the same age as us and looked like he was built from God's divine hand and gifted with the personality of a mule.

"Do you want a drink?" Maria asks with a bright smile.

"I think she may already be drunk." There's that voice again.

Without thinking, I swing my head around to him and narrow my gaze.

"I am not. I was just mad," I say matter-of-factly.

He lifts his glass to me and nods his head. "If you say so, milady." I cringe at that word and then turn back to Maria.

"I'm going to go. I just wanted to stop in and see how everything was going." I turn around, giving her friends and family my back as I look out at the sea of patrons celebrating.

"Oh. Okay." Maria looks disappointed. "In that case, just wait here for a minute. I have something for you."

She's gone before I can say anything, so I watch the people on the dance floor instead, purposely ignoring the direction of her brother. There's a couple basically humping on the floor while two girls next to them are throwing their hands up in the air and dancing.

"So, you're clever as well as pretty," someone says from beside me.

"I'm not sleeping with you," I reply, knowing without looking that it's him. And to be honest, I don't want to look his way for the sole fact I'm afraid those eyes will hypnotize me. Because maybe, just maybe, a small part of me is still a little tipsy.

"Damn, milady, that was an arrow straight to my bloody heart." I roll my eyes. "At least show us your tits." This gets my attention, and I face him. "There she is. I didn't actually mean for you to show me, but if the offer is there." His gaze falls to my cleavage before rising to my face again.

"I should slap you right now."

"It might turn me on." He winks as his tongue darts out and he licks his top teeth. How can someone so pretty, who looks like they just strutted off a runaway, entice my wildest fantasies yet also make me want to commit murder?

"Alina." Maria walks back over and holds out a

present. She eyes her brother first before looking at me. "Please excuse my brother; he has no filter. I swear they forgot it when he was born. I apologize for whatever he may have said when I wasn't here."

I smile and take the present.

"You didn't have to get me anything," I tell her, trying my best to ignore said brother. "You did pay me."

"You should up your prices. Some people pay triple for the magic you performed and don't even put in the same amount of work you do."

"Thank you." I look around the club one last time, satisfied. "I have to go, but I'll open this and text you when I'm home. I'm so happy you love it." I lean in and kiss her cheek. Looking to her brother, I'm as polite as possible, giving him a sharp smile and nod before walking off. Some might call me petty, but I consider myself more or less a calculated woman.

As I step out into the fresh air, the bouncer eyes me, I twist my lips into a smile and flash him his name badge I'd unclipped from his pocket earlier and hid in my bag.

I throw it on the ground beside him. "You dropped something, asshole," I say, feeling rather smug as he accidently steps on it, looking confused as to how it got on the ground in the first place.

It puts a pep in my step as I leave. When I'm out of his sight line, I pull out the wallet I'd stolen from his pocket on the way in. He'd been so distracted by Maria that he hadn't even noticed.

I flick through it, amused by the two hundred pounds in it. I don't need the money, but it serves the asshole right.

Where some might have a moral compass, I don't —at least when it comes to revenge. If you want to get in my way, I'll make you regret it.

I round the corner, where a homeless woman is sitting with a cute puppy. I throw the bundled cash into her beanie, and her eyes grow wide.

I continue walking and toss the wallet into a trash can before waving down a cab.

Tonight was a good night indeed.

CHAPTER 2
Will

"You scared her off," Maria scolds, hitting my shoulder. I watch Alina as she walks out, not even a stumble indicating how drunk she is. And I know she was at least tipsy because I could smell the alcohol on her, but it was mixed with an underlying vanilla scent.

"I did no such thing," I reply.

She was... interesting. Pretty. Calculating. Very drunk.

"Stop watching her." My sister throws her arms in the air and storms off. I stare until the designer makes it all the way out the front door, her ass swaying in that tight dress, which is punishable in its own right.

When my sister told me she was hiring a professional to design the bar's interior, I didn't think much of it. But the money was well spent. Alina did a fantastic job, and she's easy on the eyes.

Alina is clearly not from around here; her accent is very American. And while I just left the US after completing a job, I didn't think the next woman I would be eyeing would be from there.

Had she not so obviously despised me, I might've even tried to fuck her tonight. I hide the smirk on my face, so very tempted to seek out the designer and do so. But I follow my sister to the bar instead. The bartender is already serving her, and I tap the top of my glass to indicate the same for myself.

"So, how close are you two?"

Maria rolls her eyes. "Will, you are not fucking another one of my friends."

"You two are friends?" My eyebrows perk.

"I'm not telling you anymore about her," she says adamantly, and I smirk.

"Maria, you know I can find out anything I want about her with my own resources. I just want to make sure my baby sister isn't hanging out with anyone shady." I nudge her shoulder, and she rolls her eyes.

She might tell people that our parents never beat the smartass from me, but they'd never smacked the sass out of her either.

"The only shady person here is you," she deadpans.

"Touché."

Although my sister suspects I might be involved in some not-so-above-board business arrangements, she never pushes me about it. As far as the family is concerned, I'm a businessman. Granted, I might be one of the best trackers in the world and get my hands dirty from time to time, but they don't need the small details of such affairs.

The bartender slides over both of our drinks, and Maria and I admire the crowd together. "Did I tell you how proud of you I am?" I ask, saluting her with my glass. She smiles appreciatively, looking around, and clinks her glass against mine.

"Thank you for believing in me," she says.

Maria was too scared to ask our parents for a loan, and, apparently, I was the easier option or biggest sucker. I don't mind which one it was. I support my sister by spoiling her to make up for my not being here in London often enough.

"How long will you be in town for?" she asks.

I think on it a moment. I returned to London for a job, and it usually doesn't take me too long to find my target. In the meantime, I can have some fun.

"I'm not sure yet. Maybe a few weeks. What about your friend, is she living here?"

Maria rolls her eyes and steps away from the bar.

"Come on, help your big brother out," I call out after her, but she just flips me the bird.

Damn, it's good to be home.

CHAPTER 3
Alina

It's been over a month since I've seen Maria. After the grand opening of her club, I moved on to a new project for a café in Manchester. I've been back in London for two days now and spoiled myself with some well-deserved retail therapy after doing two big back-to-back projects.

Maria's been busy with the club, but we've prioritized meeting up for dinner tonight before I fly out to New York early tomorrow to consult with a new client. When she warned me that her brother would be joining us, I reconsidered our dinner plans until she reluctantly admitted it was because of her brother's connections that I got my next consultation in New York.

A lingerie company was after a new show floor

design, and apparently, her asshole of a brother knows people and suggested my services with raving reviews after I helped his baby sister. As ecstatic as I am by the opportunity to possibly have this contract, it's also difficult for me to swallow my pride and thank him directly.

I hold a bottle of whiskey in my hand as I walk into the restaurant, reminding myself to play nice. It's been a month since I met him; perhaps it was a one-off bad impression?

I can see them sitting at a table near the back. The hostess takes me to them, and when they notice me, Will stands to pull out my chair. I offer a tight smile and hand him the bottle, which he seems confused by.

"Whatever is this for, milady?" he asks. And when his striking blue eyes meet mine, I'm already annoyed. No man can be that good looking, have mischief dance in their eyes like stars, and also use a nickname on me that seriously pisses me the fuck off. It's a turbulent set of feelings he stirs within me that I'd rather not experience.

I push the bottle into his hands, my smile growing wider as I try to force it. "Maria told me you got me the opportunity in New York."

He takes it, smirking. "Yes. Yes, I did."

Why do I so badly want to punch his face?

William Walker inexcusably has an air of assholery around him.

"Thank you, I appreciate it." I'm still smiling, and I'm certain he can read between the lines of what I'm actually thinking because his own smile grows wider.

"It's no problem at all. You may suck when it comes to etiquette, but you do excel in your work at the very least," he says, purposefully provoking me. I can feel my temple pulse as I don't so much as bat an eye at his insult, and instead turn to his sister.

Maria pulls me in for a hug. "I'm sorry about him. This is why he will forever be a fuck boy," she says, locking eyes with her brother.

"I'm surprised people have sex with you," I can't help but tack on.

"You'd be surprised by how many women find me quite charming," he replies.

"Loneliness plays terrible tricks on peoples' minds. Sometimes an actual personality isn't required."

"Is that what bothers you about me, darling, my personality? Or are you certain it's not other things that rile you?"

"What the fuck is happening right now?" Maria interjects.

Heat scorches my cheeks. I've been so entranced in bantering with Will that I completely forgot where I am. Will smirks as I look away from him, trying to rein in my temper.

"Sorry. Let's sit and eat," I suggest, internally reprimanding myself. I'd told myself to show gratitude, and within the first two minutes of being in the same room as this insufferable asshole, we're verbally stripping one another.

"Behave yourself," Maria chastises her brother as they both sit.

Will is still smug as he places the bottle of whiskey on the table and grabs the bottle of wine already there to pour me a glass. I make no move to touch it. Last thing I want is to be hungover on my flight, even if they are flying me business class. That, and I definitely don't trust myself around this man after a single drop of liquor hits my lips.

"Anyway, I hope you don't mind, but I already ordered for us. I come here all the time, and the chef knows me," Maria gushes as Will rolls his eyes at her.

With the affectionate way she sounds when mentioning the chef, it's obvious she likes him, and so I can't help but whisper across the table. "Did you two…" Maybe I missed out on something while I was gone in Manchester.

"No!" Maria snaps.

At the same time, Will says, "Yes." He swishes the wine in his glass, unimpressed.

Red spreads across Maria's face. "We're not having this conversation while you're here," she says pointedly to Will, and he looks away as if bored.

I bite the inside of my cheek, trying not to laugh at the two. I've never seen Maria like this. She's so bubbly and outspoken that it's fascinating to see her get embarrassed. I also envied those who had siblings. As an only child, I always wished I had one myself.

Two waitresses bring out an array of pastas and pizzas. I almost drool at how good it smells. *Yes, please* to cheese all day, every day.

"Leon." Maria perks up as the chef walks out behind the waiters. I try not to smile as he shyly offers the table an awkward introduction.

"I thought I'd come and greet everyone. You must be Alina. Maria's told me great things about you. And you must be the brother, Will?" he says, extending out his hand.

"Nah, I'm the new guy, and this makes for an awkward date," Will says, making no move to shake his hand.

"Eww, never say that again." Maria goes red. "He's joking. I'm sorry about my brother. How has your night been?" She's quick to block her brother's view of Leon.

Leon gives a halfhearted laugh as he retracts his outstretched hand and begins speaking now only to Maria.

Well, this is starting off to be a weird-ass night. I pick up a glass of water and go to take a sip. Before I do, I notice Will staring at me. His hand is lazily hooked around the arm of the chair as he watches me like a predator.

I take a sniff of the water. "Did you do something to my water?" I ask him.

He arches an eyebrow. "Did you want me to do something to it?"

"Depends how much longer I have to sit at the same table as you," I'm quick to reply.

"How quickly can you eat, then?"

Without even looking at the formidable amount of food, I say deadpan, "Impressively so." I then take a sip of my water.

"I'd rather see that skillset on my cock."

I choke on the water and splutter it back into the glass. Tears leak down my cheeks as Leon's and Maria's attention snap my way.

"Oh my gosh, are you okay?" Maria asks, offering me a napkin, but I wave her away.

The asshole sitting across from me is chuckling, and I can't even get the words out to bite back at him. "I'm okay," I gasp out. "Just went down the wrong hole."

"That's what she said," Will says quietly under his breath.

"Will!" Maria snaps.

I'm baffled by Will. For a successful man in what I'm assuming to be his thirties, it catches me off guard. And I don't think it's because he's immature, although that's what he's showcasing. He has an aura around him that dictates he's all sophistication and calculation but it's as if he purposefully doesn't want to be taken seriously. Or he's just really good at pissing everyone around him off. I'm leaning especially toward the later.

"Well, I hope you all enjoy your night. I have to head back to the kitchen," Leon says amid the awkward tension, excusing himself, then adds for Maria, "I'll send you a text later, okay?"

"I don't like him," Will's quick to announce before Leon's even left the table. And I wonder if he purposefully put this crude display on to... deter the man from his sister?

I have my hand over my chest as my breathing settles and Maria's attention snaps to him. "Can you please just start eating and stay quiet? You agreed you'd be on your best behavior tonight."

"I'm not hungry. I just came for the show," he says with a slow smile as he brings the wine to his lips, still looking at me.

This motherfucker is winding me up on purpose. Here I thought it was a personal thing. Turns out he's just an asshole to everyone. Maria looks furious, and so I begin to scoop pasta onto my plate.

"Well, I, for one, am starving," I defiantly say, then make a point to ignore Will. Surprisingly, he remains quiet from then on and simply watches us. It's unnerving, but I remind myself how "grateful" I should be since he got me my next gig.

Lucky for me, I'll never have to see this asshole again after tonight.

CHAPTER 4
Alina

I try not to make it obvious that it's my first time flying in business class, but I'm certain if I have even one piece of hair out place, people will know I'm a fraud. When I first flew to London from Los Angeles I flew economy, and to be honest, I always thought I would. But here I am, with a ticket to New York—business class both ways. And I must confess, I like what I see so far.

Okay, so I may not have been subtle about my excitement since I boarded. Of course, I wanted to experience everything, so the minute they said to board, I was one of the first in line.

"Champagne?" the flight attendant offers me after I've gotten settled in my seat.

"No, thank you, water will do." She hands me a

glass before she walks off, and I sit back and watch as others board. I see men in suits, several women with designer bags, and even some kids, take seats in the rows in front of me. Wow. I feel like if I experienced this as a kid, I would never be able to fly economy again.

Someone in a sharp blue suit blocks my view. At first, I'm annoyed, then my gaze drops to his ass. Shit, he has a nice ass. I can definitely get used to business class.

I'm sinking deeper into my seat and looking over the rim of my glass, trying to be subtle, as I scan farther up the man's body, when he removes his jacket and hands it to the flight attendant. She takes it with a smile, obviously admiring the view from the front, and now I'm curious about that angle too. He has a well-defined back, and even in that blue button-up I can tell he has muscles. *Is it me or is it hot in here?* Fuck, it's really been too long since I've been with a man if I'm drooling like this. I take a sip of water. When the flight attendant walks away, I'm startled as he speaks.

"Do you stare at all passengers with those fuck-me eyes, milady?" he says and turns to face me.

Water involuntarily sprays out of my mouth and all over him. His blue shirt, which I was just admiring, is now slightly see-through. His blue eyes narrow on me, and as he looks down at his shirt, his gaze twinkles with mischief again.

You've got to be fucking kidding me.
This man is bad news.

"If I wanted to get wet, I'm sure I could think of other ways to do it," he says, and looks me over with a smirk. Heat scorches my cheeks, and I convince myself it's from the humiliation as the woman across from me stares in horror. He blocks her from my view so I'm only focusing on him.

"I'm pretty sure stalking is poor etiquette," I whisper shout.

His eyebrows raise and he looks down at his shirt pointedly. "Do you really want to discuss lessons on etiquette right now?"

I cross my arms over my chest. What did I do in a past life to deserve this torture?

"It's time to take your seat, sir." The flight attendant taps Will on the shoulder. I roll my eyes, pissed to realize I'm stuck with this asshole sitting in front of me for the entire flight. He cocks a boyish grin at me before taking his seat.

As the flight attendant walks by again with the tray of drinks, I stop her.

"I'll take the champagne now."

She smiles and hands me a glass. I gulp it down as we prepare for take-off.

This will be fine. At least, that's what I keep telling myself.

We're served a meal, and I don't see him. He doesn't get up. He doesn't even turn around.

I put on a movie and take another glass of champagne, and that's when he decides to stand up. He opens the overhead compartment, and I watch him over my glass as his shirt rides up slightly.

He's such an ass, but damn, there's no denying the Gods were generous when they sculpted him. He looks good. Fucking smells good too.

I press the call button to order another glass of champagne. Once I finish ordering, he looks down at me and then proceeds to lean over and invade my space. *What cheek he has!* I'm trying my hardest to focus on my tablet, looking at new designs and materials I've been curious to use.

He doesn't speak, just takes me in with those blue eyes, and it makes me squirm in my seat. I can't fucking concentrate.

"Can I help you?" I growl at him.

He quirks a cocky smile and innocently says, "No, I was just stretching," before stepping back and sitting down.

Gah. This asshole knows how to get under my skin.

I drink another glass of bubbly to try to ease my frustration.

Now, I need to go to the toilet, and I can feel the alcohol kicking in. I didn't plan to drink alcohol during the flight, but his presence required it. It's a miracle I didn't drink myself into oblivion last night at dinner. But asking me to have the amount of strength to tolerate him two days in a row is a no-go. As I stand, so does he, and we come face-to-face. He may be taller than me, but I stare down my nose at him.

"Fancy seeing you here—" I lift my finger to his lips to shut him up.

"Do not call me milady again. Do I look old to you?" His lips curve under my finger into a slow and steady smirk. He opens his mouth to speak, but my finger is still there. *What am I doing?* I quickly pull it away, embarrassed, and turn away to move through the lightly dimmed cabin as I make my way to the bathroom.

Just as I reach the bathroom door, a hand grabs me and pushes me inside. I'm startled but know it's him even before I turn and my head slams into his chest. I gape in shocked horror as he shuts the door behind us, locking us in. The bathroom is bigger than the ones in economy, but it's still close quarters.

"Alina," he says, and I stare at his lips as my name leaves his mouth. They're audaciously pink, and I know how soft they feel because I was touching them only moments before. "You prefer me to call you that?" My gaze is still pinned to his mouth. His hand lifts and his thumb touches my bottom lip. I take in a sharp breath, knowing I should pull out of his reach.

I don't like this man.

I don't know this man.

But I like his touch, even if the man is an ass.

"You should answer me; we don't have long." He glances at his expensive wristwatch. "I wonder if you can come on my fingers within two minutes," he purrs, and my breath rattles as I'm sucked out of my thoughts. When he removes his thumb from my bottom lip, I stifle a small moan. His smirk grows and he pushes up against me.

My heart hammers in my chest when his body presses against mine, my face nestled in his neck, and I can *feel* him.

"Do you want me to slide my hand up your skirt right now, Alina?" he whispers in my ear, and my heart is fucking pounding like a treacherous bitch. And then a low ache begins between my legs at the insinuation.

No.

No.

No.

The pulsing between my thighs intensifies as his feather-light touch glides along my elbow.

Yes.

No.

Maybe?

Fuck it.

My head nods of its own accord.

"Oh, what a good girl you are," he croons, sliding his hand from my elbow, until it's between us. He reaches down and lifts my skirt, his cock still firmly pushing against my leg through his pants.

My hips move back just a little to give him more access as he slides his hand up, and I am so thankful right now that I have on a skirt. My hands stay at my sides, unsure if I should touch him.

Should I?

Probably not.

Am I out of my fucking mind doing this?

Yes.

Am I elated about it? Also fucking yes.

He moves my panties to the side, and as his fingers slide between my folds, he presses on my clit, then moves his finger again, dancing down to where I'm throbbing.

I suck in a breath as I stare into his blue eyes that seem to be attuned to my every twist in expression.

The energy around us is charged.

He's intense.

I blame the alcohol. Or maybe the lack of having sex with someone for so many months.

I want him to touch me all over and to absolutely ravish me.

I inevitably fall forward, my face pressing against his blue button-up shirt, as he slides the first finger in. I grab his other wrist, my hand clenching around his watch, to center myself. A small moan escapes me, a mixture of relief and demand for more. Especially when I can feel his very hard cock between us. I'm so hyper-focused on what he's doing, that I can't think straight.

What is even happening?

I hate this man, don't I?

He slides in and out with a perfect rhythm. His thumb circles my clit, applying just the right amount of pressure, but I feel greedy for more as I rub against him. I can't help myself. The champagne has gone straight to my head, but fuck, this feels so good.

My head lolls back as he inserts a second finger,

and now I'm shamelessly riding his hand. Fuck, I hate this man so much. But the way he makes me feel...

"I've never seen you so quiet," he says smugly.

My eyes burst open at his comment, but neither of us change the rhythm.

"Shut up. Your personality is still off-putting," I whisper shout as I ride his hand to oblivion.

He chuckles, and it does something to me. It's like it runs down my spine and almost snaps me in two as he says, "But you like my fingers?"

"Very much," I breathlessly admit as he picks up the pace, as if rewarding me for telling the truth.

Oh fuck.

His lips brush against my neck, and I lean back, basking in the bliss as he kisses down my throat. I feel the pressure of his lips on my skin as he continues finger fucking me. One of my hands snakes into his hair, drawing him closer to me. Wanting his lips and body firmly pressed against me.

Fuck, I'm so close.

I place my other hand against the basin behind my back to support me.

I'm so close.

A moan slips free as I come undone on his fingers. My grip tightens in his hair as I hold him in place, riding the wave of pure bliss. My entire body convulses, and I sigh with relief.

The minute I do, he pulls back, and I realize my mistake. He's smirking, those crystal blue eyes shining with mischief. Victory. He'd got what he wanted, but I supposed, in a way, so had I. I can't stand this man, but my body was an obvious beacon of sexual frustration and attraction toward him. I'd be far too stubborn to initiate anything with this man. It's as if he knows this as he smugly smiles, turns, opens the door, and closes it behind him without so much as saying another word. I lick my lips and take a deep breath, recapping what the fuck just happened.

I run my hands through my hair and look at myself in the mirror, shocked.

Did I just get fingered on the plane?

Am I part of the mile high club now?

Okay, maybe I'm part of the slutty club, because damn, that was hot.

That's when my gaze lands on the not-so-subtle red mark branded on my neck. My jaw unhinges. *Did that little fuck just give me a hickey?*

CHAPTER 5
Will

Sometimes you just can't help yourself. That was me a few moments ago in the bathroom, with a certain pretty little brunette who has the most gorgeous fuck-me eyes I've ever seen. That and her scathing tongue just gets me excited for all different types of reasons.

Did I plan to go in there to finger fuck her? Probably, yes. Hell, I'll fuck her in our seats if she'll let me, airline be damned. Watching her break apart into a million pieces all over my hand was more rewarding than I thought it would be. I just wanted to one-up her, maybe fluster her a little. But this... this is so much more rewarding, and only scratched the surface of my curiosity more, which is exactly why I walked straight back out.

That, and I'm certain she's about to give me an earful considering I branded her so perfectly. I wonder how loud she might yell and how many people she'll wake when she loses her shit at me. I can't help the shit-eating grin as I notice her walking back to her seat.

She ruffles the curtains behind her, and when I turn to face her, she pins me with a glare. Her hair, which was up in a ponytail before, now covers her shoulders, and most likely purposefully, her neck.

Her stare has a lethal edge to it as she takes her seat. She hasn't said anything, and I'm certain that's her way of punishing me. She picks up her tablet and tries to ignore me, but when she glances back up, I just can't help myself. I know I do it to stir her up. I lift my fingers that were inside of her and put them in my mouth.

Her eyes go wide and her cheeks flush pink. I pull my fingers out and lean toward her. "I wonder how pink I can make your other cheeks," I say quietly, and I'm sure she's about to snap the tablet she's holding in half.

"You left a fucking hickey on my neck," she seethes, and looks around when she realizes her whisper wasn't so quiet.

I place a hand over my heart. "I also made you

come all over my hand. I thought it was a descent trade."

I see the pulse in her temple throb and try not to laugh.

"You can stop staring now," she says, pretending to be busy with her tablet.

"So, should we get a hotel when we land?" I waggle my brows at her, then check my wristwatch until I realize it's not there.

"No fucking way." She scoffs. "I had a moment of misguided judgment. It won't happen again." With smug calmness, she opens her palm, and my wristwatch dangles from her fingers. She offers a tight smile. "Don't ever tell a woman how long she has to come. It lacks in class."

I roll my tongue in my cheek as she hands the watch over. *Very interesting.* I hadn't even noticed her remove it, but then I think about the moment she pressed against my chest and held on to my wrist. *Ah. Clever.*

She doesn't seem overly pleased with me as I readjust my watch.

"Who are you? Why are you on the same flight as me? What do you even do for work? Or are you some rich, pompous asshole? I don't know how you could even be related to Maria. She's so nice, and you're so…"

"Striking?"

"Irritating is a better word."

"Provoking?" I try again.

"Thinks highly of himself."

"That's more than one word, milady. Perhaps the word you're trying to find is self-important. I've heard that one as well."

She exhales a sigh and tries to focus on her tablet again.

I can't help but piss her off. Don't get me wrong, I enjoy pissing a lot of people off, but doing it to her in particular is entertaining and... something else.

I adjust slightly in my seat so I can twist around and stare at her. "You can say it." I wink at her. "I have amazing fingers." I pucker my lips at her. "But my mouth? Oh man, he likes to taste, lingering on the tip of his tongue as he..." I glance pointedly at her skirt, and her legs snap shut.

"You need to stop," she says in a hushed tone. I shrug and answer her question about my job. It's not public knowledge what I do for a living, but, for some reason, I have the urge to tell her.

"Hmmm, you can say that my job is to locate people."

"What, like a bounty hunter?" she asks.

My expression twists. "No, that has no class.

Simply stated, I can find anyone when paid the right amount of money. It's my specialty. You have someone who wants to hide; I will find them," I tell her. "And I get paid very handsomely to do so."

"Are you taking the piss? It's safe to confess that you still play Xbox in your parents' basement, okay?"

"Taking the piss?" He seems amused by the adopted language I'd picked up in London. "You think my fingers were that good at gameplay?" I ask seriously.

"Oh my gosh, you're so obnoxious," she spits.

A smile splits my face. "You can believe whatever you like about my work. But there's only one way to describe this friction between us."

"There is no us!" she's quick to snap, and the woman next to her shushes her. Red streaks her cheeks.

I shake my head at her disapprovingly, trying not to laugh. It only infuriates her further. "Okay, then it's my hand and your sweet little pussy. That's all there is to tell." I lift my hands defensively.

She places the tablet down. "There's nothing to tell. I'm serious, don't you dare tell a soul."

I arrogantly shrug. "Who would listen to me anyway? I'm... irritating and exhausting, wasn't it?"

"And self-important," she adds.

"And good with my fingers," I remind her as I

blow her a kiss and then face forward in my seat again. I can feel the heat of her anger radiating behind me as I curve a smile and kick back, feeling much more refreshed.

Pissing people off is my specialty but I very much feel like I've found a new toy to torment.

CHAPTER 6
Alina

I try my damn hardest to not look back over my shoulder at him even though I know he's walking behind me and I can feel his gaze on my ass. I bet my next hundred dollars that he's smirking.

Unable to help myself, I take a deep breath and glance back to find exactly what I thought I would: him staring at my ass, smirking. He doesn't catch me looking, so I quickly turn away. I want to wipe away my own smile. Yes, he's attractive and it's flattering having someone that hot appreciate my ass. It's a confidence boost, but it's just a shame that the guy's a complete asshole.

I feel revitalized when the breeze hits my face as we step out of the airport. It's been over a year since I last visited home soil, and, to be honest, I didn't think I'd come back this soon, but the opportunity was too good to pass up.

Mr. Blue Eyes comes to a stop beside me. I try to take another calming breath as he checks his wristwatch.

"Lift?" he asks as a black car pulls up to the curb. The driver steps out and greets him, and begins grabbing his bags.

"No, thank you." I pull out my phone to order an Uber. "Even if it was the last cab available, I'd rather walk."

"Come on, milady, I don't bite—that hard." He winks, and I immediately point to the hickey that says otherwise. He chuckles as he encroaches on my space. I freeze as he lifts a piece of my hair, and heat flushes over the spot where he branded me. "We could play again."

I place my hand on his chest and smile as I push him away. "Play with yourself. Remember how magical your fingers are?" I say, stepping back and waving with all five fingers before turning and flicking him the bird.

I don't look back, because if I did, he'd notice me smiling. And he can't know that anything he says or does makes me smile.

I'm afraid it would just encourage his bad behavior.

I'm biting my bottom lip as I think about what we got up to in the bathroom. Though it was rather thrilling, it can't happen again. And it won't because, luckily for me, I won't ever see this fucker again.

As soon as I'm in the back of my Uber, I call my mother to let her know I've landed. My mother raised me as a single parent, and she has supported everything I do, so I try to call her every day. She asks me if I plan to visit her while I'm back in the States, but I'm not sure what my schedule will be like yet, so I don't make any promises. I won't know unless I definitely get this contract, but I'm hopeful that if they are willing to buy me business-class flights, that they can put their money where their mouth is. I mean, surely, they wouldn't spend that type of money just to turn me down, right?

My mother also isn't the biggest fan of flying, and I haven't been able to afford to fly her business class. I feel that's the only way I'm going to get her on the plane, not because she's fancy, just for the sole fact that she can freak out in her own cubicle.

"So, have you met any men yet? You can't stay single forever, Alina," she says. She's always telling me I shouldn't be single now that I'm at a different stage in my life. She thinks I should be considering marriage and children more seriously. Though I'm not sure if that's entirely something I want anymore. Years ago, I thought I found the love of my life, but it got messy to say the least. Since then, I've discovered how much I enjoy my own company. And besides having a few flings to meet my needs, I don't know if I want anything past that.

Why opt for a relationship when it offers no amount of security, whereas my toys can always meet my needs like most men can't? It just makes sense to me.

"No, and you know I'm not looking," I remind her.

"You're pushing thirty, Alina. I want grandkids." She huffs. I roll my eyes, grateful she can't see it.

I've told her I don't know if I even want children. I saw how tough it was for her to raise me on a single income. And while, yes, I make good money now, that could change if I'm unavailable to work due to pregnancy or a newborn.

It's so easy for men to just up and leave. It was different for my mom and me since my father didn't leave us willingly, he passed away, but it didn't take away from the noticeable absence of his presence.

She goes on to tell me about work at the same job

she's had, and loved, since I was a child, and the new neighbors who just moved in. It's nice to check up on her and know that she's doing well.

The Uber driver stops in front of a blacked-out storefront, and I realize we've arrived at the destination. "Hey, Mom, I've just arrived to meet the potential clients. I'll call you back tonight, okay?"

"Of course. Tell me all about the space. Sounds a little bit raunchy doing a lingerie store."

I laugh. "Calm down. We don't know if I've got the contract yet."

She scoffs. "As if they flew you all this way not to hire you. You're the best of the best."

I'm stepping out of the Uber with my carry-on suitcase as I say, "Thanks, Mom. Love you."

I hang up and admire the building. It's a bigger space than I expected, especially for a lingerie store. A tingle of excitement begins in my stomach.

I thought I'd stop by before going to the hotel because I'm just too excited to see the space that I'll potentially be working with. If they don't choose me, then at least I get to return to New York for a week, I suppose.

I push that type of negativity away. I know what I'm capable of, and a smile touches my lips at my mother's words. *You're the best of the best.*

The smile doesn't last long when my Uber driver leaves, and I realize the black car parked in front of it eerily looks like the same one Will got into. *Surely, it's not.*

I swallow hard as I walk to the front door that's been left open. When I step inside, the first thing I see is a shirtless Will, standing next to the front counter and doing up his belt. My gaze inevitably roams down the front of his body, scanning over every ridge and dip. *Fuck me.*

Another man holds out a shirt for him. When Will looks up to take the shirt, he notices me, and a devilish smile appears on his lips, that singular dimple forming.

"Milady, you made it." I cringe at the word, and at this point I know he uses it just to piss me off. But I don't let it show as I lock eyes with the second man. He offers a brilliant, charismatic smile but briefly glances between Will and me before approaching. He's well dressed in a very expensive white suit. And dare I say he's prettier than Will?

Will is definitely attractive. He's just a different type of attractive, a little rougher around the edges, whereas this man standing in front of me is very cleancut and oozes power and money.

"I'm Dawson Taylor. Will has told me all about your work. And I'm looking forward to working with you." He offers me his hand and I shake it, purposefully ignoring Will, who is moving to join us.

Why the fuck is he actually here?

"It's lovely to finally meet you, and I'm excited to see what potential this baby has," I say, looking around the shop. That's when Will steps into my space, because Lord forbid this fucker is ever ignored.

"You're not going to ask why I was half naked when you walked in?" he asks.

My gaze flicks to Dawson, who watches us as if it's the most casual exchange transpiring in front of him. If he's acquainted with Will he's probably already acquainted with his less then desirable shit stirring personality.

I smooth a hand over my hair and make sure my long locks are covering the big fucking hickey on my neck from a certain asshole.

"Not particularly. I'm here for work. And why are you here?" I ask, trying my best to remain professional.

"You seemed interested when you were staring for so long," he says with an arrogant smile, and I pin him with a lethal stare. "Haven't seen a man without his shirt on in a long time, milady?" His top four buttons are still casually undone, revealing the tight muscles beneath, and I notice a scar on his shoulder.

I grind my teeth with a tight smile as I turn back to

Dawson, ignoring Will. I don't know what the relationship is between these two. At best, I hope they're friends because this is the most awkward consultation I've done. Especially considering all I want to do is fucking strangle Will.

"So this is the space we're working with?" I ask Dawson, purposefully stepping away from Will, who seems to enjoy invading my personal space. I can hear him chuckling behind me.

"Yes, this is the one." Dawson ignores Will in the same fashion.

I'm looking at the space, but I'm also distracted by my mind rattling as to why the fuck Will is here. Is it because he got me a foot in the door? There's no need for him to be here, though. I thought I'd never have to see this guy again, so why am I still having to deal with him? I try to push down the warmth flooding my core as I think back on our encounter on the plane.

The back door opens, and a petite woman with long, honey-colored hair walks in. "I'm sorry I'm late. A few customers lingered at the café." When she notices me, she smiles, and I'm dazzled by her beauty. Did I just step into runway model Grand Central Station or something?

Dawson and the woman move toward one another —gravitate is probably a better word—and he leans down and kisses her passionately. I look away, realizing I'm watching something I shouldn't be.

"It's like that every time," Will says over my shoulder.

"I didn't ask you," I whisper shout back. "And why are you even here?"

"This is my wife, Honey," Dawson says as they walk over hand in hand. I ignore Will and smile at them.

"It's lovely to meet you," Honey says. I offer my hand, and she absolutely beams. "I've been following you on social media ever since Will suggested your services. Your designs are beautiful. It's incredible to meet the artist behind the work."

A blush heats my cheeks, and I can't help the smile that teases my lips. "Wow, thank you so much. I'm really excited to work with you both." I can't help but side-eye Will, who seems rather smug. Okay, so the fucker really did help me out on this one, but I hate he knows it and is making me feel like I'm in debt to him or something.

"Do you mind if I get my camera out and take some photos of the space?" I ask, already reaching for my bag.

"Of course. Take as much time as you need," Dawson offers, already preoccupied by his wife. I go to open my bag, but Will picks it up and carries it to the counter for me. I offer him a tight smile. Yes, it's chivalrous. Is it also annoying? Yes, but only because it's this man.

I get another glimpse of the tight muscles beneath his shirt and whisper, "Do your shirt up."

"Why does it bother you so much? Does it turn you on?" Honey coughs, and I know they heard him. "Your cheeks are pink again, and not the ones I want to see."

Fucking hell.

"Can you leave?" I turn away from him as I open my bag and pull out my camera.

"Why? Can't contain yourself around me?" he casually says as he leans against the counter, surprisingly doing up his shirt buttons. I can't help but notice the veins in his hands and internally slap myself because they should not look so fucking hot.

"I'm trying to work here. Look, I appreciate you recommending my services to your friends, but I don't understand why you're here." I step into his space and lower my voice. "I really want this job, and I don't want it ruined because you're here being an ass."

A smile curves his lips, and he looks down at his shirt. "It was a stain."

"What?" I ask, confused.

"On my shirt." He leans in closer, and my body tenses. "It had lipstick marks on it, most likely from when a certain brunette was panting harshly into my chest as she fell apart all over my fingers."

Heat flushes my face again and my pussy starts pounding.

No, no, no.

We are not going down memory lane right now. He pushes off the counter, and I'm relieved as I look down at my camera and take my first photo of the space. I just want to hide and die behind my lens right now.

I don't pay much attention to the others as they speak among themselves. I'm already too captivated by ideas. The space is massive, and the layout somewhat basic, but it's nothing that can't be fixed. I notice the fitting rooms are quite large, and there's even a powder room.

This isn't just any old lingerie store; this place sells an experience. And experiences are what I create best.

Back in the front of the shop, I notice the three of them standing and talking by the counter. They're immaculately dressed and ooze with a type of wealth I'm not familiar with. But they're all captivating in their own way. I raise my camera and take a photo for reference. You can tell a lot about an owner from the way they style and present themself, and I'm sure there are certain elements of Honey and Dawson I can put into this store.

Will's gaze slides to me the moment I've taken the photo, and he grins as he says, "I've killed people for less." I'm shocked because there's something menacing about that statement. He's saying it as a joke, but... Surely, he hasn't actually killed anyone.

Why am I even thinking about that? I must be tired from the flight.

I turn away and continue taking photos when a man with a shaved head, wearing all black comes into the shop. A ripple of unease rolls through me as he enters. This man definitely looks the part of a killer. There's something wild to his demeanor. And it's not at all surprising when Will bursts into excitement to see him, his English accent thickening.

"You bloody bastard! Missed me that much you had to make a visit? Couldn't even help yourself." He goes to throw his arm over the man's shoulder, but the newcomer flings his arm away.

"Fuck off," the man says with a slight accent. I think it's Russian. "I've come to see Dawson. We have some business we need to discuss."

Will whistles as if the meeting is foreboding.

"I didn't expect you to come find me personally,

Alek," Dawson says with a charismatic smile that doesn't reach his gaze. The tension is palpable, and the newcomer—Alek—doesn't say anything further. I have the distinct impression he's a man of few words.

"I've got everything I need now," I announce, doing my best to leave this awkward tension. "When I get back to the hotel I'll start putting some ideas together. Will tomorrow work for you if I send through a rough draft?" I ask Dawson.

"Oh, you only just flew in. You can take a few days. Please don't rush," Honey says with a bright smile, and Dawson agrees with her. I can't help but smile back; it's nice to see such a powerful man be what I dare say is "wrapped around his wife's pinkie."

"It's fine, really. It's why you flew me out." I place my camera back in my bag. "I have your email, so I'll send ideas through. Let me know if you have inspirations or ideas you'd like me to incorporate. And if you don't like certain aspects of the concept, please let me know."

"It's all on you. We trust your judgment, so go with what you feel is best," Dawson says as he places his hand on Honey's lower back.

"What if you don't like what I have in mind?" I ask, because I really want this job.

"Oh, I will. Honey has shown me quite a few of

your videos, and I haven't disliked any work you've done so far. We're excited to see what you come up with."

"Oh, and here's my card." Honey hands me a business card for what looks like a bakery. "If you're in the area, stop by. And if you need anything, let me know."

"Thank you, I appreciate that." I pocket the card. "Well, enjoy your afternoon, and I'll send through some ideas shortly."

I go to grab my bag but Will picks it up. My temple pulses as I grit my teeth and smile, not wanting to make a scene in front of his friends. *Why is this fucker so persistent?*

I walk out, and Will follows me.

CHAPTER 7
Will

"I'll call you later, lover boy." I wave to Alek who shoots me a death stare. I know he secretly loves me. He proved it that one time he shot me in the shoulder. I call it our love bite.

He calls it a fuck off bite.

Each to their own, but we all know I'm right.

Alina's standing on the sidewalk with her arms crossed over her chest as she orders an Uber. Meanwhile, my car is sitting there, waiting.

"Let me drive you," I insist as I stop beside her and place the suitcase between us.

"You have a driver, so it's technically not you driving," she retorts, not looking away from her phone.

"Okay, let my driver take you. We can get handsy in the car." I wink at her.

Her green eyes find mine and narrow. "No."

I lean into her and enjoy the way she's acutely aware of my every move, despite her venomous tongue, her body always betrays her, especially when I get this close. She can push me away as much as she wants, but her body reacts to me each and every time. Just like mine does hers.

"I can still taste you on my lips," I whisper, and she gasps.

When she turns, our mouths are close, and I'm tempted to grab her jaw and pull her to me. But she steps away.

"Why are you here? I really want this contract. I get that maybe you were catching up with your pals or something, but this is my job and I take it very seriously."

"I can see that," I say with a smirk. "I have a job here in New York as well. Timing just worked out like that."

She pins me with a stare. "Look, the plane thing was fun, but it ends here. I'm not fucking you."

"What about that mouth of yours, then?" I ask, staring at her lips. I can just imagine how she'd look with tears streaming down her face, gagging on my cock.

Her mouth snaps shut and she looks away. She's absolutely perfect.

The front door of the shop opens behind us. Alina takes another step away as Alek walks out and his scathing glare hits me.

"Do you need a lift to get away from him?" Alek asks her, and I grin at him.

"Alek, come on. If you wanted me in your car, all you had to do was ask." I wink at him and he seems unimpressed.

"You seem to piss a lot of people off," Alina says under her breath.

"I also *get* a lot of people off," I'm quick to reply.

Her cutting glare hits me, and she seems relieved as a car rounds the corner. The truth is, I haven't been able to have an honest conversation for years. It kept everyone at an arm's distant so they wouldn't look too closely and eventually they stopped asking questions.

"Thank you for the offer, but my Uber is here," Alina directs to Alek, then grabs her luggage and strides off without looking back.

I hate that she doesn't look back even once.

I watch as she gets in the car and take note of the license plate. It's a habit, really.

Alek steps up beside me, adjusting his gloves. "Seems you've found your own type of trouble."

"If I really wanted trouble, I'd pull your gloves off and force you to touch me."

An obvious shiver runs down his spine, and I laugh. It's general knowledge the hitman and black-market auctioneer only let's one person touch him—his wife. That man hates the world and everyone in it, with two exceptions: his twin sister, Anya, who is probably crazier than him, and his wife, Lena.

To this day, I still don't know why he doesn't like people touching him, but I respect him enough to let his demons remain in his past. If I wanted badly enough, I could obtain the information, but we all have things we'd rather take to the grave. I supposed in some strange way, Alek and I were on opposite personality spectrums, he was cold and quiet toward others to keep the world at a distance and I was never to be taken seriously. Except for my work of course.

I was warned early on not to piss him off, but I find it comical now to mess with him, so I doubt I'll ever stop.

"Why are you so interested in the designer?" Alek asks, and I'm almost shocked by how much he's talking today. He's usually a man of few words. Maybe he really is beginning to fall for me.

"You're awfully chatty today."

"And you're avoiding the question."

Fair.

I pocket my hands and casually shrug. "I'm curious about her."

"It's never a good thing when you're curious." *True.* "Your last job took longer in London than you anticipated. Trouble finding your target? Becoming senile?"

I laugh at that. I imagine it's very few who discover Aleksandr Ivanov has a personality, let alone a sense of humor. "I found my target. I just also discovered something to entertain me in the meantime," I say, gesturing to where Alina was standing.

"As long as she keeps you entertained while you're back instead of me having to do it, I'm all too happy for her to stay," he says before walking toward his car.

I smirk, wondering how true that is. To what lengths am I willing to go to purge this curiosity?

No one has grabbed my attention in years. So when it comes to satisfying my interest, I've concluded that I'll go to any lengths necessary... at least for a certain brunette anyway.

CHAPTER 8
Alina

You've got to be fucking kidding me.

It's like I can't get away from this man.

I'm receiving my room key from the receptionist at the hotel when Will enters the lobby with his bags.

My jaw clenches as I politely thank the woman behind the desk and beeline for the elevator. My foot is tapping and I'm making it a point to not look his way. Now I'm starting to believe his whole "tracking people" business. Or is this just outright stalking? How did he know Dawson and Honey put me up in this hotel? Did he ask them?

Surely, it's not a coincidence. Or am I just being conceited? New York has hotels everywhere, so what would be the chances that we both end up at the same one?

The more I stand here waiting, the more furious I become. A part of me wants to turn around and unleash my irritation at him, while the other part is scared that if I do, I'll let him touch me again. And the worst part about that is I would enjoy it.

This asshole.

When the elevator doors open and an elderly couple walk out, I sigh as I step in. When the doors begin to close, I'm instantly relieved, that is until they open when a hand pushes through to stop them. Mr. Blue Eyes stands there wearing a devilish smirk.

If anyone asked me to describe Will, I would find it easy to do. He's very charismatic, charming even. But when he was hiking up my skirt in that bathroom, I saw the way those blue eyes turned ice cold and something came over him. He is beautiful—in every sense of the word. Anyone would look at him and think, *fuck, that is a gorgeous man*. He dresses to impress, his eyes will hypnotize you, and that smirk that he's trying to charm me with right now would make you drop your panties. But I also sense there's a darker side to him he doesn't really let others see. Above all, he's persistent in his efforts to piss me the fuck off.

I've been with the bad boy, and I've been with the businessman. Hell, I've even been with the funny man. None of those relationships worked at all. I don't know if it was just me. I mean, it could've been. I'm a very picky person. But I haven't been with anyone as self-assured as this man standing in front of me. And all I want to do is wipe that smug expression off his face.

"Anyone would think you were running away from me," he says, stepping into the elevator. He stands beside me as the doors close, and the small space feels electrically charged with tension.

"Anyone would think you're tracking me," I fire back. "Or maybe you're a stalker."

"Oh, I could track you anywhere in the world. I told you, milady, it's what I do."

My temple pulses every time he calls me milady.

"Here I thought you were someone with too much time on your hands since you won't leave me the fuck alone."

"I don't think you want me to leave you alone," he purrs, and this time, I look at him. He's confident, and his gaze dips to my lips. The tension around us becomes heavier, and I remember all the ways his body made me feel on the plane.

I step into his space now, grazing my hand up his

stomach. Fuck me if he doesn't feel divine beneath this shirt, but I smile sweetly as I peer up at him. "Is this what you do to all your sister's friends? Try to tick them off the list or something?"

He leans in, his lips ever so close to mine. "Is it so bad to find you attractive and want to fuck you?"

I brush my lips against his jaw as I go up on my tiptoes to get closer. "Yes, because you ruin it every time you open your mouth."

He chuckles. "Do you want to gag me, love?"

My heart is racing because, damn it, though I wanted to tease him, I'm feeling the tension in equal measure. It'd be so easy to thread my fingers through his hair. To kiss him. To fuck him.

Fuck, do I want it.

But then I step back as the doors open. "I want you to play with yourself as you think about me. Because that's all I'll be to you—a fantasy."

He licks his lips and then a slow smile stretches across his expression. "You're playing with fire, milady."

I casually shrug and shoot a pointed look to the door. "Don't you have to be somewhere? Run along."

He seems almost confused in a pleased way about being rejected as he steps out. Just as the doors go to close, he puts his hand in to stop it. "Room is four ten, in case you're bored later and need another release."

I flip him the bird as he removes his hand and the doors close.

When he's gone, I can't help but smile. I'd never give him the satisfaction of going to his room.

The problem is, I'm not satisfied at all. My pussy is pounding and my skin feels like it's dancing with electricity. I don't know how I pulled any of that off without mounting the man, and it makes no sense considering how much I can't stand him.

The doors open on the sixth floor, and I'm even more flustered by the time I get to my door. My key isn't working, and I frustratingly keep swiping it until it unlocks. The room is beautiful, and I can tell they didn't cut any corners on the budget. But I can't think of work right now because my mind is focused on a certain Englishman with blue eyes, and the acute awareness of all the things I could do with a man like that.

Fuck, do I need a release, but I won't give him the satisfaction. I throw my stuff on the bed and collapse on the mattress, not even bothering to change as I try to push away a multitude of bombarding memories.

Him kissing down my neck.

His hand up my skirt.

Fuck.

I toss back and forth, wanting and needing more.

But that would be a mistake, and so I let sleep take over, exhausted from the day.

And I dream of that asshole.

Fucking Will.

CHAPTER 9
Alina

I jolt awake when I hear knocking on my door. I rub my eyes, searching for my phone, and realize it's morning. The knocking continues, and I groan because I don't want to get out of this bed. Last night I had every intention of working on the project after having a nap, but it turns out I passed out cold. This is the comfiest bed I have ever slept on in my life, and when I travel from now on, I only want to stay in these hotels.

Getting up, I yawn and glance down at my wrinkled clothes from the day before. Sighing, I open the door, rubbing my eyes, and when I properly open them, I grimace at the shit-eating smirk Will wears.

He gives me a once-over with a raised eyebrow but

says nothing as he draws my attention to the two cups of coffee in his hands.

"Wild night, huh?" He offers me a coffee. "Good morning by the way."

I yawn again as I take the coffee, step back, and shut the door in his face. He chuckles on the other side of the door. When the coffee hits my lips, I all but moan.

Damn, that tastes good.

"Usually women say thank you," he calls through the door.

"Go and die," I shout back as I rub my eyes again. When I say I'm not a morning person, it's an understatement. Especially with a shit-eating grinning asshole who flares my immaturity so easily. He frustrates me but I can't also deny the fact that I bite on his every challenge. I want to throttle him as much as I want to play. And I fucking hate the way he's gotten under my skin. Infuriatingly so.

"But you'd miss me way too much, considering only my hands have been between your legs and not my mouth." He pauses. "Yet."

I squint in the direction of the door, because despite my mood, I'm certain even if I ignore him, he won't go away. As I take another sip, I realize it's exactly how I like my coffee. And how the fuck did he get my room number?

Pulling the door back open, I find him leaning against the doorframe, still smirking, raising his coffee to his lips.

"How did you know my coffee order and room number?" I ask.

"I don't know. I just spend all day playing with my cock and thinking of you, remember?" I roll my eyes at his response.

This man is insufferable.

"How about we spend the day together?" he suggests.

"Why would I willingly choose that for myself?" I scoff. It's flattering to be chased by a man such as Will. But I know this in no way will end well. Even if I have thought about the encounter on the flight more than once. Not that I would ever admit that to this arrogant prick.

"So you don't feel so detached when I fuck you later on."

I might not be fully awake yet, but even when alert I can't believe the confidence this guy boasts. Especially with that ever-present smirk. The one I want to slap off his face. Potentially also fuck off his face. I internally growl; this man is insufferable and I shouldn't fall for this charm.

"Does that work on other women?"

He shrugs casually. "To be honest, I haven't really tried it on anyone else. You seem to be a special case."

I throw my head back and laugh, clutching my coffee.

This man.

When I stop, I wipe the tears from my face.

"Special? Oh, you're right there. I am special." I shut the door in his face again. I can hear him chuckle, and I can't help but feel mixed emotions about him.

Is he hot? Yes.

Is he a serial killer? Possibly.

He said he was a tracker, and I don't really know what that means, but I don't want to be intrigued about this man. It's been years now that I only do sex, and I certainly don't hang out with men for the day. Especially not when I have a new project to focus on.

I sit down at the edge of my bed and flick through the photos I took of the shop. I wonder if I should call Maria to tell her about her brother and ask her to have him back off. But if I do, could it possibly ruin my chances of getting this job?

He irritates me beyond measure, and that's because

I haven't decided whether I want to punch him or fuck him.

I'm certain it's a bit of both.

I take another sip of coffee as my mind starts bubbling with ideas for the space. I reach over to my bag and pull out my tablet. As I flick through different color schemes and palettes, a few ideas start forming.

This is where the magic starts.

The shower can wait for later.

CHAPTER 10
Will

She's a spicy one, that's for sure. And I like it. I'm humming her praise all morning.

"Will you stop smiling? It's freaking me out more than usual," River says as he inspects his new shipment.

I've been working with River Bentley for years. If he needed someone found, I was his guy. I'd recently spent the past year here in the States, predominantly in New York, because there was a lot of money to be made here. But I also take great pleasure in pissing him —and Alek, especially—off. It was also the most settled I'd been in years, even if I still lived out of a suitcase. If I didn't stay anywhere for too long no one asked questions, no one tried to delve deeper. The only other person who knew about my demons was River but never asked about them. If he did, I'm not so sure I'd stay around.

"Did you get laid or something?" he asks as he leans down and opens a crate with a crowbar.

"Nope," I reply with a shit-eating grin.

He looks up at me then. "Alek told me you have your eyes on some brunette who's working for Dawson. Is that true?"

I lean back against one of the other boxes. "For a man of few words, he seems to like to gossip a bit. Do you think he's jealous?"

River shakes his head and chuckles. "Just don't piss my wife's brother off too much, okay? So, what, you like this woman? More than just wanting to fuck her?" he asks.

"Not particularly. She just won't fuck me."

"Ah. Not used to hearing no?" he teases as he drops the crowbar. Reaching into the crate, he pulls out a gun and inspects it appreciatively.

"I'm quite used to hearing no, considering Alek still hasn't taken me up on my offer," I reply, and River just laughs, shaking his head.

"You and Alek have a weird relationship, one I don't care to understand."

The truth is, I just absolutely love winding Alek up because it's so easy to do.

"It's not weird, it's just taking longer for him to realize he loves me." I wink as he sets the gun back down and goes to the next crate and repeats the process.

"If you say so." He shakes his head. "You got her the job too. Does she know that?"

"How did *you* know that?"

"Alek," he says. "You know Alek and Dawson are business partners."

"Hmm."

"Also heard you paid for her flight and hotel room. Very sweet of you. All this just to fuck her?"

"Something like that."

His forehead crinkles, but he doesn't press me with any more questions. I didn't take him for a romantic who cared about other's affairs. Then again, his and his wife Anya's way of foreplay seems to be her lighting his cars on fire, so I'm definitely not ever turning to him for dating advice.

"Are you actually going to help or stand there looking pretty?" he asks, just as my phone begins to buzz in my pocket.

"Oooh, I really do want to help, but I need to take this call first," I lie. In fact, I've avoided this call for the last week, but it seems like as good an excuse as any to get out of doing the heavy lifting. Besides,

River's a big enough guy, and they're his guns. He'll be fine.

I step away and answer the call.

"Finally. I've been calling you for a week," the man on the other end of the line seethes. I pick up one of the guns from an open crate and admire it.

"Mr. Percy, to what do I owe the pleasure?" I ask. I don't like this asshole one bit.

"Have you found my bitch yet? I paid you a fuck ton of money, so you better have results, punk."

I try not to laugh. *Punk?* Who even says that anymore? "What you paid me was a deposit for my services. So I'm assuming you're calling to tell me you have the rest of the money."

"I told you I can get it for you as long as you bring her to me."

I snort. I'd found his woman in London months ago. It was the reason I had to fly there in the first place. This wasn't the first messy breakup I'd had to deal with. This guy is a no-one who could easily be knocked off within minutes if I wanted it. I was just bored at the time and it seemed like easy money.

Him not having the money now changes that, of course.

"There's a difference between 'I can get you the money' and 'I have the money' Mr. Percy."

"You upped your price after the fact."

I shrug. "You delayed the payments. Now I'm starting to think you can't fulfill our agreement. No money, no location of your ex."

I hang up the phone.

When I turn, River is looking in my direction.

"Is that the job you went to London for?" he asks.

I shrug. "More or less. Fucker's trying to underpay me."

"Want me to handle him?" he asks, admiring the next gun.

I laugh. "That might make Anya hot and sweaty, but I can handle a guy like him myself, thanks. I was sick of waiting for his money, so I came back here in the meantime."

I have more money than I know what to do with. I'm the best of the best. I really could retire at any moment, but it's the business of this role that keeps me distracted from things I'd rather leave in the past.

Maybe that's why I find Alina a delightful new distraction.

CHAPTER 11
Alina

I present Dawson and Honey the drawings and sit down with them for over an hour, explaining what I have in mind. I want to give their clients an experience, make them feel something special as they come in. Create a connection. As I go through all the details with them, even the ones that include their line of sex toys, Dawson looks impressed and Honey stares at me in shock.

"When Will said you were good, I didn't fully believe him. Then I saw your videos, and thought, *she has talent*. But this"—Dawson waves a hand at the sketches on my iPad—"is amazing."

"Thank you. I was nervous with this one," I admit.

"Okay, you have done amazing, and we need to celebrate," Honey chirps as she stands.

"You can't, you're pregnant," Dawson says to her.

She blushes, and I look down to her belly.

"We only found out a few weeks ago. It seems I wasn't paying attention," she says.

"Congrats. How far along are you?"

"Almost twenty weeks." She presses her shirt to her belly, and I can see a small bump. It's so tiny, but I guess she is too. "My sister has been dying for a night out, and while I can't drink, I can watch."

"Honey," Dawson warns.

"You have, what, three nights left here?" Honey ignores him, looking at me expectantly, and I nod.

"Okay, good. Give me a second while I call her. She has a six-month-old and hasn't left the house in a while. Crue—that's her big, scary husband—hasn't been able to get her to leave either." She laughs as she steps away with the phone to her ear.

I turn to Dawson.

"I should say I have plans," I tell him. He smirks and shakes his head.

"No, it's fine. I trust her. It's just I hate being away from her." He looks over his shoulder to where she's pacing before he turns back to me. "I'll email you all my contractors' contacts and you can start as soon as possible?"

"You want to hire me? For real?"

"Yes, and I will pay you double the original offer."

I gasp. "You don't have to, honestly. I've enjoyed creating it."

"I'll pay you double to stay," he says. "To handle it all from start to finish. This is not my expertise. I handle other things." He doesn't say what, but I get the feeling it's not legal. "And Honey has her own business. So we need someone to oversee it all. Can you do that?"

"Of course. I'll find somewhere to stay while the work is being done."

"Good. My contractors will know to take orders from you."

Honey comes back over and says, "Okay, so girls' night. Do you need clothes? I know you only came with a small bag."

"It's fine. I'm staying for the duration of the project, so I'll run out to grab a few things and some new outfits," I tell her.

"Oh, you accepted!" She beams at me, then turns to her husband. "You offered her double, right?" He rolls his eyes and looks to me. It's not a sign of annoyance; you can see he loves her.

"He did," I answer. "And I'm excited to get started."

* * *

I managed to get a few things to hold me over in the short term, but I'll have to look for somewhere else to stay soon, as I don't think they'll want to cover a hotel for the whole time I'll be here.

Honey texted me the address of where we're meeting and told me it was just around the corner from my hotel. I step out onto the sidewalk dressed in jeans with a brown belt, a small white shirt that shows my midriff, and a pair of heels. It takes me less than five minutes to find the bar, and when I walk in, I spot Honey straight away. She stands from her seat and pulls me in for a quick hug before pointing to the lady behind her.

"This is Rya, my sister." I give Rya a wave and then take a seat.

"I ordered you a drink," Honey tells me, and I note a glass of water by her hand.

"Thank you."

"Honey was showing me your videos," Rya says, a drink already in front of her. "You're really good; I can see why Dawson hired you."

"Thank you. And what is it that you do?" I ask her as the bartender walks over with a French martini. I smile and take a sip of it. *Yum.*

"At the moment, I'm a breastfeeding machine. But I'm a criminal lawyer and own my own firm." She smiles.

"Wow, that's impressive."

"The breastfeeding? Yeah, I know." She winks, and Honey spits out her water, laughing.

"She doesn't mean to be rude, but it's just Rya," Honey says, then stands and heads to the bar, calling out over her shoulder, "I'm getting you both some shots."

"Who has the baby tonight?" I ask Rya.

"His father. Eli is the best baby," she gushes, picking up her drink. "He loves his father as much as he loves me, which I think helps."

Honey comes back with a tray full of shots. I stare at it, shocked.

She picks up two shot glasses and places one in front of me and one in front of Rya. "Since I can't drink, you two will do it for me," she says, picking up another set and placing them in front of us. She sits down and claps her hands. "Drink."

Rya looks at me with raised brows, shrugs, then throws back the shot. I lift mine up and do the same. It burns as it goes down. We both pick up the next shots at the same time, and the bartender approaches with two cocktails and a plate of dips and bread. Not sure how much alcohol that's going to soak up, but I'm willing to try.

"So, what does your husband do?" I ask Rya, trying to not throw up as I grab a piece of bread.

"Oh, you know, he kills people, runs a lot of businesses, and is probably one of the most dangerous men I know." She leans in and whispers, "But I can make him get on his knees and beg. Maybe I'm more dangerous than he is." She throws her head back and laughs. I'm not sure if she's joking or not. She definitely has a dry sense of humor, which I can appreciate. She gives me a knowing look when she adds, "And I worked with Will once. He assisted me in finding a client. He has a knack for hunting, that one."

"Yeah, he mentioned his job is to track people down," I tell her. Rya looks at Honey, then back at me. There seems to be a silent conversation between the two, one I don't entirely understand. It's as if they're deliberating telling me something maybe. Or perhaps I misread something?

"Do you know what type of world you're in right now?" she asks. I look at her, confused. "It's all good. Just keep it that way. Do your job and then go home. Trust me." Honey offers me a small smile and no further explanation. It's unsettling in a way and also creates more questions. I know these people are different. They have a particular aura around them. I've dealt with people who work in what might be considered the underworld before but part of me wonders if I'm wrong. Surely I am right? They seem far classier and put together then those who I've dealt with in the past.

But when Rya and Honey go to the bathroom my curiosity gets the best of me. I can read between the lines of Honey wanting to tell me something but deciding it's better not to. With that said, left to my own devices even if only for a few minutes I want to know exactly what I'm involving myself with. I pull out my phone and Google Rya, then Google her husband. At first, I'm in shock about what I find, I thought maybe they dabbled in questionable affairs but as I flick through and read, I realize Rya wasn't joking when she said her husband kills people.

The first thing I find about Crue Monti is that he is a known mafia leader but has never been charged with a crime. There are many theories regarding certain events but no solid evidence of anything at all.

I search Dawson then, and gape when I find that he's suspected of being a human trafficker. But it's nothing but allegations.

Is that what they're doing? Getting me drunk to kidnap and traffic me?

Oh, God.

Standing, I wonder if I can leave without getting caught, but Honey comes over and sits back down. When I don't sit straight away, she looks up at me confused.

"Do you want to change the venue? I know of a cute little bar down the road."

"Do you plan to traffic me?" I blurt.

"Traffic you? What the actual fuck?" Rya says, walking up to the table and about to take her own seat.

"I Googled your husbands," I say, my gaze darting between them. I mean surely she didn't think giving me an ominous warning like that wouldn't spark my curiosity to delve deeper.

"Sit down, Alina. And, no, we don't traffic people," Honey says, tapping the table. "You honestly thought that?" She sounds surprised, and honestly, a little hurt.

"Well, your husband—"

"Do you believe everything you read on the internet?" Rya asks me.

"No, it's just..."

"Yes, it's true that my husband is part of the Mafia," Rya admits. "Now, sit down. We don't plan to traffic you or hurt you in any way." She rolls her eyes.

"Dawson runs exclusive auctions that are sex related, but he doesn't traffic anyone," Honey explains.

"I'm sorry, it's just..." I shake my head.

"It's fine. You're vanilla," Rya says.

"Vanilla?" I ask and it immediately snaps me out of my frantic thoughts and I'm not sure if she's joking and teasing me.

"You weren't brought up in this world. We were, so we weren't thrown off. Our father is very powerful, and so are our husbands. But they won't hurt you, unless you hurt us." Rya smiles and sits back.

I take a breath. The experience I've had in this world...although short and fleeting was what destroyed my previous relationship and he was far from a powerful man. He was just a piece of shit caught up in drugs. I should be scared but when I sit across from them... they seem like normal women. Besides wearing designer everything, we're just three women out for a girls' night. It's jarring almost, but I trust my instinct that they genuinely aren't here to hurt me, and my instinct has never led me astray. But it immediately forms another question.

"Is Will part of that world?" I ask.

The sisters look between one another again, a silent conversation happening. I'm somewhat envious of their ability to do that without even speaking but don't all siblings have that relationship? I wouldn't know.

"I think that's something you should ask Will," Honey says and I feel like all of a sudden I've stepped over a line. I also feel bad accusing them of potentially trafficking me when I know they'd never hurt me.

"I'm sorry," I say, turning to Honey. "Really, I am. I read stuff and just got..."

"It's fine. But don't feel like you have to stay here with us if you feel unsafe. You can stop drinking and head back to the hotel." She's saddened as she says it. I wonder how often they have to draw a line in relationships not to let them get so close or to discover this part of their world. Shouldn't I be flattered in the least that they piqued my curiosity so much to let me ask the question?

"Fuck that. I'm not stopping until I have to crawl home," Rya exclaims, downing the last of her cocktail and sauntering back toward the bar. I kick up a smile, a wave of relief washing over me that despite the awkward exchange and swirling questions they're acting as if nothing strange has happened at all. I can process this later, but for now, I'm enjoying myself, and who am I to stop myself from having a good time?

"Get me one?" I yell out, to which she winks approvingly, and I notice the wave of relief run through Honey. Where Rya might be more direct, Honey is sweet and easy to read. At this point, I know two things. One, I can trust them. Two, I might not remember much of tonight, the way we're ordering drinks. And I'm fucking down for it.

CHAPTER 12
Will

I knocked on her door for a good ten minutes with no answer. It's past midnight, and she hasn't come back to the hotel. I know because I'm sitting in the lobby waiting for her.

Maybe she's with a guy. I did hack the security footage to see her walking out in tight-ass jeans and a tiny shirt.

I consider my options. It's too easy to track her phone, and the temptation is there.

I've become outright fixated on her. I tell myself it's because I'm stalling in between jobs, but the truth of the matter is, I'm intrigued by her, even though I already know almost everything there is to know about her.

It's my job to know these things.

And I took great pleasure in learning about her.

It's the first time I've become fixated on a woman since... well, some memories are best left to the past. I seriously just have to get her out of my system.

Just as I pull my phone out to track hers, I hear her laughter flutter through the lobby.

I stand and call her name.

She pauses, and her laugh cuts off when she sees me. The doorman is discreetly checking her out.

I get it; she's beautiful. In a stunningly classical kind of way.

"You." Her eyes narrow as she says it, then she lifts her finger and points it at me. "You." She slurs the word this time.

"How much have you had to drink?" I ask, amused. Because there's nothing more entertaining than the drunk, unfiltered version of Alina.

She gets in my space and looks down her nose at me. I don't even know how it's possible considering she's so much shorter than me. My nostrils flare with the mixture of her perfume and the alcohol on her breath. She pokes her perfectly manicured nail into my chest and leans in with a sneer.

"Why are you always here?" she asks. "You just poof out of nowhere like a magician."

I try to contain my laugh.

If I answer her, she'll just call me a stalker. And, hell, I probably am.

But right now, *her* hands are on *me*.

"Do you think... because I let you finger fuck me... that I'll fall at your feet?" she stammers. The doorman coughs behind her, and he's quick to step back to his post by the door.

"I was hoping," I reply. Then we can clear whatever this thing is between us and be done with it.

"Whatever." She flips her hair over her shoulder and heads to the elevator. I follow her into the car and press the button for my floor. She tries to stand but ends up leaning against the wall for support.

"Do you intend to come to my room?" I ask curiously.

"Oh my God, why would you even say that?"

When the elevator begins to rise, she loses balance and stumbles. I catch her and press her against the wall.

"You didn't press the button for your floor," I tell her, and her eyes go wide. The elevator stops, and the doors open to my floor, but I make no move to exit.

She stares up at me through thick eyelashes with those big fuck-me eyes. I raise my hand to rub against her lower lip, smearing lipstick along my thumb. These fuckable lips. Just thinking about them gets me hard.

I could take her now. Taste her and fuck her as I please. But there's something about how drunk she is that has me reluctant to make a move.

When the fuck am I ever a gentleman?

The energy shifts and she speaks. "Aren't you going to get out since this is your floor?" She breaks the tension and moves past me to press her floor number. I lean against the wall and wait for the doors to close. She seems confused.

"Aren't you meant to get off?"

I tuck my hands into my pockets casually. "I'm just making sure you get to your room safely, love."

The doors open and I hold them for her.

"You aren't allowed to come to my room," she says, stumbling off and searching through her purse. I hold the door open, watching her.

"Fuck!" she curses, then looks over her shoulder at me. "I've lost my room key."

This one is more trouble than she realizes; she's practically asking me to be her knight in shining armor. And now I have to get off the elevator to help her with her door. The temptation just keeps increasing. I push out of the elevator, amused, and approach her room as she stumbles behind me. "We need to go downstairs to get a new key."

"We?" I ask with raised eyebrows.

"No, not as in *we*. Shut up. You know what I mean." She folds her arms across her chest, and my gaze dips to her cleavage.

Too much fucking trouble.

I pull out my card and swipe it. Her door opens, and her jaw unhinges as she stares at it and I place the card back in my pocket.

"How the fuck do you have access to my room?"

"I have access to everyone's room. I told you. If I need to find people or things, there's no stopping me. I can gain access to any key for any type of room or treasure."

She stares at me, her face scrunched up.

"That's really fucking weird. And don't ever come into my room without my permission." I kick up a smile as she pushes past me. "But I really need to pee, so whatever."

"I believe you owe me a favor for this." She swings around in shocked horror, and again I try not to laugh.

"For saving me from five minutes and a bill for requesting another room key?"

"In your state, it would've been a lot longer than five minutes."

Her lips curve into a wicked grin as she saunters up to me. I know what she's doing, and it's fucking working. She grabs the lapels of my jacket. "And what type of state might I be in, Mr. Blue Eyes?"

My eyebrows shoot up. "Mr. Blue Eyes?" I repeat. My cock twitches as I stare at her lips. Fuck, I want her so badly.

"It's better than asshole, isn't it?" she asks innocently, and pouts. My cock jumps again at those beautiful, full lips.

Too fucking temping. When I slowly lean in, she pulls back with a smile. Teasing me. I grab her by the throat, and her grin widens. I want her. Fuck, do I want her. But I want *her* to come to *me*. Sober.

"And I thought you so badly needed to pee?" I ask.

It's as if she's just remembered as the urgency sparks again, and she flips me the bird over her shoulder. "Whatever. I owe you one."

I call out behind her, "See you in the morning, milady."

"Fuck you," I hear her say, and I chuckle as I close the door.

I'm certain that whatever she drank tonight, she'll regret it tomorrow. Or more likely, she'll regret agreeing to owing me a favor.

I step into the elevator and select my floor. It's not until the doors open and I step off that I go to grab my key. Except, I realize it's not in my pocket anymore.

I can't help the smile that spreads over my lips. That conniving little vixen. She pickpocketed my card. A grand little thief who can't hold back on her own temptations and part of me already has suspicions as to why. But right now, all I can think about and imagine is her self-satisfied smile in her room.

CHAPTER 13
Alina

My head hurts. A lot.

I groan at the headache pounding in my skull.

Shit, what did I say to Honey and Rya last night?

Oh gosh, I accused them of wanting to traffic me.

I bury my head deeper into my pillow when there's knocking on my door.

Is that what woke me up?

I bet it's him again, but this time I welcome the coffee. I fell asleep in my clothes again and don't even bother finding anything else to change into as I pull the door open.

"You better—" The words die on my lips when I discover room service waiting at the door with a tray.

"Good morning. I have your breakfast order," he says. I politely smile and step back so he can enter.

I stand to the side as the waiter carries the tray in and begins setting covered plates on the table. Wow, this is definitely better than just coffee, but I don't recall ordering it.

Maybe I ordered it before I fell asleep?

"How much do I owe you?" I ask.

"It's all been paid for plus the tip," he says, then leaves with the tray tucked under his arm.

Okay. I'm not going to say no to free food or caffeine first thing in the morning.

I shut the door behind him and then walk to the table to sit down. Stumble might be more of an accurate word, as I realize I'm still possibly drunk. My head is hazy as I groan in pain.

Eggs, bacon, bread, orange juice, plus a coffee are arranged neatly in front of me. My stomach starts to growl as I pick at a piece of bacon.

I sigh as I recap the night, focusing mostly on seeing Will.

I wonder how I should thank him for breakfast, because I know it was him. I don't know how I know it, but I do.

Strange. He's an arrogant, cocky prick, but then he does things such as pulling out my chair, carrying my bags, and ordering me breakfast. I don't think I'm ready to look further into the fact that perhaps he isn't that bad of a guy.

Wow, I really am still drunk.

Reaching for my phone, that is almost dead, I call Honey. She answers straight away.

"So, I think I should start by apologizing for last night," I blurt.

"No need. I had so much fun. And Rya did as well."

"But the things I said..."

"It's fine, really. I'd be more skeptical of you if you didn't question it. How are you doing this morning?"

"I feel a little dead, but I got room service, which I didn't order. I have a feeling Will ordered it for me. He was waiting for me last night in the lobby when I got back."

"Was he just?" she says and I can imagine her biting back a smile. I groan as my headache intensifies

"Do you have his number?" I ask. "It's fine if you don't want to share it, but I want to thank him for helping me into my room last night," I say, eating another piece of bacon. "Not in that way!" I quickly snap before she can look into it any further. "I lost my card."

"If you say so." She chuckles on the other side of the phone.

My phone dings, and I pull it away from my ear.

"That's Dawson's number, he sent it to you," she explains.

"Thank you." And I'm grateful that she doesn't prod me any further about the strangeness of whatever is happening between me and Will.

She asks to meet up later to look at an apartment she said I can stay in while I'm here. It looks like I'll be here for at least another month, and her old apartment is apparently available.

Deciding the best action is to shower before I call Will, I make sure I eat everything on my plate before I do. Once I'm clean and dressed in clothes that I haven't slept in, I dial his number.

He answers straight away.

"Milady," he croons. I still cringe at the word and I'm certain he's used it ever since he realizes how much I hate it–always purposefully winding me up, baiting me for a reaction.

"My name is Alina," I remind him. And to think, for a second, I was considering him to be anything but annoying.

"If you say so." He chuckles.

"Did you send me breakfast?" I ask, exasperated

because I'm really not in the mood for his quick responses this morning. More or less I'm not sure if I can keep up with them while I'm in such a vulnerable state.

"Of course I did. I hear the way to get between a woman's legs is to feed her, so I'm feeding you."

I sag back into bed, shaking my head with a sigh. "You really have no shame."

"I do not," he confesses. "Now, meet me downstairs. I need a shopping partner, and I know you'll give me your honest opinion."

"Shopping? I don't know if I'm in the mood to go anywhere today."

"You owe me a favor, remember?"

"A favor for wh—"

He hangs up, and I curse under my breath. *Motherfucker*.

Considering I don't meet with the contractors until Monday, I do technically have the day off. I might feel like death, but it'd also been a while since I explored New York. And the very vague memory of him helping me into my room resurfaces.

Fuck. Fine.

I change clothes, grab my purse, and head downstairs. When I reach the lobby ten minutes after the call, he's waiting for me, dressed in a clean, pressed suit.

His baby blue eyes look up from his phone screen, and that dimply smile kicks up my heart rate.

I get flashes of him pressing against me in the elevator from last night and a low ache begins between my thighs keeping tempo with my headache.

I'm pretty sure we didn't do anything last night.

Am I disappointed that nothing happened?

I push away that irrational thought and remind myself I'm still drunk... I think.

"So, what do you need help with?" I ask as he strides along beside me. The doorman greets me with a smile, and I'm not sure if I missed out on something, because he seems to be very familiar with me.

"I figured you, who has impeccable taste, were the right person to call."

"That I do," I agree. "But you still haven't told me what we're shopping for."

When we reach the sidewalk, a black car is already waiting for us at the curb. Will steps in front of me to open the back door. He closes it behind me, then he circles the back of the car and gets in beside me, angling himself to give me his full attention.

It's intimidating.

Even with his smartass mouth, there is something dangerous that lurks inside him.

I kind of like it.

And I want to slap myself because of it.

I've dated the bad boy before, and that was the worst relationship I've had. I can't fall for that type of charm again.

"I'm not telling you what we're shopping for. It's a surprise."

"Are you sure you're not kidnapping me?" I say, rolling my eyes at him.

"If I were kidnapping you, you'd be tied to my bed already," he says matter-of-factly.

Heat swarms to my core, and the visual of that has me curling my nails into my palms. He smirks knowingly. Fuck, why does my body react to him so profoundly.

Maybe I just need to get laid—by anyone—and it'll shake this temptation off.

The driver pulls out and follows the traffic.

"How did you get my number?" he asks. "I would have gladly given it to you if you had asked." When I don't reply, he leans in. Damn, he smells good. "Is it so you can send me naughty messages at night?"

"You are so full of yourself," I'm quick to say.

"You, too, could be full of me." He winks, and my eyes go wide.

He did not just say that.

I don't know why I'm shocked every time he says something so promiscuous.

"Does this seriously work on other women?"

"You've asked me this before, love. I don't try this hard on other women."

"Oh, that makes me feel special."

"You are special," he says, continuing to stare at me. I stare back. Something passes between us, and it makes us both uncomfortable. I don't like the way he looks at me at times like these. Like he can see me. The *real* me. The *ugly* me.

"You have ten freckles on your nose," he says seriously.

"Did you just count my freckles?"

"Yes. And your lips form this sad heart shape when you're mad, like right now." He nods to my lips.

"What do you want from me?" I ask, frustrated and tired with not understanding this man. Before, I wanted nothing to do with him. But now I'm noticing I'm becoming interested. And being interested is a bad thing. "Is it just sex?"

"Just sex..." he ponders. His accent thick when he says it. "At first, yes. I wanted to fuck you because you didn't want me, and I liked that. Now? Well, now I just want to fuck you."

"That's sweet, but I'm still not fucking you," I say,

looking outside the window, feigning boredom. The thing with Will is he's defiantly the person your mother as a child would've told you not to play with. He's mischievous and most likely will get you into all sorts of trouble. The problem being I was that child as well. I was just never *caught.* I inwardly smirk. I'd never admit it to him, but he brings out a playful side of me that I haven't had for quite some years. He is as refreshing as he is irritating.

"I bet I can get you to fuck me," he says matter-of-fact. I turn to him now. This man knows how to challenge me in ways no one has been daring enough before or more specially I was always in control of the game we played.

"You really think you can make a bet like that?" Unfortunately, I'm nothing short of competitive, and I think this asshole knows it because his arrogant smile kicks up, forming that single dimple.

"I'm counting on it, love."

CHAPTER 14
Alina

The car slows down, and I realize we're at an air strip.

Will gets out first and then opens my door. We didn't speak much after the betting comment. The ride has been sexually charged ever since. A small part of me reminds me that he's my friend's brother and I so shouldn't be looking at him this way. The plane incident I could knock off as a onetime thing. But whatever we're heading toward is a train wreck.

And part of me wants in on that.

When I step out of the car, I notice two men in suits waiting for our arrival. A red carpet is laid out to the staircases of two airplanes.

"Mr. Walker, it's a pleasure to see you again." The men look at me expectantly.

"This is Alina, she'll be assisting me today on picking an aircraft."

Is he for real? Has he really brought me to help him purchase his own fucking plane?

They smile and we shake hands. Will is watching me through the lenses of his dark sunglasses. I might not be able to see his eyes, but I always know when his gaze is on me.

When the first man offers to take us on a tour of the first plane, I fall back a few steps to Will's side.

"Is this a joke?" I hiss under my breath.

He chuckles. "Why would I bring you here as a joke? I consider my humor in better taste."

I gawk at him now. I knew he was loaded but come on. A fucking private plane?

"Still think I sit at home playing video games with my dick in my hand?" he asks with an arrogant smile as he waves for me to step onto the staircase of the first aircraft.

Who the fuck is this guy?

And why do I have an unhealthy curiosity about men I should stay away from?

I have never been on a private plane, let alone had a viewing of one. The gentleman points out things that are alluring and shocking. Well, shocking for someone like me, who just came out of economy class for the first time. How is this shit even real?

We move on to the next plane. The first one had a champagne colored interior, while this one has more dark features. Both are beautiful. Both equally mind-blowing.

When we're done with the tours, Will speaks to the men before joining me again.

"Which one?" he asks.

"You can't seriously be asking me. I flew business class for the first time coming here, and not because I can afford it but because it was paid for me. I know fuck all about airplanes," I confess.

And I don't know if he's purposefully pushing me—to try and make me uncomfortable—or if he genuinely trusts my taste that much. But this is a significant investment and I don't want any responsibility for the decision.

"Which one?" he pushes. "I wouldn't have asked you here if I didn't think you were capable of giving me an unfiltered and honest opinion. Don't disappoint me now," he teases.

I fold my arms over my chest, annoyed. This asshole really knows how to make me bite.

"I liked the darker one," I admit. "It's more

comforting, and I feel like the darker tones would make it easier if I wanted to sleep."

I don't understand why he brought me out here or cares at all for my tastes. I know I have good judgment, which is why I'm paid for it, but this is the most peculiar "favor" I've ever been called out on.

"Perfect. Give me a few minutes."

He strides back over to speak to the men, and I pull out my phone, scrolling through my work emails. I reply to one from the contractor, confirming time and place to begin on Monday.

I then switch over to my personal email, and delete a few spammy messages, but one grabs my attention. When I open it, my heart sinks.

You still owe me, bitch. Did you really think you'd get away with it?

A lump forms in my throat. Even without them signing their name, I know exactly who it's from. Chills runs down my spine, and I delete the email and block the address.

I thought they'd given up. I haven't heard from

them in months, and I fell into a sense of security. But the harassment hasn't seemed to cease.

"Everything okay?" Will asks, and I look up, startled. I hadn't even realized he was standing in front of me. I push my phone back into my pocket with a forced smile.

"Yeah, of course. I was just emailing the contractors," I reply as we fall into step on the way back to the car. "So, what? You just have money lying around to purchase a plane?"

His arrogant smile appears, and that single dimple forms. "No, I have it tucked away in an account like all trust fund babies. That's what you expect from me, isn't it?"

I scoff. "Would make sense as to why you have so much time to stalk me."

"I'll have you know, I worked for my money, and now I have more than I know what to do with."

"Thus the plane?" I say with an eyeroll. He opens the door for me, and I slide inside.

"Thus the plane," he replies as he closes the door.

When he shuts the door behind me, I let out a shaky breath. Suddenly, my hangover has very much cleared.

I can sense the driver watching me through the rearview mirror, but I don't care. I hate how much power that email has over me. How unsettled it makes me feel.

Will slides in beside me, and the driver pulls away from the air strip. I don't like how Will is looking at me now, and maybe it's because I'm paranoid. I push away the email. My past has no hold over me anymore. I've started a new life.

"Where are we going now?" I ask with another tight smile. And I realize my mistake. Perhaps it's because I'm feigning kindness that he senses something is off.

But much to my relief, he replies with, "Lunch."

Luckily for him, I'm hungry.

CHAPTER 15
Will

Alina was chattier than normal on the drive to the restaurant, which was unnerving. I'm used to her ignoring, teasing, or snapping at me, the latter being my favorite. She asked questions about the plane, but I know she's not interested in it. Something put her off, and I suspect it might've been an email or message she received because it only happened after she checked her phone.

We're in the restaurant now, one that I must confess I've frequented quite a few times. She's eaten half of her pasta with copious amounts of cheese and is nursing a glass of water. Ever since we sat down, she's been quiet. That makes me even more uncomfortable than the chattier version of her from the car.

"So, let's make a bet," I suggest as the waiter brings

over a side salad. I offer him a courteous smile as I reach for my water.

She takes another forkful and stares at me as she wipes her mouth. I see the spark of life appear in her eyes. This woman, if nothing else, likes a challenge.

"What type of bet?" she asks from behind the napkin.

The restaurant is filled with men in suits, which is perfect for the idea that comes to mind. I clock a man sitting at the bar. In fact, I noticed him the moment we walked into the restaurant. He happens to be the owner. A mischievous idea comes to me, and I can't help but smirk.

"Let's have some fun with it. If you fail, you come back to my room with me tonight."

Her green gaze pins me. Honestly, I think that kind of loss is really a win for her, and it goes without saying it's a win for me.

"What do I get out of this bet? I mean, you get me, but what do I get?" She taps her finger on her lip, and it draws my attention to that come-fuck-me mouth. I'm certain she's doing it on purpose. "I can't really think of anything worth it."

I smirk with full confidence that I'm going to win this bet. "How about the plane?"

She chokes on her water, and I chuckle. If I'm

being honest, I did intentionally wait until she was taking a sip because she chokes almost every time I say something shocking. I fucking love it.

When she looks up, she seems almost angry, and I'm not sure if it's because of my perfect timing or the terms of the bet. She wipes at her mouth. "You can't play that type of game."

"I can and I will," I assert as I lean in. "Come on, you know you want to."

I can see it in her eyes. This little vixen is coaxed by danger. I imagine it's gotten her into trouble a few times, which is perhaps why she's so cautious. Rightly so, especially when it comes to men like me.

She leans in, as if we naturally gravitate toward one another in mischief. "What's the bet?"

I pretend to casually search the room, but I already know who my target is.

I lick my lips, knowing full well she's going to be in my bed on her back tonight.

I point to the man sitting at the bar. "I dare you to get the phone number of one of the men at the bar. If you succeed, I won't have the pleasure of tasting you tonight and you'll get a plane."

She looks at me skeptically. "You're really not joking, are you?" She sits back in disbelief. "What would I even do with a plane?"

"You sound so sure that you'll win," I taunt, because I know she can't help but take the dangling bait.

"Have you seen me? Of course I'll win." She scoffs, and my cock twitches at her confidence. Because, yes, I have seen her, and she's been the bane of my existence ever since.

"I have seen you, and I would personally give you my number in a heartbeat. So, are you up for the bet?"

She defiantly holds out her hand. "You're on."

I offer my hand in return. "But I get to choose whose number you get." She squints but casually shrugs and shakes on it. Her eyes twinkle with certain victory, and I imagine mine mirror the same. She can't help but smile, and my cock hardens at her arrogant confidence.

She will be mine tonight. Of that much, I'm certain.

"So who's my target?" she asks, twisting around to look at those sitting at the bar.

"You really want the plane, huh?" I tease. "See that man sitting over there?" I point to the owner, who is sitting by himself. He's dressed in a nice suit and is easy on the eyes. "Get his number. Oh, and did I mention you have a time limit?" I look down at my watch. "You have ten minutes. I'd get moving if I were you."

She stands up and brushes her hands down her skirt as she leans down to me and smiles. "You're on. I'm going to win that plane."

"I'm going to win that," I say, dropping my gaze to her cleavage, and I have every intention of staring at her ass as she walks away.

"No, you're going to keep fantasizing, and don't stare at my ass when I walk away," she spits as she turns and heads to the bar.

I grin as my gaze dips to her ass and I secretly know she loves it.

This should be interesting...

CHAPTER 16
Alina

I can do this. I mean, it's for a fucking plane.

Not sure what I would do with a plane, but I'm willing to find out.

Shit, do I have to pay to maintain a plane?

Maybe I should have asked questions first.

Fuck it.

I brush my hands down my skirt and approach the man Will pointed out. When I step up next to him, he's removing his suit jacket. I notice a few tattoos that skate up his arms beneath the rolled-up shirt.

"Excuse me," I say, and he lifts his head and meets my eyes.

Oh, he's beautiful. His eyes are a mix of blue and hazel, his hair is dark, and he watches me as if he can see straight through me. And he also gives me the vibe that I shouldn't be approaching him.

"Yes?" he answers, looking me up and down. Not in a leering way, more as if to make sure I have nothing on me.

Weird, but okay.

"So, I have this guy over there." I point behind me. "Just don't look, okay?" He nods, and I pull out a seat next to him. "Anyway, we made a bet. I was hoping you could help me fulfill this deal," I explain.

He picks up the silver knife beside him. At first, I think it's strange, until I realize he's shifting it back and forth to get a glimpse at Will. When he does, a small sigh escapes him.

"What type of deal?" he asks, leaning back into his seat.

His phone lights up, but he makes no move to touch it.

"I want you to give me your number," I tell him. He raises a brow. "And in doing so, I'll pay you."

"You'll pay me?" he asks, somewhat amused. "For my number?"

"Yes. Not right now because it'll be obvious to my friend, but I can transfer the money afterward because I'll have your number anyway," I state, smiling.

"Just one issue," he replies, raising one finger. "Not

that I don't want to help you, but if you turn around right now, you'll see my wife standing behind you. I suggest you don't speak, because she has a habit of stabbing people." I tense.

He stands and holds out his hand, gesturing toward his wife. I sit frozen in place, realizing I've probably taken her seat. In my periphery, a delicate hand with red painted nails clasps his hand, and as he pulls her into him, piercing green eyes glare at me.

"This is Anya Ivanov, my wife," he says. "And I'm River Bentley. Now, let me get my number for you." He reaches for a napkin.

"N-no, please. It's fine," I stammer.

"You said you had a bet with him, didn't you?" he asks.

"A bet?" Anya asks with a slight Russian accent, her gaze narrowing. When I look at her properly, I realize her red hair is impeccable, slicked back in a tight bun, and she's clad in a dress with a slit up the side. And she definitely looks like she could stab me. But she also reminds me of someone I've met before.

"Yes, I'm so sorry. I wasn't hitting on your husband. The man I'm dining with made a bet with me." I clear my throat. "If I got your husband's number, he would give me a plane." Her gaze immediately drifts over to Will, even though I hadn't told her which man. *Fuck, am I going to get us both killed?* Her gaze narrows and her high heels click-clack as she approaches Will. He just sits there and waves.

"You," she says, looking over her shoulder at me. "Come with me." She indicates with her finger and turns back to Will's table. If she's not going to slap the smug expression off his face, then I fucking will.

That's if she doesn't murder us first.

I'm not intimidated by too many people, but I would avoid this woman at all costs.

In a few short steps she reaches Will. I come up behind her and look down at him apologetically, that is until she speaks.

"You set this up, now give the fucking woman her plane," she demands, and Will adjusts his glass on the table with a shit-eating grin.

Realization dawns on me then.

He knows her.

That means…

I look over my shoulder to find River smiling as he watches his wife. He's sitting back down, as if getting comfortable, as he takes in the show.

"Come on, Anya. It's a little funny. I had to see her try, even though I knew he wouldn't give it to her."

"I'll chop off your fucking cock and feed it to my

dogs if you pull a stunt like this again," she replies, her Russian accent thickening with her anger.

"Your dogs love me."

What the fuck?

"You know each other?" I ask, my own irritation spiking. At him, as usual.

"Yes. River and I go way back, and as you can see, Anya is quite fond of me too. Unfortunately for you, it looks like you lost the bet, milady," Will says in mock apology. "My hotel room or yours?"

I snap. I'm so fed up with this man and his games.

"Fuck you." I reach for my glass of water and throw it at him, glass and all. He moves out of the way and it misses him. His smirk never leaves his face.

"You're more well-tempered than me, I would've gone for a knife," Anya interjects, and I'm reminded that I'm in a restaurant. People are staring now, but River and Anya don't seem particularly bothered.

Anya reaches into her pocket, pulls out a card, and hands it to me.

"This is my husband's number." I stare at the card. Then she turns back to Will. "Now, give her the fucking plane," she orders, then returns to her husband.

I grab my purse from the table and walk away. Fuck this guy and his games. I pass River and Anya, who are watching us, on my way out. I don't make eye contact, just in case she decides it's time to kill me after all.

"Alina," Will calls out after me, but I ignore him as I step out into the crowded entranceway where people are lining up for the restaurant. I don't know where exactly I am or where I'm going, but it doesn't matter, as long as I'm storming away from that asshole.

My phone starts ringing, and I look down to his sister's name on the screen. I'm fucking furious, and I know that answering isn't a good idea. But I'm so fucking mad at this asshole.

I answer it, growling, "Your brother is a total asshole."

Maria laughs as I seethe. "Yeah, that's the impression he gives people," she says. "Why what did he do this time? And why are you two even hanging out? Did you have to do a group dinner with his friends that own the store or something?"

Where do I even start? The bet? Staying at the same hotel room? The—

My phone is snatched from my hand as I try to wave down a cab.

"Hi, baby sis, I'll call you back. Right now, I have to calm down my date," Will says, then he hangs up the phone.

"Date?" I bark at him as I try to reach for my phone, but he dangles it above me. "I am *not* your date, you fucking idiot."

"Calm down," he soothes with that half-cocked smile.

"No woman has ever calmed down in the history of calming down with a man telling her to do so. You are such a fucking idiot," I scream, and people around us stop and watch. They begin to whisper, but I don't give a shit.

Today was a mistake.

"Are you done?" he asks patiently, his eyes never leaving mine.

"No. Give me my phone before I break that fucking nose of yours."

His eyebrows perk up as he whistles. I've never been like this with anyone before, but I'm so fucking mad. I just can't control my irritation around this man.

"I'm sorry," he says, and hands my phone over. I snatch it out of his hand. "Let me take you home."

"Go eat a dick and die," I spit back, turning on my heels and walking the other way.

I'm relieved, if only slightly, when he doesn't follow.

Sometimes threatening to break a pretty boy's nose is effective.

CHAPTER 17

Will

"You fucked that one up." I'm clipped in the back of the head, and when I turn around, Anya is standing there with her arms crossed over her chest.

"What?" I say, shrugging my shoulders.

"You thought you could get her into bed with that stupid game?" Her gaze moves to River, who's stepping out of the restaurant. "And you!" She points to him. "You shouldn't have entertained this stupid game in the first place." She shakes her head before she stomps off to the waiting car.

"Man, you made my wife mad," River says, although I can tell he's amused.

"To be fair, I didn't think both of them would be this angry. It was just a little cheek."

He shakes his head. "For someone so smart, you're really dense when it comes to women. Maybe more so because you don't know how to deal with them outside of fucking them."

My phone buzzes, and I see it's my sister. I ignore it. "That might be true, but I'm certain I can win the next bet."

River looks at me in disbelief. "I don't think you have a second plane to spare. And besides, I don't think she's going to play that game twice."

I casually shrug. "So I let her choose the guy next time."

River laughs. "You're out of your mind if you think she'll fall for that a second time. And it's not as if you would let her take any other man's number anyway."

I'm quiet for a moment as his words sink in. Alina and I aren't anything. But neither would I let her go home with another man. Would I? It shouldn't affect me. So why does just the thought bother me so much?

River's smiling now. "Grovel, my friend. It's all you have time for. I'd watch that one, actually, she was pretty smooth. Good luck with her ever speaking to you again."

"Fuck off." I flip him off and he laughs.

"Anyway, now I gotta suck up to my wife because she's mad," he says as he waves and heads to his car.

I watch as he gets in, and they drive off just as my phone starts buzzing again.

Maria.

Fuck. I approach my car that's waiting at the curb. I know she'll continue calling until I answer. Persistence is the one thing we have equal footing on.

I sit in the back of the car but don't offer my driver direction as I answer my phone.

"What do you want?" I huff into the phone.

"What do I want?" she asks, flabbergasted "What did you do?" she screams. "I warned you to not fuck up my relationships with my friends. Why are you even hanging around Alina? I thought you went to New York for work."

"She's a paid contractor working for my friend. We run into one another from time to time."

"And she is *my* friend," she warns. "I'll tell Mom. Is that what you want? Me to go and tell her you're trying to sleep with my friends?"

"I did that once."

Shit, maybe more than once.

But who's counting?

The juvenile threat of dobbing on me to my mother shouldn't be as effective as it is. But the truth was we both adored our parents, and no one could be more relentless than my mother. It'd only cause more of a headache as she theatrically claimed she raised a brute of a son.

"And are they still my friends?" she asks pointedly.

"I don't know, Maria." I sigh. "But do not go to our mother." The last thing I want is her badgering me as well. My mother looks at me differently these days. Like she pities me. I don't need to add ammunition to cause her to worry about me more, or worse, to try to convince me to come back to London; she has tried that already.

"Well, stay away from Alina."

I'm surprised when my phone beeps to indicate another call. I check the screen and see Alek's name. It's not too often he calls.

"I haven't slept with her anyway. I have to go, work and all. Don't worry, I'll make it up to Alina."

"No, you stay away from her, Will," she demands.

"Love you too," I say, hanging up and answering Alek's call.

"Aren't I Mr. Popular today? It's not like you to call me. You must've really missed me," I tease as I bring up the tracker I put on Alina's phone. I'd be the furthest thing from a gentleman if I didn't make sure she got back to the hotel safely.

"Do you answer your phone like that all the time?" Alek asks, irritated.

"You're special to me," I say, and I can just imagine his jaw ticking.

"I need you to find someone for me," he states.

My eyebrows perk in surprise. It's not often Alek calls upon my services. For the most part he's efficient enough on his own.

"I'm kind of between jobs at the moment and staying in New York for a bit," I tell him.

"Between jobs?" He sounds shocked. I suppose that makes two of us considering I've never taken a break. "I'll pay you double. It's local, but I need the person found within a day."

A challenge. I do like challenges. And local... it's tempting.

"Why can't you find him yourself?" I ask, curious now.

Alek is silent for a moment. Without his body language to read, I simply wait until he's a big boy and uses his words. "I haven't found him yet. But it's Lena's birthday in two days and I want this guy dead."

"Ah." I click my tongue. "Can't be late for wifey's birthday." I laugh, knowing how much it pisses him off. But the truth is, as I say it, it brings up something uncomfortable in my own chest.

It reminds me of my previous life, of things that were precious to me before they were taken away. Suddenly, nothing seems funny anymore.

And I'm left with the dire realization that I seriously fucked up with Alina.

"Send me the details. I'll find him for you."

I watch the pinpoint of Alina's tracker. I can't dispute her accusation that I'm an asshole. And perhaps I should give it a little bit of time before I grovel.

Grovel? Me?

I try not to laugh at myself.

How the fuck did I end up in this situation when I haven't even fucked this woman yet?

CHAPTER 18
Alina

Monday can't come soon enough. I was even more furious with Will by the time I returned to the hotel, and no matter how much I tried to lose myself in work, I was constantly distracted by the thought of him.

I toss and turn for an hour, trying to get to sleep with no luck. Frustrated, I kick off the blankets, throw on some jeans, and put my hair into a messy bun before taking the elevator down to the lobby and stepping out onto the street.

The air is refreshing, and I pocket my hands in the hoodie I'm wearing. I just need a walk or something. It's not like me to get so bothered by some guy. So why am I now? I round the corner and step into the convenience store.

I don't know exactly what I'm looking for, but I'll know it when I see it. I'm scanning the chocolates when my phone pings. I open my emails, and a cold shiver runs over my skin.

A new email. A simpler message this time.

You stole from me.

I swallow as I delete the email as if I never saw it.

That's two emails in two days when I haven't heard from them in months. I internally curse as I close my eyes and push away all the imposing thoughts. What if they found me? I thought it was all behind me now.

I grab a chocolate bar with caramel in it and continue down the aisle.

It's close to midnight, so there's only a few customers. I walk past the cosmetics section and pause as I look at the red lipsticks. I look around, noticing that I'm alone. I discretely look up at the ceilings and don't see any cameras.

My fingers curl around the lipstick, and my heart

pounds with the thrill and thought of pocketing it. It's an impulse. A need. A want.

It'd be so easy too. It always has been.

As a child I learned I had a knack for taking what wasn't mine, as a teenager and even in my early adult years it became an impulse. I'd never been caught and I close my eyes and try to push away the thrill. That was the old me. Part of my past and what haunts me now.

I take the lipstick and round the corner. When I approach the counter, I place the chocolate bar on the counter followed by the lipstick. The cashier absentmindedly rings up the items as I stare at the lipstick. When was the last time I wore red? Why did I stop?

I've worked so hard to get to where I am now, and I refuse to let my demons catch up with me. Once I'm done with this job, I'll go back to London, because being back on American soil doesn't feel entirely safe.

These emails might just be harassment. But I can't help but be paranoid that it'll become something more. And I'm not willing to risk everything I've built being ruined by the same man who ruined me all those years ago.

CHAPTER 19
Alina

It's nearing the end of the day and I'm absolutely buzzing as I go back and forth among the construction workers. I'm in a small office that's going to be the last room they touch. I look over the plans, impressed. I can't wait to see this come to life.

Jerry, one of the workers, pops his head in. "Miss, there's someone here to see you."

"Is it the tiler?" I ask, looking at my watch. I wasn't expecting him until Tuesday.

Jerry shrugs. "I don't know, he just said he has to see you."

"Okay, no problem. I'll be there in one second." I scan my reflection in my laptop screen and quickly adjust my ponytail. I admire my red lipstick, appreciating the new purchase, and take one last sip of my coffee before I go out onto the shop floor. Chaos is erupting around me as men busily work away.

I come to a stop the moment I see Will standing at the door. He looks out of place in his freshly pressed attire considering all the dust and dirt fluttering about him.

This guy has got to be kidding me. I stalk up to him, and his arrogant smile pops that dimple into life. "You haven't replied to my text messages."

I grab him by the elbow and usher him out to the front of the store, where there are fewer workers. The moment we step outside, and the door closes behind us, I snap at him.

"Can you leave me the fuck alone?" are the first words out of my mouth. I could throttle him. And had I not met him before, I'd be in absolute disbelief by his sheer audacity at being here right now.

"Alina," he drawls arrogantly.

"Wow, it seems like you've finally remembered my name with that one brain cell of yours," I say with a vicious smile. "Now, leave."

The door opens, and the contractor who I'd been speaking to ten minutes ago, starts to speak but stops when he notices the way Will and I are facing off.

"He was just leaving," I tell the contractor.

"No, I wasn't, and we're not done," Will argues,

and there's a threatening edge in his tone that catches both me and the contractor off guard.

"It's not urgent, miss, I can wait inside," the contractor says in a thick Boston accent and all but runs back inside.

I turn on Will with my finger in his face. "You can't just show up here. This is my job, and you need to kindly fuck off. Whether these are your friends or not, it doesn't give you the right to piss me off whenever you please."

"Alina, I came to apologize."

I try not to laugh as I place a hand on my hip. He's deadly serious now. "For what, exactly? Humiliating me? Almost getting me killed? Because I'm pretty sure Anya is capable of it. Stalking me? Pissing me off every chance you get? Interrupting me at work? Shall I continue?"

"It's a rather impressive list, isn't it?" Will acknowledges.

I throw my hands up in the air, exasperated. "Can you take anything seriously?"

"I'm taking *you* seriously," he says, and it catches us both off guard. He frowns at what he just said. "Come on. I know as much as I piss you off you also enjoy the challenge. I know that despite it, we have fun, don't we? Please let me make it up to you."

I shake my head in disbelief. I don't know why he's so focused on me, and yes, it's flattering; yes, I do like the challenge. Yes, we're sexually charged around one another, but I can't make out what this connection is exactly. I know there's depth to Will despite him hiding behind his humor and wit. I know this well because he's not the only one who hides behind a mask and keeps everyone at an arm's length. And it's that intrigue making me want to discover more about him, to unravel him as much as he's probably trying to figure out me, that's the problem. What if I'm wrong? What if there is no depth and I'm wasting my time?

That startling realization brings me to a halt. Because why do I care about his layers? wasn't it only physical attraction and a little banter and fun before he stepped too far?

I have to cut whatever this is here and now. I already have enough to think about without my friend's brother chasing my skirt. "Thanks for the apology, but no, thank you."

"How about another bet?" he suggests.

My mouth falls open in shock. I clearly didn't hear him correctly, right?

Did he just suggest another bet?

He's either deadly serious or absolutely trying to

get another bite out of me. And it works. Every fucking time.

"So you can rig the next one too?"

"Nope. You pick the terms and the prizes this time. And I'll play along like a good boy."

"How would that benefit you? Win or lose, I could choose that you fuck off either way."

"I think you'll be fair. I mean, my prize should still stand. You let me have you for one night. And for yours, you pick what happens if you win."

"Not if, *when*," I correct him.

Damn, I just played right into his game.

I hate that I'm so competitive.

I hate that I want to play any type of game with him.

I just can't shake him. Is it just sex? Is that what we need to do to end this? Just fuck already?

That's when a car pulls up to the curb and Dawson and Honey climb out. Honey is carrying a bag of what looks like baked sweets.

"Well?" Will asks.

"You need to leave. I have work to do. And shouldn't you be chasing someone down and getting your bounty money somewhere or something?" I wave him off as Honey approaches me. I ignore Will as he and Dawson begin talking.

"Why does it look like we just walked into something we shouldn't be a part of?" Honey whispers as we enter the shop.

I sigh, exhausted and somewhat perplexed. Honey has been very vocal about becoming friends, but I don't know where to draw a line since I'm working for both her and Dawson. But it's the same feeling I have with Maria, that it's an immediate friendship and surely they know more about Will than I do being his friend. She's already prodded me so many times about what's happening between us, and I want answers, too. Why is he so persistent? But I don't want whatever is happening between Will and me to ruin this gig for me. "He just won't leave me alone," I tell her with a casual shrug, trying to probe casually. When she looks over her shoulder, he's staring at me while still in conversation with Dawson.

"Looks like he doesn't intend to leave you alone. He seems mesmerized." She laughs. "These are for the workers, by the way. I made them fresh today for everyone."

Jerry is walking past when I tap him on the shoulder and point to the baked goods. His eyes go wide as he happily takes them from Honey and whistles to the other guys working. I've never seen men stop so quickly, and they meet in the middle of the room to look through the bag.

Honey seems pleased with herself.

"I didn't know there was anything between you two before he recommended you to redesign the shop," she quietly whispers.

I roll my eyes. "There is no us. And I don't know why he won't leave me alone. Yesterday he almost got me murdered by a beautiful Russian woman. I've never been more terrified in my life. If looks could kill, I'd be dead."

"You aren't talking about Anya Ivanov, are you?"

My head whips around. "Do you know her?"

"Of course. And if Anya wanted you dead, you would be dead without a doubt." She pauses, raising a brow. "What did you do?"

I scoff and head to the back of the shop so I can get farther away from Will. I'm somewhat reluctant to speak with Honey since her husband hired me, but she also has that immediate "you can tell me and trust me with anything" vibe. Damn her for being so kind.

I lean against the counter and pull out my camera. I take a few photos for my social media before I hesitantly say, "He made a bet with me."

"A bet?" she asks, confused. A few of the men thank her for the baked sweets, and she smiles brightly at them. I have the distinct feeling if her husband saw her smiling at other guys, he'd sack them all in an instant. What is it with these men?

I can't imagine Will being possessive, but then I think about how he spoke to the contractor. I push the thought away, reinforcing to myself that Will and I aren't anything.

I pick a piece of lint off my shirt, then explain, "Yes. You see, I have issues with saying no to things I could win and I also love a challenge." I give my best eye roll. "Anyway, he bet me I couldn't get some guy's number." Her eyes go wide, as if already knowing where I'm going with this. "Turns out he was married."

"You tried to get River Bentley's number and you're still alive?" She laughs, quickly covering her mouth as she tries to stop herself. "I'm sorry, but she's killed for far less."

I don't know if she means in the literal sense, but it wouldn't surprise me. Which makes her one hell of a dangerous woman, and yet I find myself confessing, "I kind of liked her. She went over to Will and tore him a new one."

"Yep, that would be Anya. River and Will have been friends for a long time."

"Of course they have." I sigh. He must've planned the bet the moment he spotted River at the bar.

"I don't know Will too well, but River and Dawson seem fond of him. From what I've heard, he's never taken interest in a woman. Serious interest, that is."

I roll my eyes, because I don't think Will is taking me seriously, at least I hope not because I don't do serious. I'm certain this is just sexual tension we both need to exploit.

I have very mixed feelings regarding Will. I must confess that I haven't had any man try this hard to be with me. It kind of gives me a small boost of serotonin. But part of me thinks it's absolutely crazy to entertain the idea of us, and that I should stay as far away from him as possible.

But what could it hurt? He could turn out to be my best lay ever. He could fuck like a god. Hell, he could give me multiple orgasms, which I have a feeling he knows how to do for the simple fact that he made me come with his fingers alone.

That in itself is a hard task. The only way I have ever been able to come prior to our encounter was with vibration on my clit. And yet, this man traps us both in the tiniest bathroom and manages to do it all within five minutes—with only his fingers. So yes, there is a small part of me that wonders if I should lose this bet. I would be stupid to give him that power over me.

But I think it's a game I want to play. And I may very well lose on purpose just to get him away from me —or better yet, on top of me.

"I can see you thinking. You like him," Honey says.

"No. No, I don't," I reply, baffled as to how she even came to that conclusion. She hums as her husband walks in, and I notice Will has finally taken a hint and left.

"I hear you've met almost everyone," Dawson says, and I sag in defeat. It's becoming rather difficult to keep the professionalism here. Will gossips just as much as any woman. Even though I'd just been doing the same.

"He told you about River and Anya?" I clarify.

"Oh, he sure did. Interesting, really."

"I don't think 'interesting' is the right word. Stalker might be the right one though."

"Some of the greatest love stories start off with stalkers," Honey gushes.

"You read too many romance books," Dawson says, putting his arm around her waist and scanning the space.

"I feel like I see him every day since he's at the same

hotel," I say absentmindedly as I flick through the photos I just took.

"Really?" Honey sounds surprised.

I look up and see they both have puzzled expressions. I thought they knew since they paid for my hotel.

"Yep. He apparently has access to open my room too," I tell them, shaking my head.

Honey bites her bottom lip, and she and Dawson exchange a look.

"What?" I ask, not understanding what I'm missing. I feel guilty now. I hope they don't think I'm ungrateful for them paying for my stay.

"He seems like he's got it bad," Honey says, then waves it off and goes on. "Well, anyway, if you'd like my old apartment, it's vacant. At least that way you'll have your own kitchen. And it's in a good neighborhood not far from here."

"I couldn't impose," I gush.

"Honestly, I haven't been there for well over a year, so it'll be nice to know someone is using it. Only if that'll make the next few weeks more comfortable for you, that is."

"Ah, sure, if you don't mind. I mean, that sounds really nice, actually."

She clasps her hands together. "No problem. I'll

bring in some keys tomorrow and give you the address. I told you, we're friends now."

Dawson kisses the top of her head almost as if adoring her kindness. I wonder if it's what he gravitated toward at first, but Honey has a charm about her that I imagine is very difficult for anyone to ignore.

I admire what they have.

It doesn't mean I want it though.

No, what I want is hard fucking.

And if I'm checking out of the hotel tomorrow, maybe I should make the most of tonight with a man who is far from sweet and adoring.

It doesn't hurt to have a taste. Only once. Right?

CHAPTER 20
Will

Sometimes in life you just fuck up. I don't normally fuck up. But with her, I can't seem to get it right.

Maybe because she's better than me?

Can't say I've met many people who are.

Yes, I'm cocky.

Yes, I know I look good. But I look good because I take great pride in doing so.

I look after myself to look good, and when I look good, I feel good.

So why is she so resistant to my charm? And why am I so hellbent on fucking my sisters' friend?

I even apologized for fuck's sake.

I'm not clueless about women, but I've never had to put this much effort into them in a very long time.

"Are you just going to continue staring at yourself in the mirror?" Alek asks. I'm sitting in the passenger seat of his car. Because a certain brunette didn't want to speak with me, I made it a condition that I go with Alek in exchange for the location of the person he wanted me to find.

I close the mirror and turn to him. "It's my favorite way to pass time."

He exhales loudly, and it brings a smile to my face. It's just so easy to piss this guy off.

"Here." I point to an old, decaying house. "This is the place. What did the guy do to piss you off?"

He gives me a scathing look, and I shrug. Fair enough. He doesn't want me to know too much about his business. I get it.

"Stay in the car," Alek grits out, and I frown, disappointed.

"Come on. I thought we'd have some fun together. Besides, it wouldn't be the first time I've saved your ass."

Alek steps out of the car, glaring at me as he snaps the door shut. I chuckle. *Whatever*.

When he leaves, I scroll through my recent photos of Alina. At first, I convinced myself it was part of my job, to do a background check on the person with whom my sister was conducting business. But it's beyond that point now; it's my personal obsession. I'm only a man after all. And besides, I remind myself, it's my job to be obsessive.

My phone lights up, and I grimace. This fucker again.

"Mr. Percy. I'm assuming you're calling because you have the rest of my money," I say as I flip open the mirror again and admire myself.

"I told you I'm not giving you the rest of the money until you give me my ex's location," he snarls.

I sigh, irritated, until I see a man running for his life out of the same house Alek just walked into. The man's only wearing his strawberry printed boxers, and Alek is storming out behind him, looking seriously pissed.

He's just lucky this neighborhood is mostly deserted, which is most likely why this guy is hiding here in the first place.

"Are you there?" Jack Percy demands. I didn't even hear what he said before because I'm so fascinated as Alek's target runs toward the car.

I grin as, with perfect timing, I push open the car door and the man slams into it. I then step out smugly, and Alek looks all foreboding and pissed that I ended up helping him anyway.

The man on the ground is disoriented but tries to

get up. I adjust my neck tie slightly as I say into the phone, "You're lucky I'm so generous as of late, Mr. Percy. If you don't have the remainder of my money sent to me in four weeks, we cease communication."

"What about my deposit?!" he demands.

The groggy man on the ground tries to stand back up again. I cover the phone's speaker as I say to Alek, "See, I told you, you need me. I'm quite the handsome sidekick, if I do say so myself."

The glare he pins me with is murderous, until he shifts it to the man at my feet and yanks him off the ground.

"Are you there?" Mr. Percy shouts.

"Yes, I hear you. And that deposit is mine because the work's already been done. You should've figured out a better way to ensure you had the money to receive the goods."

"She has something of mine that is worth ten times more than what I owe you. If I have that, paying you will be easy."

Alek steps behind the man and without remorse or mercy, slits his throat. Blood sprays my shirt and suit coat, and I'm shocked. Not by the fact that I'm almost certain he fucked with my suit but because I swear, I see a glimmer of amusement reach his gaze because he did it on purpose.

"Four weeks, Mr. Percy," I reiterate as I watch Alek drag the body to the back of the car. "Oh, come on, Alek. You can't just dump a body in such a nice car." I sigh. "Goodbye, Mr. Percy."

I hang up and look at my suit. Damn, this was one of my favorite suits too. It's not like it's the first one to get bloody, but because I'm certain Alek did it on purpose, it's now sentimental to me.

The car sags with the weight of the body. Alek adjusts his gloves as he comes around from the trunk. He might not like touching people, but he doesn't seem as concerned when they're dead.

He pulls out a fresh pair of gloves, and I'm shocked as I watch him remove the bloody ones and exchange them. "Wow, I thought your hands would be hideous or something. Well-manicured nails." I applaud.

"Do you ever shut up?" he growls as he throws me a sealed bag. When I peer into it, I notice a clean dress shirt and suit, and I sigh romantically.

"I didn't think we were at the stage of sharing clothes yet. You do love me," I gush jokingly, and he rolls his eyes as he slams the trunk shut.

This is why I enjoy my time with Alek. He's always two seconds away from exploding, and it just so happens that I enjoy playing with danger.

CHAPTER 21
Alina

I'm waiting for him in the hotel lobby.

Call me crazy, but whatever this is between us needs to end. I'm certain the moment we have sex it'll flush out this weird tension we seem to be forming. I've already decided I'll be staying in Honey's old apartment, so tonight might be the last chance to get it out of my system. It might be a mistake, but I'd made plenty of those in the past, so what's one more? Isn't that what life is meant for?

And besides, he still owes me something. If I can use my body to obtain it, so be it.

It's late, and I'm not entirely sure if I want to know what he could be up to at this hour. One thing I'm certain of is that he's always around. Wherever I am, he'll be there.

With serendipitous timing, he walks in looking slightly more tired than I've seen him before. He stops when he sees me, and a slow and steady smirk finds its way to his lips. I don't bother standing, instead waiting for him to come to a stop in front of me. He's changed his suit since I saw him earlier, and there's an electrical charge around us as he looks down at me.

"I could get used to being greeted like this," he says with that single dimple forming.

I stay where I am, pinning him with what he would most likely call a "come fuck me" look. He steps closer, never having issue entering my personal space. It's almost a challenge for him to see how close he can get to me. When the tip of his shoes meet my heels and his cock is at my eye level, I stand and smirk up at him.

"The bet," I say.

"Yes, the bet," he muses as he slowly grabs a lock of my hair that frames my face, even with the rest of it put up in a ponytail.

"You stick to our original agreement and give me the plane, and you can win our last bet. Without having to play again."

"You want the plane?" he asks, seeming preoccupied and fascinated by my hair.

"Yes."

It's as if that snaps the last of his control, because he grabs my hand and pulls me toward the elevators.

"Done," he grits out, and the moment we're in the elevator, he doesn't even wait for the doors to close before he's on me. He pushes me against the wall as he presses the button for his floor, and his lips crash into mine.

My brain immediately short circuits as all inhibition snaps, and I feather my fingers through his hair. My body is on fire as he presses against me. Fuck, I want this. Fuck, do I need this.

He pulls one of my legs over his hip, and I'm already grinding against him, the tease of his very hard cock pressing against his pants. I'm shamelessly using it as friction.

The doors open and, for the first time since we entered the elevator, I can breathe as he pulls away and drags me by the hand into his room, keeping a tight hold on me, as if I'll run.

I may.

But he doesn't need to know that.

I had a few glasses of wine earlier to hype myself up, not for the fact that I'm more than likely going to be sleeping with him but to follow through with it.

Because for all his charm, Will is dangerous. I know that, which is why I've tried to avoid this, even though it almost feels inevitable. And I hope he'll be bored with me once he's had his fix. And hopefully, that works for me, too.

And I really want the plane.

Why?

Because I can, and I want to sell it and open an actual office. Somewhere I can meet clients, spoil my mother, and offer her early retirement, if she wants that. Why wouldn't I seize this opportunity?

When we reach his room, he unlocks the door with one swift movement. His room is slightly bigger than mine but with a similar layout. What does grab my attention is the three monitors and laptop on the desk. He says he's tracker. I say he's a gamer.

The door shuts behind us, and it's then that he drops my hand. As if he finally has me caged. Electricity dances along my skin, and suddenly, everything I'm wearing feels too tight.

At first, we just stand there, staring at each other. I don't know why I'm nervous. I've never been nervous when it comes to pleasing men, but instinctually I know Will is on a completely different level. He slowly removes his jacket, that sensual, arrogant smile kicking up his lips.

"Last chance to back out," he warns.

"I could say the same to you. It's a pretty expensive

fuck, wouldn't you say?" I answer, pointing my nose higher in the air.

"Worth every penny. And besides, I do owe you that plane. You did win the bet," he says as he removes his shirt and then kicks off his shoes. Now he stands before me in only his socks and pants.

He doesn't make a move to touch me, and I stand there, eyeing his body. It's hard not to. It's very evident that he takes great care of himself and how he looks. He's perfectly sculpted. I've seen him without a shirt before, but having him an arm's length away, within touching distance, draws my skin tighter and causes a heated thrumming in my core.

"Can I touch you?" he asks, stepping into my space so we're toe-to-toe again.

"You're asking?" I'm surprised.

I slowly trail my fingers over his chest and land on what looks to be a scar from a bullet wound on his shoulder.

"Yes. I want your permission before you submit to me and scream my name." His gaze flicks down to my curious one. I run my finger over the scar.

"How did you get this?" I ask.

"Alek shot me," he says casually.

"By accident?" *Aren't they friends?*

"On purpose," he says proudly. "I was tracking him for a job and got too close. It's our love bite."

I don't even know how to process that, and I'm not entirely sure if I want to dive deeper into the weirdness of that statement. Instead, I step closer so his hard cock is pressing against my lower stomach, and it curls my toes, thinking of all the things this man can most likely do. "You have a lot of confidence that you can make me scream."

The smirk doesn't leave his face as he reaches for my jacket and pulls it down my arms and then drops it to the floor with a light thud.

"I know I will." His confidence is sexy.

He leans in, and at first, I think he's going to kiss me. But he doesn't; he just moves in so close that I can smell his minty breath on my lips.

"Do you want me to undress you?" he purrs.

"Yes," I whisper, not sure if my hands will shake if I do it myself. I don't know what it is about this man, but he makes me nervous. Maybe it's the sexual attraction. Or the sense of danger he emits. Or it could be that pompous intimidation he carries with him.

He comes up behind me, and I feel him at my back. He doesn't touch me at first, but I can feel his breath on my neck. I wait, as I don't plan to move first. When he finally touches me, it's to pull the tie from my hair, which leaves the locks loose and heavy down my back. Then I feel his fingers on my upper back, where the zipper to my dress is. He slides it down to the top of my ass, revealing my G-string. The dress slips down my upper body to bunch at my waist. He waits a beat before he reaches for my hips and slides the dress to the floor.

When he doesn't speak or move, I glance behind me to see him eyeing my ass. I bite my bottom lip, feeling rather smug.

"Do you plan to stare at my ass all day?" His blue eyes find mine, and I track his movements as he circles me appreciatively and comes to a stop in front of me.

He admires my breasts, which are covered in a matching bra to my G-string. I feel oddly exposed with the way he devours me with his gaze alone, yet it produces a ripple of confidence to wash through me.

"Fuck me, you're better than I could've ever imagined." He drops to his knees in front of me and caresses my ankle. I still have my heels on, and when he gestures for me to lift my leg, I do, surprised when he drops a gentle kiss to my ankle.

Then his kisses start to move up my leg, higher and higher, until my leg is over his shoulder and his mouth is on my inner thigh. My heart is pounding as I watch this powerful man on his knees, and I take in a sharp breath as he reaches my G-string.

He pauses for a moment, then his tongue darts out and he licks me through my panties. When I gasp, he takes that as invitation and moves the material to the side so his tongue can slide between my folds and straight to my core.

I was already wet, but having his tongue there makes me flush with heated desire.

Fuck.

One of his hands is roaming up and down my leg, stroking it as his mouth works wonders between my thighs. I grip my fingers in his hair to keep my balance. His other hand has found its way to my ass, and he squeezes it, hard.

Oh my God.

He suddenly pulls back, my leg dropping from his shoulder and his hands abandoning me. He's staring up at me now, a lethal edge to his blue gaze even when on his knees. I swallow hard as I catch another glimpse of his cock pressing against his trousers.

"Turn around, get on your knees, and press your hands on the floor," he commands.

I do as he says, my ass now display. He kisses my ass cheeks appreciatively before sliding my G-string to the side again and angling my hips back so I'm more bent over. I'm completely exposed to him, and when I look over my shoulder at him, I'm pulled back to pure bliss as his mouth lands on my hole and his finger circles my asshole before pressing in.

I gasp in pleasure, the buildup making me feel too weak to hold myself in this position. His tongue is rapidly licking me, and his other hand moves to my front, where he begins circling my clit.

Fuck me.

I'm certain I'm already soaking wet.

His mouth doesn't stop, moving over me like I'm his last meal, while his hands work magic in a way I didn't know was possible.

I feel my legs start to tremble, but he doesn't stop. No, he keeps going, pleasuring me in both holes, and I only want more and more.

Oh my gosh, he really is good with his fingers, because I'm going to come soon.

The buildup begins at the tips of my toes and slowly moves its way up to where he's eating me out.

Fuck. I try to remember to breathe.

The finger that was in my asshole vanishes, and I moan at its absence until I realize he's undoing his belt and pants. My heart and core are fucking pounding, and he's devouring everything I'm able to give, his tongue unrelenting.

The buildup continues, and I can only focus on my own bliss.

His mouth continues fucking me, and I don't want him to stop. But I can't take this much longer.

"That's it," he says against my flesh. He doesn't rush his rhythm, keeping up the perfect pace. My pleasure is about to cause me to snap in two as my nails curl into the carpet, and I moan as the wave crashes over me. My legs are trembling as he devours me, licking up everything as he continues to finger fuck my asshole.

It takes me a few moments to gather enough energy to stand. Only then does he pull away. When he does, I catch my breath before I turn around to see him pulling his trousers off. I gulp at the size of his large and very hard cock.

"I..."

"Yes, you can call me master anytime you please." He winks and pulls me against him. His cock is pressing against my lower stomach as he walks me backward toward the bed. "Do you want to know how amazing you taste?" he asks, and before I give him an answer, his lips are on mine, his tongue pushing into my mouth, devouring me. As I wrap my arms around him, I'm lost to him, wanting and needing more.

Part of me is terrified, because how could anyone

not be ruined by sex like this? But the moment my mind momentarily drifts away, he's drawing me back into him by being ever more demanding.

I feel the back of my legs hit the mattress as he keeps kissing me.

Wow, he can kiss.

I knew that already, but damn.

His hands are on my hips, his blunt nails digging into my skin. His hands sensually glide up my sides and around to my back, where he unclips my bra. He pulls back and removes it from me, then stares with pure bewilderment.

"Are you enjoying yourself as much as I am?" he asks.

Who even asks that in the middle of sex?

"Tell me honestly," he says, his gaze flicking back up to meet my eyes.

"You're weird. You know that, right?"

"Yes, I guess I do. But, Alina..." He leans in and pinches my nipple. "I'll be whatever fucking weird you need me to be to get off," he states as he presses his hand against my shoulder and pushes me back on the bed.

He climbs over me, and I admire the flex of his muscles as he kicks my legs apart. I look down between us—mostly at his huge cock—appreciating every inch of him.

When he's hovering over me, I wrap my legs around his waist. He smirks down at me, his cock nudging at my entrance. He moves the tip of it up and down, coating himself, soaking his cock in my juices.

"Will," I say breathlessly.

"When you scream, you will call me William," he orders before sliding straight into me to the hilt. My back arches at the contact, and my hands find his shoulders, my nails digging in hard. "That's it, baby, fucking mark me." He slides out and back in again.

I don't hold back, feeling my nails cut through his skin, but I don't stop.

I need this.

As much as he does, it seems.

He moves at a perfect rhythm while his hand disappears between us, and his fingers rub my sensitive clit softly.

Oh gosh.

"Alina."

"Hmmm?"

"You can start screaming now." He picks up speed, removing his fingers from my clit. And as he gets to his knees, he takes me with him, holding on to me and pounding me from the inside.

My hands find the sheets and clench them tightly.

He doesn't stop.

And I don't want him to stop.

"Now," he orders, and the words leave me on command, as if I can't stop them.

"William, fuck."

"That's my girl. Now, tell me what a fucking god I am to your pussy. How you'll come back night after night so I can service her." When I don't speak, he slaps my clit, and I scream his name again, unable to stop myself as I come. He jerks beneath me as he begins to come inside of me, and I can't but help wriggle my hips back and forth, wanting to milk him of every drop. Fuck, this man feels so good. He rolls into me at a lazy pace now, as if we're not yet done with each other.

When I open my eyes, I realize he's watching me. His hand trails down my chest and stomach, and the way he looks at me—as if he worships me—makes me feel powerful.

He pulls out, then stands with a smirk. He saunters to the bathroom, and I can't help but bite my bottom lip. Fuck me, that was the best sex of my life. Not that I'd ever admit that to him. So when he comes back out with a damp towel to clean me up, I put on a sweet smile and ask, "So, when can I get the plane?"

CHAPTER 22
Will

She is lying naked before me on the bed, looking like a fucking goddess.

And my cock starts getting hard again just from staring at her. She's leaning back on her elbows, a smirk curving her lips, as she asks me about the plane.

Fuck, the plane.

"How do you have so much money in the first place?" she asks, sitting up and taking the towel from me. "And so help me God, if you have any diseases, I will find you and chop your cock off myself," she adds, which makes me laugh.

"I don't usually fuck women without protection, so no, I don't have diseases."

"Good. I'm on birth control," she informs me as she cleans herself up.

"Pity," I mutter, and her eyes shoot up to mine and narrow. Because having her milk my cock was the hottest thing I've ever experienced. And for a moment, I considered what it would be like to trap this woman. To feed her my cum until her belly was swollen with my child.

I smirk as I step closer to the bed, amused at her glare. "My tongue can clean you up, if you wish." Those eyes, that were narrowed just a moment ago, open wider, and she hesitates to give me anything to read off. She's a nice girl, a good girl. At least that's what I think until she opens her legs and discards the towel.

Oh boy, she's a bad girl.

So fucking bad.

I waste no time crawling over and burying my head between her thighs. I take one taste and then do it again. A soft moan slips from her lips, and I smile as I lick her again. I could listen to that forever.

What the actual fuck?

Listen to that forever?

Am I fucking drunk?

No, I'm high on pussy.

And do I stop eating said pussy, which is making me delusional?

No. That answer is no.

Her hand slides down to my hair. She grips it and takes control.

Fuck.

Her legs spread a little wider, and I move my hand between her legs and slip one finger straight into her. Her hips start moving faster, and I add another finger. Her hips don't slow down as she rides my face.

Soon, both her hands are in my hair, pulling me in whichever direction she wants me.

I let her.

Because this is all about her.

I knew I would love the taste of her.

But fuck.

I'm eating her pussy like it's my last meal.

And I'm already thinking about when I can have it again.

I'm royally fucked.

As soon as she comes, her hands tighten in my hair. She lets out a scream and closes her legs, telling me to stop, as she pushes my head away. When I sit up, I wipe my mouth, and find her trying to catch her breath, her chest heaving up and down.

"My turn," I say. She smiles lazily and shakes her head.

"No, I think it's time I leave."

My hand falls to my cock, and her eyes follow. I start to stroke it as she gets off the bed, not taking her eyes off me.

I grip my cock harder as she opens her mouth just a little bit before she shakes her head and meets my eyes.

"You don't want to sit on it?" I ask. She shakes her head, but her gaze drifts back to my cock. "Bounce on it, perhaps?" She moves to where I stand at the end of the bed, and I turn so I'm facing her. Her eyes lock on me as she smiles, and I feel her covering my hand with her own. I move my hand slightly so she can touch me. At the feel of her soft palm on my dick, I lean in to kiss her, but she pulls back.

"This was fun," she says as I try to kiss her again. But she leans away, still stroking me. "But it has to end. Thanks for the orgasms. I think I'll sleep well tonight." She releases my cock and smiles before finding her clothes and quickly dressing. I watch as she collects her jacket and goes straight to the door. When she pulls it open, room service is standing there with a bottle of champagne, and her eyes go wide, but she doesn't bother shutting the door as she turns back to me.

"I'll expect a plane tomorrow afternoon." She plucks the bottle of the champagne out of the shocked hotel employee's hand.

"It's a date," I call out after her, and she flips me off, leaving the door open—and the hotel employee still staring at me in shock—as she walks away.

CHAPTER 23
Alina

My phone has been ringing all morning, and every time I look at it, I see his name.

I let it ring.

I don't plan to get up early. I did tell him this afternoon after all. I might have purposefully left out the information that I won't be at the shop today. Since the tilers are starting their work, it means no one but them can be on-site until they're done. Of course, I'm a call away, as I focus on other aspects of the job, but he doesn't need to know that.

Part of me is somewhat curious as to how long it will take for him to realize I haven't left the hotel yet. I do plan on checking out later today before I meet with Honey to get the keys to her apartment.

When my phone rings again, I don't even bother checking who's calling before I answer, as I'm online shopping for certain fixtures I'm going to need.

"I told you the afternoon!" I yell into the phone.

"Alina?" my mother gasps on the other end of the line.

"Shit, sorry, Mom. I thought it was someone else."

"Who got you so mad?" she asks.

"A man." I laugh, adjusting how I'm sitting in bed and moving my laptop to the side.

"Well, I hope he does other things than just make you mad." I smile as I think of the other things he can do... with his mouth and hands and cock, and how very gifted he is with said body parts.

I dreamed of him and what we did.

A part of me wants to do it again. He is by far the best in bed I have ever had.

Maybe his cockiness is actually earned.

I believe so.

But I've been with cocky assholes before, and their game in the bedroom consisted of doggie style, nothing else.

I guess that made them feel macho.

Whatever.

"How is New York? Are you having fun? You're

due to head back to London soon, yes? Do you think you can stop here to see me?"

So many questions.

"Well, I'm staying here longer than originally planned. As of now, I think it should only take me about eight weeks, but I don't think I'll be free to leave for more than a few hours at the moment. I could try to fly you here, if you think you're able?"

"No, I don't want to fly," she's quick to say, and I can hear her throat constrict. She only tried to fly once, as a child. That was the first and last time.

"Okay. I'll try to fly out to see you for a weekend, but I'm not sure when yet."

"That sounds wonderful. I miss you," she admits. "Now, are you going to tell me about this man who's made you so mad?"

"I miss you too," I reply as a knock sounds on the door. "And he's more like a boy than a man. Not much to discuss," I add as I absentmindedly get up, wearing only a baggy shirt over my G-string. It's long enough to cover me, so I'm not too concerned about answering the door to get the coffee I ordered from room service. But when I pull open the door, it's not room service greeting me but Will, and he's in a suit.

"I think I should be part of the debate as to whether I'm a boy or man, wouldn't you agree?" he says with an arrogant smirk and if it were anyone else I might've been embarrassed that he heard that last part through the door. "Ready to collect your plane?"

"Who is that?" my mother asks.

"No one, Mother," I tell her before I place my hand over the speaker to hiss at Will, "I said afternoon."

Ignoring me, he looks at the phone, and his brows pinch before he reaches forward and takes it from my grasp.

"Hey!" I trying to jump up and grab it, but there's a significant height difference between us today now that I'm not wearing my heels.

"Hello, Mrs. Harper, it's lovely to meet you. I'm William, the gentleman your daughter is seeing."

"Like hell. I am not seeing you," I bite back, but he chuckles as he pushes out of my way so I can't reach my phone.

He raises a brow and pointedly says, "You're in front of me; therefore, I see you." He winks and listens to whatever it is my mother says, then smiles. I try wrestling him to steal my phone back.

That's when I notice his phone in his back pocket, and I swipe it.

He doesn't notice at first. They never do.

That is until he turns around and I'm holding it

in front of him. His eyebrows raise appraisingly as I take a few steps back and toward the bathroom. He follows me each step, his smile growing wider as I open the toilet lid and dangle his phone over the bowl.

He now wears a face-splitting grin.

"Give me my phone back. I imagine it'd suck if you had to buy a new phone and redownload all of your little games on here, wouldn't it, gamer boy?"

He chuckles and leans against the doorframe. "It was lovely to speak with you, and yes, I would love to accompany Alina out to visit you. It would be my pleasure."

Fucking hell.

But he hands my phone back to me as he quietly says, "You have no idea how much money has been invested in that phone for tracking, not gaming."

I don't trust him as I slowly pluck my phone out of his fingers, and he catches my wrist as I go to drop his phone into the bowl anyway. I bite on my lower lip as I step into the shower, as if the glass might protect me from him. He's smiling as he pockets his phone again and watches me like a predator toying with its prey. It creates goose bumps all over my skin.

I pointedly say into the phone, "He's not coming, Mother."

"Oh, darling, it's been so long since you brought a man home." She pauses. "Bring him."

"Goodbye, Mother. I'll talk to you later." I hang up and look him dead in the eye.

"Do you really think that shower door will keep me away from you?" he asks, his gaze roaming over my body.

"Room service," someone calls out from the hallway, and I remember that my door is open.

I open the shower door, and he chuckles and steps to the side as I walk into the bedroom and toward the front door. He admires my ass as he says, "I should give you one of my shirts to wear. I hear that makes a man's cock as hard as a rock, though it's pretty hard just seeing you in this." He nods to my shirt.

I really hope the guy delivering my coffee didn't hear that.

I thank and tip him before I close the door and shoot a smile at Will. "It's my ex's," I lie.

"I can cut it off, then," he growls, stepping closer. I move farther back, pressing against the door.

"Or you can leave," I tell him as I casually sip the coffee. But fuck me if my pussy isn't pounding in anticipation over what this man can make me feel. "We agreed to one time."

It's hard to ignore his imposing presence when I

just want to rip his clothes off. But if I do, then I might not get the plane. It still blows my mind that he might be serious about handing it over, but neither do I think he's a liar.

"Is that what you really want?" he asks, leaning in so his breath caresses my neck. "For me to leave?" I bite the inside of my cheek to stop myself from saying no. Because I would very much like him to throw me on the bed and have his way with me.

"Get dressed. We'll go see the plane and do the paperwork," he says, then grabs the top of my shirt and tears it straight down the middle before he turns, letting it fall from my body to the floor. I'm shocked, standing there in my G-string, as he offers an arrogant and appreciative smile before stepping back and opening the door, basically kicking me out of the way so he can leave.

What an asshole.

But my heart is still pounding from how fucking hot that was.

This man is as terrifying as he is beautiful and insufferable.

CHAPTER 24
Will

I rest my hand on her knee, gliding my thumb up her inner thigh as I let her work. I'm driving us to meet with my lawyer, who I've spent all morning with, putting all my affairs in order.

She's been reading the same page on her tablet for the last five minutes, and I'm certain it has something to do with my thumb that continues rolling over her jeans, but she doesn't say anything, as I'm on speaker with one of my men.

Tracking is how I made my fortune, but it doesn't mean I haven't invested my wealth in other avenues of businesses all across the world. This particular venture is based back home in London.

I don't often deal with issues personally, since I've hired the right people to handle things for me, but because of a recent fire that burned one of my buildings to the ground, we have to go over some finer details.

Being completely honest, I'm only half listening, as the only thing I can focus on is how good Alina's pussy tastes. By the time I've finished with the call we've already reached the airstrip.

"You've been staring at that same page for a while. Eavesdropping on my call?" I ask with a smirk.

"No. But... isn't it serious that one of your buildings burned to the ground?"

I shrug as I stop on the tarmac. "Not really. No one was hurt, and I just put more money in for it to be rebuilt. Worried about my fortune, love?"

She folds her arms over her chest and looks away. "You wish. The only thing I care about is you holding up your end of the bargain."

I can tell she's still doesn't believe I'll go through with giving her the plane. I may be many things, but a liar I'm not. And I'm curious as to what this little vixen plans to do with it.

"Shall we go transfer the plane into your name, or would you like to bounce on my cock again?" I ask, readjusting myself. Her gaze immediately drops to my cock, and she bites her bottom lip before looking away. I chuckle, loving the way she can't help herself. She's attracted to me just as much as I am to her, and I thought last night would be enough to get her out of my system. But I haven't had nearly enough.

I step out of the car and go around to her side to open the door. I offer my hand, and she seems hesitant to hold it but does. We walk toward the airstrip's office, where I know my lawyer will be waiting.

When I spot him, I don't drop Alina's hand.

"You have the contracts?" I ask my lawyer, who stands to attention and adjusts his suit when he sees us.

"Yes. Strange requests, but it's all here," he says, pointing to the papers. The moment Alina walked out of my room last night and I jacked off one more time when she left me high and dry, I called him to put him to work on this immediately. Black rings circle under his eyes as he pushes the contract across the table. I've already gone over the virtual copy, and so I pass it to Alina.

We haven't even sat down and she's already wide-eyed.

"The plane is yours." I nod to the paperwork. "Sign it and it's a done deal."

She licks her lips as she takes a seat. "Are you really giving me your plane?" She looks between me and the lawyer, and I smirk as I take a seat beside her. She pushed for this, and yet is in disbelief that's happening.

I lean in and whisper, "Yes. A bet is a bet. But I'm not against earning brownie points, and perhaps that sweet pussy of yours milking my cock again."

The lawyer clears his throat. "I'll remove myself for the time being while you go over the contract together."

Alina's cheeks are bright red as he leaves. "Why would you say that in front of him?"

"Because I can, Alina, and I don't care. The only person I focus my attention on in this room is you."

Her breath hitches, and I notice how uncomfortable she is. She always resists me if I say things like that. And I like how it makes her squirm.

"Can you afford to give me this plane? If this is going to make you broke or—"

I laugh and pout. "I could easily afford twenty of these. I can see you second guessing yourself. Are you telling me your pussy isn't worth millions?"

Her cheeks go red again, as if we still have an audience.

I lean toward her, guiding her hand and pen. "All you have to do is sign." She smells good and fuck me if it's not tempting to fuck her all over again. "You know your worth. Don't second guess it again," I tell her in a hushed tone.

"I know my worth." I see the spark and challenge

coming back to life in her. "But I'll read the fine print first, thank you very much."

I smirk. "Please do. I'll wait."

As she reviews the contract, my phone begins buzzing in my pocket, and my forehead crinkles at the name that appears on the screen.

"I just need to take this call," I tell her, then step out of the room and wave for my lawyer to go back in, in case she has any questions.

I might've been okay with answering the previous call in the car, but this one has no place for Alina overhearing.

When I'm outside, I answer the call. "Thomas, this is unexpected. What's it been, seven years?"

"William. I need your help," he says breathlessly. "My daughter's gone missing."

My stomach drops at the frantic tone of my old colleague's voice. He's the only person from my past I'd answer a call from because he was the only person who helped me back then. But it isn't enough to motivate me to leave Alina's side. I'm determined to see this through.

"Have you gone to the local authorities? What have you done to search for her?" I ask, because Thomas was effective in his own way at hunting people down.

"Please, Will. I can't find her. It's been a week. I'm begging you." His voice cracks.

"Are you sure she hasn't run away? People go missing all the time—"

"Don't you dare recite the stats for disappearances to me. Come on, Will, please. You, of all people, know what it feels like to lose a loved one. I'm calling in the favor." My heart sinks as he brings back my demons. Of ghosts, I've been running away from for so many years.

But I also remember the insufferable desperation to find them before it's too late. And sometimes—more often than not—it is. I lick my lips and look back toward the building where Alina waits for me.

"Please, Will. You're my last resort. No matter your price, I'll pay it."

I know Thomas doesn't have the money to pay my rates, but he is one of the few to whom I owe a sliver of loyalty because he was one of the few who was with me back then.

"Send me all the information you have so far," I say.

"Thank you, Will. Thank you." He chokes on a sob, and I grind my jaw, listening to the tears that are about to break this man who was never moved by much.

I hang up and fight back the ghosts of my past. Of a woman I once loved, who was taken from me far too soon.

Why now is she coming back to haunt me when I've been able to outrun the pain for so long?

I pocket my phone and walk back into the office. My lawyer and the plane salesmen are smiling and chatting idly with Alina.

She notices immediately when I enter. "Are you sure you can afford this before I sign on the dotted line?" she teases, and my lawyer coughs in shock. He knows too well what I can afford.

Her expression changes when I produce a dimpled smile. "It's all yours, love."

She seems perplexed, and I imagine it has much to do with my changed demeanor. But once I'm given a job, I'll stop at nothing to find my target. Especially this one.

She signs the dotted line, and I turn to the salesmen. "Done. Show her the plane."

"There's no need," she says, raising her hand to stop them. "How soon can you sell it?"

"S-sell it?" my lawyer stutters, shooting me a look.

"It's her plane." I shrug, amused and not at all surprised.

"And how quickly can you sell it?" she demands.

My phone begins buzzing, and information threads through from Thomas.

I grimace as I step up behind Alina and kiss her on top of the head goodbye. She seems surprised but equally suspicious, and I simply explain, "I just got a new job. I'll have my driver pick you up and return you home. Sorry, I can't drive you myself."

"That's fine," she replies, perplexed. "I can get an Uber." She twists completely in her chair and says in a hushed tone, "Is everything okay?"

"Of course." And then I look to my lawyer. "Whatever she asks for, provide it for her."

My phone starts buzzing again, and Thomas's name appears on the screen.

I don't have a good feeling about this at all.

I answer it as I walk out, leaving Alina behind with a bet won and a new plane to sell.

CHAPTER 25
Alina

I haven't seen Will for two weeks, which surprisingly leaves me with mixed emotions and ultimately pisses me off. I knew it was only sex, and that's what we signed up for. It was a stupid bet where I somehow ended up with a plane. But it's the way he left and then up and vanished. Considering how persistent he'd been previously, I thought I'd see him at least one more time.

But I'm not here for Will; I'm here to focus on my project, which is coming along swimmingly. Without Will's presence, I've been able to focus almost every waking hour on it. I moved from the hotel into Honey's old apartment, which I absolutely adore.

I never knew where I'd end up permanently. I was

ecstatic that my job took me to all kinds of places in the world. But a small part of me thought I'd somehow end up in London and living there for the rest of my life. But in Honey's apartment in the heart of New York... I can see myself living right here. I love this place.

While the construction continues in the shop, it gives me time to focus on future projects. I've been sought out by another club back in London, and I'm seriously considering taking the job. I'm inclined to because there's nothing keeping me here after the project.

I've also become close to Honey and Rya in my time here. I'm currently sitting across from them, picking at my lasagna. For some reason, I feel off. I love pasta, and I feel like my funk has everything to do with the fact that I haven't heard from Will.

"Is everything okay?" Honey asks, concerned. Her stomach seems more prominent tonight, but that could be because I haven't really seen her in the last week, with all the heavy construction happening in the store.

I look up, realizing she and Rya are both staring at me. "Yeah, of course" I say, defiantly taking a bite of lasagna.

"You look like you need a night out," Rya suggests,

biting into her lentil salad, and I'm not sure if she's suggesting it more for me or herself.

"And your husband would be okay with you going out on the town?" I ask somewhat mockingly.

Her lips tip up into a smile. "I'm past the days of enjoying clubbing. But to piss my overbearing husband off, I might be so inclined."

We both laugh at her.

"So did you sell the plane?" Honey asks curiously.

I put the fork down and take a sip of my red wine. "Yeah. It was actually a lot easier than I thought it would be. Sold it within a week." The money has since been sitting in my account, and I've stared at all those zeros, thinking about all the things I can use it on. I could never work a day in my life again if I wanted to now, but I have no intention of stopping. I enjoy what I do, but there's a strange profoundness around my future.

I bite my bottom lip and finally build the courage to ask, "Have either of you heard from Will recently?" I don't enjoy inquiring about him, in case they think he means more to me than he does, but it also doesn't sit right with me that he up and vanished right after he literally gave me a plane to sell.

Honey and Rya look at one another. "He's probably on a job. He dips out of contact from time to time. He gets pretty laser-focused."

I can't imagine it. But then I remember how focused he was, giving me multiple orgasms.

Honey adds, "Dawson also mentioned that this is the longest he's probably stayed in one city. He seems to jump around a lot on jobs."

"Why do you ask? Missing the sex?" Rya asks with a provocative smile.

"No," I reply far too sharply before taking a sip of wine, and she chuckles.

I told them Will and I hooked up for one night. I did not tell them how many times that one night. But I'm not really one to overshare my business. Maybe that's part of being an only child. Honey and Rya seem to share everything with one another, and I like seeing how they interact with one another.

They've made me curious about children again. If women this powerful can still maintain their careers and goals and build a family, why do I think the same can't happen for me? If I found a man who was as obsessed with me as their husbands are obsessed with them, I feel like it would be doable. Thus, the weirdness surrounding my sudden fortune. I can literally buy anything I want, and now I'm not really sure what I want.

Not all of us are that lucky to marry someone so head over heels, and I've momentarily fantasized what it might be like to still have their own space from their partners, basically their own identity, and not get lost in their relationship. I've had a lot of friends who, once they get a partner, basically discard everyone around them and only focus on that one person. And to be honest, none of those relationships have ever really worked. So, yes, I want both. Actually, I want it all. I want a man to be obsessed with me, and I still want my own identity. I don't think that's asking too much.

Yet it sounds easier than finding Mr. Right. I internally growl, hating that I'm succumbing to the "Mr. Right" idea in the first place. I'm very much happy on my own, so why am I even thinking about these things?

"Earth to Alina." Honey is waving in front of me, and I look up from my lasagna.

"Oh, sorry." I laugh.

The sisters exchange another glance.

"I'm sure Will is going to turn up soon. He always does," Honey assures with a tentative smile, and it makes me feel uncomfortable.

I don't want them thinking I'm curious about Will, but I also can't help myself from leaning in and asking, "So, like, his tracking job. It's not really dangerous, is it? He just hides behind some screens to find people, right?"

"You two haven't spoken about this?" Rya asks, wiping at her mouth and placing down her fork.

"Will's line of work can be dangerous. Some of the people who hire him aren't always good people. He also gets his hands dirty, the same as Crue and Dawson. He might be a goofball at times, but he takes his job very seriously."

I try to absorb that information. "So, like, theoretically, he could just go missing for a few weeks and never come back?" I ask.

Rya sighs and crosses her arms over her chest. "They all could. It's the world they live in."

"But they're also highly intelligent. The risk factor doesn't get any easier, but you just learn to embrace this part of them as much as they embrace certain parts of you," Honey says.

I want to laugh. I don't know if anyone would be so inclined to accept all of me. Especially if they knew about my past. Who I am today is very different to the woman I was those many years ago.

"You seem to have a lot of questions for someone who's not overly interested," Rya teases.

I smirk and pick up my fork again. "I just want to

make sure we're not on bad terms. You know, after selling his plane and all."

"Can't say Dawson's ever bought me a plane," Honey says with a chuckle as she places her hand on her stomach. "I'm sure Will is going to be back in no time. Until then, you'll just have to get by with your toy."

"Or go out and find someone else to scratch the itch," Rya dares.

"I'm not attached to him." I wave them both off and point my fork at Rya. "And stop trying to use me as a pawn to get your husband all uppity about you hitting a club."

She casually shrugs. "Have to keep it saucy in the bedroom."

Honey gasps. "Oh my gosh, no. As if you two need any encouragement. I spent time with them before Crue gifted me the apartment on the floor below them, and I couldn't sleep because of how loud they were! No wonder you got pregnant so fast," she teases, and Rya nudges her.

"I don't need to hear about keeping it fresh in the bedroom from the woman whose husband auctioned off her virginity."

I gasp and look at Honey, whose cheeks go red. "We all have our things, okay?"

"You can do that?" I ask, intrigued.

"If you step further into this world, your mind will be blown," Honey says with wide eyes, and we all laugh. I can't imagine what it's like to know about all of these things. But what I do know is that, although the fantasy of what they have is impressive, I need to do what I have always done—focus on myself.

CHAPTER 26

Will

Thomas is driving on the outskirts of Los Angeles, following my directions. I look down at my phone and flick through the photos and video footage I have of Alina. I don't like being so far away from her. It's unsettling to live only through my devices to watch her.

Thomas glances down at the phone briefly and clears his throat. He doesn't look like he's slept a wink since his daughter went missing.

"Is that a new target of yours?" he asks.

I lazily smirk. "Something like that." I close the phone, not wanting anything from my past to mix with my present.

He sighs, and it reminds me of how defeated I'd

been those years ago. I'm exhausted, as if I've been sucked back into that vortex.

I'd tracked the car his daughter had last been seen in, and as I look around the sketchy area and what looks like a disorganized scrap yard, a sinking feeling settles low in my stomach.

Thomas pulls over and kills the headlights. We step out of the car in unison, and the scrap yard might as well be a graveyard. There's no security or even fencing, just a random spot where cars have been dumped.

"Let's see what we can find," I say as my eyes adjust to the dark. I slip my hands into my pockets as I turn left and he goes right, looking for the same license plate or make and model of the car I'd given him.

I walk through the random cars until I set my sights on one that might meet the description I have, except this one's been blown out by a fire. I look down and notice the license plates have been removed.

I shine my light on the interior, which doesn't give too much away except charred seats and smoke damage. I stop at the trunk, and I have a bad feeling as I lean over to pick the lock. It pops open, and I cover my nose from the stench that escapes.

My stomach sinks as I look down at the burned-to-a-crisp body. From what I can tell, it was most likely a woman.

Reluctantly, I blow out a shrill whistle and wait for Thomas to track back to me. I don't want him to see this. I know the feeling well, and my jaw grinds that I was too late to stop this from happening.

"Did you find something?" Thomas asks, hopeful. Before I can warn him, he looks in the trunk, and his face twists as he speaks his daughter's name. He drops to his knees as he touches the necklace that hadn't completely melted.

"My baby girl!" he cries, and I take a step back, cowering into my own memories. Of the woman I'd loved and lost and the powerlessness I felt to protect her. "My girl!" he screams, and I don't have the heart to tell him to remain quiet. I'd fight off an army for him right now if it'll give him even a moment to grieve. "Who would do this to you!" He begins to sob.

Whoever abandoned this car tried to leave no loose ends. Had they been smart, they would've dumped it into a body of water or at least not been so clumsy with the body. What I do know is that she deserves a better grave than this.

I leave Thomas for the time being and scour the area. I find what I'm looking for—a tarp covering another car. I undo the plastic sheet and return to Thomas, dumping it at his feet.

He stares at it, confused, destroyed, not really here.

"She deserves to be taken home," I say gently, putting my hand on his shoulder. "She deserves to be properly buried with her family."

He begins to sob again, crumbling under my hand.

I take a deep breath and hold my nose as I pull the body out of the trunk and then lay it down on the tarp, intending to wrap her up. There's nothing dignified about this. But it's the best we can do and the very least she deserves.

Thomas seems in shock as he watches me carry his daughter back to our car. "I told the police, but they didn't believe me at first. They took too long," he says angrily from behind me, and I recognize the pure hatred that fuels him now. Because I'd been there. It's something that still lingers so closely under my own surface. I feel like I'm looking at a reflection of myself.

"I'll find the person who did this to her. I promise you that much."

Because everyone should be found and returned to where they belong.

Some lives are just taken too soon.

CHAPTER 27

Alina

Honey invited me to a small gathering for Dawson's birthday. I considered visiting my mother instead, but with the schedule and changeover of workers on Monday for the shop, I didn't want to jeopardize anything by being out of town in case something happened at the last minute.

Tonight, I decided to dress up, considering Honey and Dawson are still technically my clients, even though they're now also my friends. I've kept most of my relationships to a professional level, but recently I seem to not have much of a choice. Starting with Maria and then Honey and Rya. But I've enjoyed it. I'm wearing a light-blue silk dress with black heels. A small part of me wonders if I'll see Will tonight, but I doubt it. I don't like that my mind keeps wondering about what he's doing and where he is. I insist it's my own paranoia after he upped and left when I won our bet. And definitely not the fact that I've dreamed about his face between my thighs almost every night since.

It's a cute restaurant that I walk into, and when I tell the hostess who I'm here for, she guides me to a private section with a few faces I recognize.

Honey stands up, waving, wearing a flowing pink dress that emphasizes her stomach. She's probably the cutest pregnant person I have ever seen. When I spot her, she sits back down, and Dawson's hand naturally gravitates to her stomach. He's always touching her, not just her belly; it could be her shoulder, her hand, or even her lower back. It's cute even though most of the men sitting at this table are deadly and anything but cute.

I met Rya's husband when I moved into Honey's old apartment. Crue barely looks my way, and I don't take it personally. I've come to realize he doesn't curry favor with many people. His gaze is only ever on his wife. With an exception for Dawson and Honey, at times. He's cold and not overly friendly, but the way he watches Rya is nothing short of uncomfortable because he devours her with his gaze.

I stop short when I see Anya and River. I didn't expect them tonight, but I keep my composure, hoping there's no bad blood with regard to the prank Will set me up for. Either way, I got a plane out of it, so it wasn't all an entirely wasted effort. The Russian beauty is eyeing me as if she wants to chop my head off, but I have the sense she's more like Crue and chose not to take it personally.

I haven't seen Anya since that day, and I gathered from that encounter she's a very powerful woman. I would say she would be someone I aspire to be, but I think I'll still be afraid of her.

"You can sit beside me," Honey chirps as she pulls me toward the chair beside her. The chair on the other side of me is empty. And although it's nice to sit among these powerful people, it's also a reminder of my single status. Something I've never been bothered about before.

"You've met everyone, yes?" Honey asks.

I nod with a smile as I eye the table.

"We were in cahoots to get her a plane. Did the little fucker honor your bet?" Anya asks, and I'm caught off guard.

"He did. I sold it."

The corner of her mouth curves up into a smile. "Apologies my brother Alek and Lena couldn't come tonight. For some reason, Alek wanted to take her on a two-week birthday holiday in France. I haven't heard from either of them since."

River laughs. "I think she's more upset about Lena's disappearance than Alek's."

Anya doesn't respond, taking a sip of her water as a mountain of food is delivered to our table.

"This is River's new restaurant, and he insisted we celebrate here," Honey whispers into my ear. "I've been dying to try it out." She smiles happily as she hums to herself over the food.

I glance up, then freeze, when I see Will walking toward us. I almost forget to breathe because, although it's only been two weeks, I forgot how beautiful he is, especially in his well-fitted suit. The hostess points to our table even though we're obviously the only guests in this part of the restaurant.

"Thought you could start the party without me?" he says with an arrogant smile.

Dawson smirks as River says, "Here I thought you were dead."

"You wouldn't get rid of me so easily," he replies cheerfully, but I can see the dark circles under his eyes. Then his gaze lands on me. I don't know what to say or do.

The table falls eerily quiet, and I can sense the others are looking between us.

"Please don't tell me you two haven't fucked yet," Anya says with an exasperated eye roll and throws her napkin. Will's smile morphs into a smirk.

"Now, Anya, do I ask the last time you took it in the ass? Be pleasant, would you?" Will retorts, his gaze never leaving mine. River shakes his head at them. I'm guessing River is very used to Will's crudeness.

"I am pleasant," Anya says, then turns to me. "Was I not?" The table goes silent, and instead of answering, I reach for my wine glass and take a sip.

"Smart woman," Rya says, her head leaning on Crue's shoulder.

"Don't just stand there. Take a seat," Dawson instructs, and Will does so, happily considering the only chair available is the one beside me.

He's here. And I don't know why I'm feeling all sorts of weird about it. I pretend to be unfazed by his presence as he takes the seat next to me.

He leans in and whispers, "Cat got your tongue, milady?"

"I was enjoying my meal," I say, rather prickly, as I scoop spaghetti onto my plate. I swear I was an Italian in a previous life because I love everything pasta and cheese.

"Your meal for tonight hasn't even started," he

assures, and I snap my attention to his arrogant, dimpled smile.

"Anyway, it was Will's idea for Alina to hit on my husband, and I'm a smart woman, so I'm mad at Will, not Alina." Her gaze falls to him, and I can't help but smile. I'm certain Anya is the type of person who, if you cross her even once, will never forget it. But Will continues to wear that shit-eating grin.

"Come on now, love, don't be mad. I had River first and let you have him," Will says to Anya, intentionally stirring her. She reaches for her glass of water and puts it to her lips, then looks to her husband.

"I'm always yours, darling. No one else's. You know that."

"Pretty little lies," Will says, shaking his head. Honey offers him a glass of red wine. He takes it, and then his gaze is back on me. I swallow, staring back at him. Tingles erupt over my skin and my dress is feeling too tight. I want it off.

Stop. I look away. How can he have this much hold over me? I told him we were only fucking once. That's it. So why am I acting like some feral cat in heat?

Everyone is reaching around the table and talking. I casually listen in on conversations, but my full attention is on the man sitting beside me, who has barely removed his gaze from me since he sat down.

Will leans in, his hot breath ghosting over my shoulder. "You look lovely tonight."

When I turn my head, his lips are close to mine, and I inhale sharply.

He's always been this imposing, hasn't he?

"Thank you," I reply, somewhat clipped. Anyone would think I'm mad at him for not contacting me for the last two weeks. *Am I?*

"Have you missed me?" His hand slides under the table and over my thigh. I try not to make my surprise obvious to the rest of the table.

"I've been busy." Fuck, he smells good. I'm hyperfocused on his hand as it trails over my silk dress and higher up my thigh.

"That wasn't a no." He smirks. I'm conscious of his wandering hand, which is making me all sorts of hungry—and not for food.

His hand pauses for a moment before it continues its path, and I feel powerless to stop him. I don't *want* to stop him. I guess he was giving me a chance to push him away or tell him no, and I did neither of those things.

Suddenly, his hand changes direction and moves down to my knee. When he reaches the hem of my dress, he pulls it up, then slides his warm palm up my bare thigh.

"How long do you think until you're finished with the shop?" Rya asks, and I slam my hand on top of Will's, trying to keep my expression neutral.

"If everything goes to schedule, in about two weeks."

"And do you plan to go back to London?" she asks. He squeezes my thigh a little tighter and ignores my hand as his fingers continue to trail between my legs. I'm acutely aware of the moment he begins to stroke the outside of my panties.

Fuck me, this man wants me to soak this fucking chair.

"Yes, I booked my flight already," I squeak.

"You did?" Will asks, and I turn to look at him.

"Yes, I did." I avoid looking down where his hand is under the table and up my dress.

"Well then, I guess you're coming with me tonight." He pulls his hand from between my legs, offering it to me as he stands. I'm staring at him, confused, trying to avoid everyone else's questioning looks and raised brows. "If we only have two weeks left to fuck, we're leaving now, milady."

"We can't just leave now; we've barely eaten." I roll my eyes at him, then glance around the table. Everyone is waiting for me to answer, and no one seems overly surprised. I forgot who I'm sitting with here.

"Yes, and I would like to eat as well. So, please stand up, and let's get going. I can't continue to slide my hand up your dress under the table all night when I know what's underneath." My cheeks go pink at his words, and Honey chuckles.

How the fuck can I stay after he's announced that to everyone?

I stand, and Will immediately grabs my hand.

"Thanks for dinner." Will waves at everyone before all but dragging me out of the restaurant.

CHAPTER 28
Will

The minute we're out of the restaurant, I push her up against the wall and my hands are on her. She doesn't stop me and or pull away when my lips smash against hers.

No, she kisses me back—feverishly, hungrily, and demandingly.

Her hands come up around my neck, and she holds on, her bag hitting my back as I assault her with my fucking lips, my body pressed up against her.

Fucking hell, why did I even think I could walk away from this? From *her*?

I can't.

It's impossible.

Two weeks of only watching her through a screen was torture.

"Will..." she says breathlessly against my lips. I lean back, but my body stays locked to hers, crushing her to the wall.

"Yes?"

"Not here."

It's the first time I realize onlookers are gawking, shocked at the show we're putting on.

I couldn't give a flying fuck. I'll have her against this wall in front of everyone if it's the only way to get my taste of her. Then again, as I notice men lining up for the restaurant, I don't like the thought of that.

"Come with me, then," I demand as I grab her hand and lead her to my car, which sits at the curb. The driver doesn't even have time to open the back door because I've already opened it for her, gotten her inside, and I'm circling the car.

When I'm in the back of the car, our lips lock together again, and my hands are all over her in this silky come-fuck-me dress. My cock aches against my pants as she moans into my mouth, and I press my thumb against her jaw as I devour her.

My driver clears his throat from the front.

"My hotel," I instruct him as I go to assault her mouth again, but this time, she laughs and presses a hand against my chest. My breaths heave in and out as she whistles.

"I'm not putting on a show for your driver," she says and shuffles away from me.

I lean back into her space. "You'll, at the very least, stay by my side." I grab her hand and cruelly place it beside my rock-hard cock.

She laughs, biting her bottom lip as she stares at me. "Where have you been?"

I curve a smile. "So you have missed me."

"No," she says defiantly. "But you upped and left after transferring the plane into my name, and I thought…"

"That I left you behind?" I ask.

When she doesn't reply, I realize it's precisely that. Fuck, I want to rip her clothes off right now and watch my cum run down her legs as I mark her.

"I'm busy tomorrow, so don't have high expectations of sleepovers or anything." She scoffs, and I shoot her a wicked grin.

"Albert." I grab my driver's attention. "Whenever and wherever Alina is, if she asks it of you, you drive her to her intended location. No questions asked."

"Yes, sir." He nods. When I look at her, she's shaking her head.

"You're so bossy," she purrs, and this time I realize she likes it.

"But you like it," I tease as I run kisses along her

bare shoulder. She shivers as she leans against the leather of the back seat and gives me better access. My hand is gliding up her dress as I trail kisses down her neck, marking her. *Mine*. Every inch. Her flavor is a delicacy I haven't been able to remove from my memory since the moment I first tasted it.

"Fuck me, you're dinner and dessert all rolled into one," I growl. "Two weeks was too long going without the taste of your sweet pussy."

She sucks in a harsh breath, and I kiss down to her collarbone, my finger feathering at the edge of her panties. Her fingers curl into my hair and she yanks my head back. I laugh at the angle.

"Maybe next time let a girl know when you plan on skipping town, or you will be replaced," she reprimands.

My eyebrows shoot up. "You didn't give anyone else this while I was gone?" I ask, already knowing the answer. I know every place she'd been to these last two weeks.

She pulls back on my hair a bit more, and I laugh as I say, "Noted. You're needier than I expected."

Her mouth opens in shock. "I am not—"

I kiss her. Needing her. Needing this.

With everything that happened while I was gone

and all the memories being brought up, I need to lose myself in her. Even if I'm in town for only one night, I made sure I'd have at least this.

    Her.

CHAPTER 29
Alina

There's an intensity to Will tonight that I don't entirely understand. I have the sense that something happened, but he's using my body, so it's left unsaid. And I get that. I've used men many times before for the same thing. But tonight, it just feels different.

"Maybe I should leave," I say as he holds the door open.

"Why?" He eyes me, waiting for me to answer him, his hand not letting go of mine.

We had sex two weeks ago, and yet there's a charge around us that I've never experienced before, and it terrifies me.

"What are we doing?" I ask.

"We're fucking," he says matter-of-factly.

"But—"

"No buts allowed. Unless you want me to fuck you in the butt." He wiggles his brows.

"Have you ever been in a serious relationship?" I ask, crossing my arms, and even I'm surprised by the question. *Why am I asking him this? Now of all times?* "You just seem... different tonight."

He lets out an exhausted breath, and it's the first time he's let me have a look at the man under the mask. A different side of Will, I doubt very many see. Hell, I wonder if even his sister sees this side of him. He's tired. Defeated.

"Should we get a drink? Is that what you want instead of me having you for dessert?" he asks earnestly.

"Yes, a drink sounds good." I don't know why it's important to me, but I feel like he needs more than just sex tonight. Or am I using that as an excuse for myself? I've thought about him every day since he disappeared, and the moment he steps back into town, I'm all over him. I've never reacted to a man like that. Now I'm asking questions about him.

Who am I?

He adjusts himself and smirks, staring at me as he does it because I can't help but dip my gaze and bite my bottom lip. He steps toward me, and I purposefully take two steps back, taking me outside of the room. Though, staying in here right now is tempting. He chuckles as he closes the door behind him. It's the same room he had before, making me assume he never checked out.

Taking my hand, he guides us back to the elevator and presses the button for the rooftop bar. He seems somewhat entertained as he stares at me and asks, "You really feel like a drink?"

I bite my bottom lip. Well, no. Now I'm regretting leaving the room and not fucking him, but I stick to my guns. "Yes. You gave me a plane and have had sex with me, and I know fuck all about you. All I know is that you have a sister."

"You also know what I do for a living," he counters.

"You're a gamer who plays with his cock all day."

He grins as he steps into my space, and his thumb finds my bottom lip as he studies it, fascinated.

"These lips are going to get you into a lot of trouble one day," he muses.

"Haven't they already?" I whisper breathlessly as I stare into his iridescent blue eyes.

He smirks and takes a step back as the elevator doors open.

It's not too crowded yet, and with the simple wave

of his hand, he has a waiter's attention. Will guides me to an available daybed by the pool where we can look out at the nightlife of New York.

It's colder up here, and when I half lie down he notices the goose bumps on my arms. He leaves and then returns with a blanket and wraps it around me. The waiter walks over with a bucket of ice, two glasses, and a bottle of champagne.

"Your favorite, isn't it?" Will asks as the waiter pops the cork.

I nod and watch the waiter pour it before I say, "Like that. How do you know it's my favorite brand of champagne?"

"Because I'm observant as well as handsome." He smirks as he picks up both glasses and hands me one. But he makes no move to sip from his.

"Be serious with me. You track people. How does that pay so well?" I'm truly curious. "Is that why you were gone these past two weeks?"

His gaze narrows slightly, and again it's strange to see this more calculating side of him. I imagine he doesn't share this information with anyone, so why do I think he'll share it with me?

He twists so he's lying on his side, casually propped up with a bent arm. He reaches over and toys with the ends of my hair. "You really want to know the answers to these questions?"

I hesitate because it feels like it's a loaded gun now. But I've never been scared of much, so I defiantly answer, "Yes."

He cocks a half grin. "Yes, I was gone for two weeks because of a job. My job pays well because my services are in very high demand. I also work for the most brutal and ruthless people in the world, and only those who can afford my fees. I'm the person you turn to as your last resort. I'm even better than the Ghostbusters."

I roll my eyes. "And are you always such a smartass to them as well?"

He chuckles. "Yes. Humor has saved my life many times, and I enjoy it. I see the way people are. I like to study them and learn about them. I always have. I just realized I was better at it than others." He still seems fascinated with my hair, and he has to adjust his cock again. I try to suppress a giggle. Knowing this man is so captivated by me definitely strokes my ego.

"You never thought of becoming a detective?" I ask. He goes quiet for a moment and then meets my eyes.

"I was a detective."

"Oh. And you stopped because…"

"Because I had to find my wife's killer, and my job didn't allow me to get dirty enough."

His words slowly sink in, and I'm frozen in place with shock.

Did he just say...

Clearly, I didn't hear him right.

His wife?

No, way.

"You were married?" I put my glass on the table and then shuffle to my side to mirror his position. He places his drink to the side as well, and he notices my outstretched hand peeking out from beneath the blanket.

He grabs it, his touch feather light as he says, "Yes."

I swallow. Hard. "How long ago?"

"High school sweethearts, married straight out of school. She stuck with me through university until I could find a job. I stayed here in the US for her, though we always spoke about spending some time in London before settling down in the small city she grew up in."

Wow. What the fuck?

"I'm sorry she died," I say earnestly as I rub my thumb back and forth over his.

He smiles, but there's no humor in it. He's uncomfortable. Vulnerable. Perhaps something he hasn't been in a long time. He looks tired. "So am I," he says. "Her death was the reason I began to live in this world."

"What do you mean?"

"River was the one who helped me. I busted one of his warehouses full of guns, but instead of taking him in, I asked for a favor. He got me my first connections, and it grew from there. I eventually found her—well, her body—and then I tracked down her murderers. And, well... you can imagine what happened."

Dead. Brutalized, most likely. This man is deadly under the surface.

"How long has it been since she passed?" I ask quietly. It feels like nothing else exists on this rooftop bar as we stare into one another's eyes with old wounds reopening. And not only his. I feel the weight like it's my own. Of former lives ,we'd prefer not bring to the light.

"Seven years."

Knowing that about him makes me look at him a little differently. I don't know why.

"No one here but River knows about her. Maria knows not to speak of her. It's better that way."

"Can I ask why?"

"It hurts less."

I nod. I don't understand, because I've never been married before or even loved someone enough to want to marry them. But I understand running away from demons.

"I don't know much about death or losing someone you love, but I hope if I die, those who love me will never stop talking about me," I say, and as I do, the world around us goes silent, and his gaze drops to our intertwined fingers. And for the first time, I don't see the happy person I'm so used to seeing.

I see a man who has been broken and is trying to put himself back together.

And I like him more.

"I'm sure anyone who loves you would never forget you, Alina." I didn't realize how much I needed to hear those words. Besides my mother, who would truly miss me? Who have I let close enough to care if I went missing?

"Thank you, Will." He nods, and we fall silent. His gaze flicks back to me. I wonder what type of man he was as a husband. Was he a good one? Was she always laughing?

I want to know all of these things. Yet there's a bitter twist I don't entirely understand.

"Do you plan to ever marry again?" I ask.

"No," he admits. "I loved her, no doubt in my head about that. And I assumed I would never meet anyone as amazing as she was." He pins me with a stare. "But marriage was something she wanted; I never wanted it." He leans back over and grabs his drink, reminding me to do the same. As soon as I do, his hand is waiting expectantly for me to place mine back in it.

"Do you want marriage?" he asks.

It wasn't something I'd seriously considered, not until recently, after watching Honey and Rya. It's inspiring but also something I'm certain happens in fairy tales. But if I met a man like that, I suppose I would want it.

"I think I do." I'm smiling as I say it, thinking of Honey and her happiness. It's all Maria talks about as well. I always thought it was a sign of weakness, but the women here in New York have proven that otherwise.

"I hope you get everything you want, Alina."

It feels kind of... done. Like that's the answer we both wanted to hear.

That what we're doing between us is just that—sex.

It offers me a bitter twist but also a foundation and understanding as to where we stand. He's a man not willing to step away from his past, and I'm a woman only looking at my future.

"I think we can go to your room now," I tell him, finishing my drink and placing it down.

"You needed liquid courage to come back to my room?" That playful side of his is back.

I laugh as I lean over and brush my lips against his. I graze my lips along his jaw and then whisper into his ear, "No, I just feel more comfortable now, knowing there are no expectations."

"Well, I did give you a plane, so I at least want some head."

I laugh, and he cockily grins and pulls me up from the day bed. I grab the bottle of champagne and say in a sing-song way, "I guess we'll see what we can manage."

CHAPTER 30
Alina

I'm pinned against the door before it even shuts behind us. His mouth is on mine, his hands curving over my figure and crumpling the soft fabric of my dress. I'm arching into him, my body an absolute whore for his touch. The only thing keeping me in this room is him, as I focus on his every touch and demand.

The bottle of champagne slips out of my hand and falls to the floor, but he ignores it; he grips my ass and lifts me. I wrap my legs around his waist, and he carries me to the bed.

We pull away from each other momentarily to appreciate one another. His beautiful blue eyes, a raging storm of desire, stare into mine, and that cocky smile forming a dimple makes me want to slap him for it. But not until after his head has been between my legs.

He shifts my weight, now holding me with only one arm, as he moves a piece of my hair out of my face. "Fuck, you're beautiful."

My heart skips, and I hate the way it twists a new sense of unease within me. Because flattery like that should only be sexual, it shouldn't make me feel any type of way. Especially after the conversation we just had.

"You still talk too much," I say as I lean down to kiss him. My manicured nails dig into his cheek as I bite and pull on his bottom lip. He chuckles as he throws me onto the bed. I jolt under the force, but before I can adjust myself, he's on his knees with his head between my legs.

I arch over him as his mouth remorsefully attacks my clit through the fabric of my panties.

"Fuck, I missed this sweet pussy," he purrs as he pushes the scrap of material to the side and his tongue strokes me. I sigh in relief, and anticipation swarms in my core. No matter how many times I've masturbated and fantasized about the first time, it's not as good as the real thing.

This man knows how to use his tongue. My fingers rake through his hair as I push him closer to me, demandingly and hungrily. He chuckles as he inserts a finger. "You're awfully greedy tonight, milady."

"Keep calling me that and I won't let you taste this sweet pussy ever again," I say as I shove his face back to work.

For once, he doesn't have a smartass comment. He just busily goes to work, eating me out as God intended for him to do. He inserts another finger, and I'm shamelessly rolling my hips into him, looking for the high of my next release.

He lifts a hand to my tit, cupping and twisting it through the light feeling fabric of my dress. I arch into him, in utter bliss, as he continues pumping his fingers into me. It's great, but I want more. I want *him*.

I open my eyes and adjust myself slightly. "I want you inside of me."

He pulls away with an arrogant smile. "If we're making requests, I want my cock in your mouth."

I bite my bottom lip and come to a sitting position. I edge the tip of my nail under his chin. "That's a special service."

"I think I'm a special kind of guy." He stands from his knees to his full height, towering over me, and I can't help but stare at him. This man is infuriatingly sexy.

"Take your dress off," he orders as he begins to

undo his shirt. My gaze dips to the bulge pressing against the fly of his pants, and I swallow hard. Expectantly. I get onto my knees and then slip off the bed. We stand, staring at each other from across the bed.

I watch as his hands trail down his buttons, my pussy still pounding from being denied an orgasm. But I want it when he's inside of me instead of his tongue. I unzip the back of my dress slowly, knowing it's torture for him.

The dress falls to the floor just as his shirt does.

"The bra and panties," he orders.

I arch an eyebrow. "How about you remove the pants first?"

He flashes an arrogant smile and takes off his pants. I admire the view, the bold muscles flexing as his suit trousers hit the floor. His eyebrow raises in challenge as I take an appreciative glance at the hard, veiny cock pointing in my direction. Fuck, I'm hungry for him.

I unclip the back of my bra and then easily slip the G-string to the floor. I go to step out of my heels, but my ankle gives out, and I bump into the desk with all the monitors.

He's across the room within seconds, catching me so I don't hurt myself. I internally laugh at myself. That is until I hear a woman moaning. I freeze as I look over my shoulder.

Was he watching porn before he left? When I see what's on the monitor though, I'm shocked to realize it's not just anyone. *It's me.*

In this very room. I spin on Will in shock as I realize he filmed us when we had sex here last time.

"What is this?" I demand. I'm in disbelief as I watch us entangled within one another. I moan on the screen again, and I'm both mortified and mesmerized as I watch him eat me out as he strokes himself.

I turn back to Will, who casually shrugs. "You did tell me to go home, play my games, and play with myself. So I did."

My eyebrows furrow. I should hate this. Be shocked. But the pounding in my pussy hasn't stopped. "Do you record all the women you bring back here?"

His naked body presses in behind me, and I can feel his cock push against my inner thigh.

"I don't bring anyone else here, Alina," he says as he kisses my shoulder, spreading a fire down my arm.

I should hate this, shouldn't I? But I can't look away.

"This is illegal, you know?" I say breathlessly, but I can't look away. And I'm once again conscious of every part of me he touches.

"Yet you can't look away," he claims as he kisses

down my neck and his cock presses firmer against my thigh. "You're a fucking goddess, Alina. Look at yourself." I can't help but do as he says, watching and hearing us fuck. I keep watching as he lines his cock up against my entrance.

I shouldn't be into this. But I am.

"Do you always record your sexual encounters?"

"With you, yes," he breathes as he points to a camera on his third monitor. His hand curls around my front and begins to circle my clit, and I'm hit with a new wave of pleasure.

"Is it recording us now?" I pant. This is dangerous. What will he do with it? What if someone else sees it?

"Yes. And you like it."

I want to disagree with him, but I can't. My body melts against him. *Fuck*.

His foot kicks one of my legs out and then the other. "Do you want this cock, sweetheart? Do you want to watch us while we fuck? Get off on your own moans and screams as I fill your pussy with my cum?" he asks as he glides the tip of his cock against my folds.

A small whimper escapes me, and I'm at his mercy. I shouldn't let him do this, right? But, somehow, I trust him with this.

This hot, unfiltered, raw version of us on display.

"Say you want my cum filling you up like a filthy

whore. That you want it dripping down your legs so I can stuff you all over again."

"I want—" *You.* The word goes unsaid as his hand moves from my clit to wrap around my throat. His other hand is on my hip as he slams into me. And, fuck me, I feel incredibly full.

He has me pinned in a position where I have nowhere else to look but at the video of us fucking.

He slams into me again, and the sound of my own moan coming from the screen makes me so incredibly wet. I moan in real life as I unapologetically stare at the screen and Will begins pumping me from behind.

"Say you want me to fill you," he growls, and his grip around my throat tightens. Oh, fuck me. I'm already a wet mess.

"I want you to fill me," I say breathlessly.

Yes, I want that.

Yes, I want this.

Yes.

Fuck, I'm so fucking wet. He's slamming into me, and I want to milk him dry. For my pussy to swallow every drop he's able to give.

Fuck, why is this turning me on so much?

I'm confused but on a completely different level to what I've ever known.

"Watch me fill you up," Will instructs, and I see

him on the screen, pounding into me, my legs around his waist.

"Yes, I want you to fill me up," I say, a little disoriented. I'm watching myself be fucked while I'm being fucked, and it's the weirdest and hottest thing I've ever done.

Will's hand trails from my hip to my clit, and he begins circling it, making my toes curl.

Oh fuck.

"I'm about to fill you to the brim. Are you watching, Alina?"

"Y-yes. I-I want it again," I stutter out as I see him thrust into me on the screen. And then I hear myself scream out "William!"

I shatter into a million pieces, bewildered that there was no climb, just a fall straight over the edge.

He's still got me pinned as he thrusts into me one final time, and I can feel him jerking inside me, filling me, as I crash against him in waves of cum. At first, I think I might be pissing myself until I realize, with shock, that I'm squirting.

Oh my gosh.

"See how your body responds to me?" Will asks into my ear. "The way you want my cum to fill you?" He pulls out, and his fingers glide against my folds, rubbing our combined mess into me.

"I want you full of me, and my cock glistening with how wet you are."

I'm shocked, mortified, and not done in the slightest.

I shouldn't want this depravity, but something in me has snapped. This is everything I've ever wanted.

I wrap my hand around his throat as I arch into his fingers that are stuffing me.

"You better be able to fuck me like that again in five minutes, or I'll never see you again."

He chuckles as he presses me against the desk.

"Should I put it on replay, love? Do you want to come to my sweet nothings all over again?"

"I want you to fill me up again and again and again."

CHAPTER 31
Will

Fucking perfect. All of her was molded and shaped especially for me. I can't get enough of her. All I want to do is repeatedly stuff her with my cum. I want to mark her from the inside. I want to fuck her so much she's filled with my babies.

Am I sick? Probably. Am I twisted? Maybe. But I feel like a depraved maniac as I fuck her. I can't stop. I won't stop. Her ankles are on my shoulders as I slam into her, and she's squirting again. The sheets are soiled, and the room's a mess, and I don't fucking care. I can see my cum all over her inner thighs.

She's a fucking goddess. *My* goddess.

I don't even know what I'm thinking right now.

She moans and cries out, as if competing with herself on the audio and video playing in the background. It's been on repeat. She's greater than any of my wildest fantasies. Had she wanted to leave when she saw the recording, I might've let her, but not now. How can I when I know how much she loves it? How much she's thirsty for my own sense of depravity.

Her nails rake down my sides, marking me, as she grabs my ass while I thrust into her again. Her marks are bruising, as if she's keeping me in place so she can swallow every drop of me.

My lips crash to hers, and she whimpers into my mouth as her hips rock back and forth.

How many hours have we been fucking like this for? I release my grip around her throat as I kiss her gently, slowly. Fatigue finally takes hold as I pull away from her, but not before she bites my bottom lip and drags it between her teeth.

She's flushed and exhausted, her hair fanning around her head where it rests on the pillow.

Beautiful.

Perfect.

Not mine, I remind myself.

Her nails release from my ass as I slowly pull out of her. I brief a glance at the clock on the side table and realize it's already past seven in the morning.

What?

"We've been fucking for hours. It's like a

marathon," I say, pressing my lips against her neck and kissing her gently. She chuckles and pushes me away. The sounds of her moans and my grunts on the video still play in the background.

"What's the time?" she asks as she lazily wraps her arms around my neck. I realize I quite like this side of Alina. For all her defenses, smartass personality, and fuckery, her body is made perfectly for me.

"Past seven," I tell her. I go to kiss her again, but she jerks under me.

"Fuck off," she bites out and awkwardly angles to check the time on the clock. "Oh shit." She tries to push me off, but I chuckle as I flip us so she's on top of me in a straddling position. "I have to go. You're an absolute monster." She giggles, and I'm disappointed when the heat of her body leaves mine. But I let her go.

She gets off the bed, and I can still see my cum dripping down her legs when she stands.

Fuck.

"Where are you going?" I ask. She looks over her shoulder, her long hair flowing down her back. Fuck, now I want it tied around my wrists while I fuck her. Again.

"Back to my apartment," she says, slipping her dress on. Pulling her hair back, she ties it up in a bun and looks over to me. "It was nice. Thank you for talking to me as well."

I sit up.

"You don't have to go, you know? I don't have to leave for a few more hours yet." And the thought of that sours my mood. Especially knowing what it is I have to work on. I'd much rather be buried deep inside this spitfire of a goddess.

She shakes her head. "First, you look like you need sleep. You probably should've been doing that instead of fucking for the last eight hours."

"Depends on whose perspective you're looking at it from," I lazily say, sitting naked in all my glory.

She laughs. "Besides, I have to go into the shop for a bit. Dawson has a local paper interviewing him about the grand reopening, and I want to make sure it doesn't look like a disaster. And I need to go back to my place to shower and change first. I'm not walking in there looking like this."

"Like a perfectly fucked doll, you mean?" I ask sincerely. She hides her smile. "And I thought the shop wasn't ready yet."

"It's not, but that doesn't mean it can look like a dump. And besides, we both know what this is. And I can't deny that it's fun, but I still have to work. There are only a few more weeks left."

I sigh, tired by her schedule and not entirely liking the idea of her heading back to London. Especially when I've just discovered how fun she is.

"Have you visited your mother yet?" I ask.

"Not yet, but I'll do that before I fly back to England," she replies, slipping her heels on.

"Your mother wanted me to come with you," I remind her teasingly as I prop myself up on an elbow.

"You are not going to visit my mother." She points a finger at me. I smile when her lips twitch.

Fuck, I could bite those lips off.

"Okay. Tell her I miss her and I plan to visit her soon." I wink, and she rolls her eyes. "What, no goodbye kiss?"

"I think you've kissed enough of my body." She heads toward the door.

This is true, and I would gladly keep on kissing all of it if she let me.

Her gaze roams down my body appreciatively, and it fills me with male pride to know it's difficult for her to walk out that door. And it's satisfying for me to know my cum is still coating her thighs.

"My driver will be outside waiting for you," I tell her.

She stands there awkwardly for a moment, then

nods and turns for the door. "Well, thanks for the mediocre sex," she shouts on her way out.

"Medio—" I start, but the door has already closed behind her. I chuckle, scanning the chaotic mess of a room. The echoing moans continue from my computer screen. I didn't expect her to see that, but the moment she bumped into it, and I went to catch her, my computer picked up on my facial recognition and, well... I was caught out.

I smirk as I stand up to pause the video, satisfied by all the new hours I've recorded of her. Fuck me. If I didn't have to get on a plane in the next three hours, I'd probably be jacking off to all the new footage. I can't seem to stop watching her. It's an obsession.

I didn't plan to tell her about Hayley; it just kind of happened. However Alina made a valid point about remembering her. Just because I want to forget, does that mean I don't want her to be remembered?

Hayley was murdered, and the police couldn't find her killer. Even as a detective myself, I could do fuck all.

It turns out she was digging into things she shouldn't have been, and a hit was put out on her. She was a police officer.

I guess what she found was bad enough for them to want her dead.

And then I found them.

Every last one of them.

And then I fucking killed them. After that, I knew I was no longer meant to be a detective.

I knew the people we were after were only the small monsters in stories. And I was after the bigger ones. I help take down the worst of the worst.

Gladly.

Sometimes I even do the shooting. I am a fucking excellent shot, that's for sure.

But if I can keep my hands clean, I will.

Unless an outlet is needed.

Something inside of me shifts. I don't know if it's because Thomas' daughter's case is too similar to Hayley's or if it has something to do with speaking about her to Alina. But I feel that chapter of my life, the old wounds, reopening. I'm not sure why, considering I'd kept them buried for so long.

I reach for my phone and pull up the number I want. She answers straight away, without a second of hesitation.

"Aww, Will, it's been so long. I've missed you. How are you?" Hayley's mother says. Hayley's parents were amazing. Still are. And now I feel bad that I haven't bothered calling even though they try to call to check in with me once a month.

"I've been good. Just in New York. Hope I didn't interrupt anything."

"No, never. Sebastian had a little girl last week, and guess what he named her." I don't have to answer to know. Hayley was close with her brother, Sebastian. "Hayley," she says.

"That's beautiful," I tell her, rubbing a hand down my face.

My hand smells of Alina, and my room smells of sex and her perfume.

"Will you visit soon? You are missed." The news of her murder was devastating, and although I never went into detail as to how she met her demise, I'm certain they have an inclination. Somehow, it was the only gift I could give them among the madness. They'd always been welcoming, and it made me run in the opposite direction because the reality was, as her husband, it was my job to protect their daughter, and I failed. Even if they didn't make me accountable for it, it was my guilt to carry.

"Hopefully, soon." I don't know if I will. But I think I'll try to call a little more often.

CHAPTER 32

Alina

When I find you, I will fucking gut you. And I will find you.

Delete.

Goose bumps erupt along my skin. Another email. It feels like he's been more persistent recently and I don't know why. But I'm definitely ignoring it. Besides, I have better things to focus on right now.

The construction of the shop is complete. This means that, as of tomorrow, the fun begins. Well, my version of fun, anyway. All the fittings and boxes of stock are due to arrive. I'm curious as to what will show up. I might be so inclined to grab a few toys and lingerie sets myself.

I know Will is going to appreciate them. Then again, the thought is stifling in itself. I don't know what was going through my mind last night, but whatever it was, I've never had such crazy sex like that in my life.

I scan the papers on my clipboard, biting at the edge of my pen thoughtfully. Unfortunately, the things running through my head don't have much to do with what I should be focusing on right now but rather a certain blue-eyed Englishman who shouldn't be consuming my thoughts as much as he is.

I didn't expect that he was previously married, but then again, he doesn't know much about my past either, and I'm keeping it that way.

"Alina," Dawson calls out from where he stands with the reporter who's noting down his answers. I look up, startled from my earlier thoughts, and then join them. "Would you mind answering a few questions? It's okay to say no."

I don't want to disappoint Dawson or the reopening in any way. "I can; I just don't like my photo being taken," I admit. My business name and last name are aliases. I didn't mind telling Honey and Dawson my real last name, but when it came to my company, I tweaked my surname slightly from Harper to Harriet.

"We can do that," the reporter says with a smile. "Can you tell us about the inspiration behind the design?" She dives straight in. That's when Honey arrives and Dawson excuses himself. I suddenly realize I might've been used as a scapegoat. The reporter stares at him starry-eyed as he leaves. Ah, definitely a scapegoat.

But Dawson only has eyes for one woman. Honey smiles as he approaches and then kisses her passionately. Anyone would think they've gone weeks or months without seeing one another.

I go through some details about what to expect at the grand reopening and how grateful I've been to work for Dawson on this new design. Then he saves me, taking the interview back over, and Honey links her elbow with mine.

"Am I allowed to go inside now?" I ask with a smile. She smiles back and hands me a coffee from her bakery.

"Oh, don't worry. Apparently, they took the photos earlier. Dawson said they took about thirty, but I know for a fact they only needed one. I've never seen that man take one bad photo from any angle." She laughs.

"You have no idea how badly I needed this coffee." I groan. The one downside of having a fuck marathon is the lack of sleep. I'm just lucky today doesn't require too much brain power.

"I thought so from the way you and Will were eye fucking one another. A long night, then?"

"Very." I laugh as I take a sip and appreciate the hot brew.

When we turn, we notice they're taking more photos of Dawson. "Wow, the feature wall is stunning!" she exclaims as she sees the intricate design I had a famous street artist lay out. "Also, you never told me why you don't like getting your photo taken. Even on your social apps, you don't post any photos."

I take another sip of coffee, avoiding answering that question. I feel guilty at times that they've all been so open with me while I've been holding back. Rya and Honey were even so bold as to let me in on the secrets of their world.

I sigh. I don't want to lie to her. But what if I say something and it somehow brings all the demons back?

She turns then and looks at me. "Is everything okay?"

"Yeah. I just..." I'm hesitant to tell her why I don't like photos. Though I have people around me, Maria included, who I have really opened up to since everything went down? In a small way, it's starting to feel lonely. I've been having a lot of those thoughts lately. I don't entirely understand why, but I say, "If I tell you something, do you promise not to tell anyone else?"

"Of course. Is everything okay?" she asks again as she joins me at the minibar with leather stools. They haven't yet been positioned correctly, but there will be a small space for cocktails for clients who are shopping for special occasions.

"Everything's fine. I just thought maybe I could tell you why I don't like having my photo taken. I haven't really told anyone before. I don't even know if I should now." It feels strange. Maybe it's because I've been fucked within an inch of my life, or lack of sleep, or I feel guilty for letting Will open up his wounds in front of me without reciprocating.

"You can tell me anything. I won't judge," Honey says, placing a hand over mine.

I sigh, already exhausted. "The quick answer is I ran away from someone a few years ago. It was before I started up my business. We weren't officially boyfriend and girlfriend, but close to that.

"He was involved in a bad crowd in LA, and... I

don't know. I was stupid. Attracted to danger. But when he got too deep into the drugs and the gangs, I knew it was time to split. The problem was, he spent all my savings, so I stole something of value from him so I could get myself out of that situation. I haven't seen him since, and I don't want to. But I don't want to risk him discovering everything I've built."

Honey doesn't say anything while I tell her my story; she just listens, and it makes it even more unnerving. More real. She's the first person I've said those words to out loud.

"Do you think he'll find you now? Because if you need help, Alina, you know you kind of have a kick-ass group of friends here in New York." We nervously laugh at that, and it feels like the weight evaporates from me. "Have you spoken to Will about this? You know he could probably find the guy just to put your mind at rest."

"No. I definitely won't be telling Will about this. We're having a fun fling. That's all. I don't want to be in debt to him in any way."

Honey ponders that. "Does he know it's just a fling?"

"We both do," I say adamantly, and I know it's not my place to tell her about his wife. That's his story, but it weighs heavily over me, and I don't entirely understand why yet. "That kind of brought down the mood." I try to laugh it off, embarrassed that I told her that. Why did I tell her that?

"No, it didn't. Thank you for telling me, and for trusting me. And you tell me if you're ever in trouble. We're friends now. I hope you realize that. I don't know if you know this about yourself, Alina, but you have a very magnetic presence about you. I'm sure you make friends wherever you go. And I may look super sweet, but I actually know how to kick ass, so if you need me, let me know."

"My wife will not be kicking anyone's ass," Dawson interrupts as he opens the door. A cold shudder runs down my spine at the thought of him hearing any of that. But luckily, he only just stepped in. "That's why you married me. And besides, wasn't it you who said just this morning that your stomach is going to be the size of a watermelon?"

"As if you don't expect your baby to be picking fights even inside the womb." She laughs, and I chuckle. I can see it. And then there's Crue and Rya's son. From what I've heard, he's a handful.

"How did the interview go?" Honey asks knowingly. She seems smug. She must be used to women staring at her husband like that, and yet it's so obvious he's devoted only to her.

"Good. Longer than expected but finally done." He glances around the space, then turns to me. "I would've never considered these colors, but I like them. It fits. So, you start setting up tomorrow?"

"Yep." I slide off the bar stool. "I have to take more photos and videos today. You know, before and after."

"Speaking of before and after, I find it strange that your lapdog isn't with you," Dawson jokes, and I realize belatedly he's referring to Will.

"Very funny," I deadpan, hand on hip as I pick up my clipboard. "And he's out on another job. Besides, I like the peace when he's not around. It means I can focus on my job without him intruding all the time."

The truth is, though, I've become used to his presence, and after him not being around for two weeks, dare I say I was a little bored.

Not that I'd ever tell that arrogant asshole that.

My phone pings with a message from Will. It's a video. When I press play, I immediately close my phone, but it was enough for a second of moaning to escape through the speaker.

My cheeks heat red as I realize he's just sent me videos of us fucking with the caption:

> This was my favorite position I had you in last night.

This fucker knows how to make an impression even when he isn't standing in the same room.

CHAPTER 33

Will

Thomas doesn't look like he's slept the entire week since I've been back in LA. The only time I excused myself from searching for his daughter's killer was the time I spent with Alina. I don't know why I craved her so much, but after seeing Thomas in that state, and his daughter... I just needed her. I even told her about my wife and I haven't spoken about her for a long time.

Tracking the killers was slightly more difficult than I expected and took me almost a week. Thomas is a detective, so this was very much a targeted attack. When I traced it back, I realized she was purposefully wooed.

The message the killers sent was clear to Thomas.

But he's already gone off the deep end. I recognize it. It's the same way I felt and looked after Hayley.

The group that targeted Thomas was small and foolishly living in Los Angeles, which made it that much easier to track them. I could've given him the location and then let him deal with them how he pleased. But I couldn't let him do it alone. I don't have loyalty to many, but because he was with me when I found Hayley, it's the least I can do.

Thomas stares at his gun as I drive us to the garage where the biker gang hangs out. They're known for drug trafficking but nothing of the same magnitude Crue Monti deals with in New York. Had they tried this in New York, he would've already dealt with them. But this was now a personal matter.

"Are you sure you can do this?" I ask, noticing how white my knuckles are from gripping the steering wheel.

He's head rolls to the side to face me. "I had to take my baby girl home in a tarp to my wife only days ago. This is all I have to do."

I get it. "I'm just reminding you that after this, if you're caught, they'll take your badge."

"They did nothing for me," he says quietly, and again I understand. It takes me back to seven years ago. But now all I can think about is returning to a certain little brunette who, right about now, is probably fluttering about her night with the Ricci sisters. And for some reason, that makes me a little jealous. It also makes me self-loath myself because I shouldn't be thinking of any other woman with remnant feelings for my wife. She is and always will be my wife. I'd never taken a woman seriously since, hell, I didn't want anyone to take me seriously altogether. But Alina is all I can think about, and it stabs at me, and I'm unable to break through the betrayal I feel like I'm committing toward Hayley. I can't entirely understand it. I've slept with plenty... but something felt different, and I didn't want to dig any further, too scared of the answers I might face. Or with the realization that the harder I thought about it, the more pain it brought up with memories of Hayley.

I pull over across the street from the garage. It looks like a full house tonight, which we anticipated. We'd already been there that morning and had also set off a small fire in one of their clubs in the city.

I don't want to draw attention to ourselves so close to a busy area, so we set up a small arson attempt, anticipating they'd have a meeting about it.

Unfortunately for them, while they had their attention on the club, we rigged a few bombs under their vehicles and around the garage, which is attached to a fuel station on a very quiet highway.

"They set the perfect scene, really," I say because it's too easy. No cameras, and for the few strays that do make it out, we'll be waiting for them.

I hand over a controller to Thomas and we step out of the car. Two men sitting out front on their bikes, smoking. They notice our arrival as we cross the street.

"There should be about twelve members inside," I murmur as another two walk outside. "Make that ten."

The bikers snicker and sneer as we approach. One of the men addresses Thomas. "You have a lot of balls coming here yourself. Didn't even bother hiding your face,"

I look at Thomas, who has tears in his eyes, rage fueling him. One of them laughs as he points a gun in Thomas's direction. "Thank you for making it easy for us to tie up some loose ends."

For a moment, I consider that Thomas isn't going to hit the button. Maybe he's reconsidering this "hero" notion. But then I see the twist of rage roll through him.

"You stole my daughter from me."

The man pointing the gun raises his eyebrows. "Oh, so you found her body. You should've been there to hear her scream and cry. *Pappa*," he says theatrically. "*Papp—*"

Boom!

Thomas presses the button, and the entire garage explodes. Then, there's a second wave as it hits the fuel tank. I turn my face away as hot wind pushes against my hair. Men go flying and screaming. The four bikers who were guarding the front are trying to stand, staggering from how disoriented they are.

Thomas hands me his gun and the controller before he storms over to one of the bikers, who is attempting to roll out the flames on his back. He picks him up and begins hitting him. It's the same man who antagonized him only moments before.

He turns into a madman. Hit after hit after hit. Another man approaches them, but I take the easy shot and shoot him in the head.

Thomas is now kicking in the man's head, tears streaming down his face as I take this moment to mourn for him because there's grief in this moment. Realizing no matter what, nothing will bring her back.

No matter how clever, rewarded, or strong in his role and talent, none of it means shit when it comes to looking after his family. I know that feeling too well.

It draws me back to my own darkness and need for escape.

A certain brunette comes to mind.

I sigh, exhausted. I convince myself it's just sex, but she's left an impression on me.

I pull out my phone and hit dial on the number from which I've purposefully ignored multiple calls.

"Mr. Percy," I say with no emotion in my voice. "Your deadline is up."

"I still have two days to get the money to you! I have it! I can get it!"

"No. You've run out of time. Our business is done."

"Is this how you conduct business!" he screams, and it's his own problem of not realizing how small of a fish he really is in the grand scheme of things. The only reason I took his job was because I was curious about *her*.

"I suggest you stop trying to find your ex, Alina Harper, Mr. Percy. I'll leave it in good faith that you understand that is a threat. Never call this number again."

I hang up.

At the start, Alina was only ever a job, but curiosity turned into something else entirely—a personal obsession.

Thomas is still on his rampage, his knuckles bloody, and no one else moving. I'll make sure to clean up any ounce of evidence. This man doesn't deserve to be behind bars. He's already imprisoned from his loss.

I look down at my phone and at the live footage of Alina getting ready in a shimmery gold top and tight jeans. I bugged her apartment while she was out working. There is no space that I can't get into. She might've thought I had no idea where she was staying, but I knew the moment Honey handed her the keys. Considering she's still under the assumption Dawson and Honey paid for her hotel, it made it all the easier for me to slip through the cracks.

When Mr. Percy phoned me about his ex, who'd stolen something from him, I didn't care. That's until my sister suggested hiring the very same brunette. At first, I thought Alina had somehow made a targeted attack against my sister. But as I studied her, I realized she was a woman running away from her past and starting afresh.

My curiosity continued as I returned her to US soil —as promised to Mr. Percy. But besides him not gathering the money, there was a part of me that wasn't done with her yet.

That curiosity turned into obsession, and now I'm not so sure I'll be able to get her out of my system at all. All of the photos, keeping her close by purchasing her flights and hotels, arriving at her work… it all started as a job. Now, I couldn't imagine myself dealing with her in any other way.

She's the first target I haven't taken out or handed over in all these years.

A smirk touches my lips at the thought of what I'll do with her when I return to New York. I'll devote myself to her. But I'll distract myself in the meantime. Try to drown out the resurfacing feelings brought on by Thomas's mourning–the ones that make me think of Hayley.

I have two women on my mind. My dead wife and the woman I was meant to hand over to another man. And I have no idea how to decipher the rolling emotions either evoke.

I don't know why, but it's her legs. I need to be buried between them tonight for me to make sense of anything. And yet nothing at all.

CHAPTER 34
Alina

I take a bite of a toast, then kick back on the couch and turn the TV on. This week has been intense, as it usually is at this stage in a project, but I'm slightly ahead of schedule, which means I've been able to book a flight to my mother's for the weekend.

I only purchased the ticket an hour ago and haven't yet told her, but I leave early tomorrow morning. I plan on surprising her.

I channel surf, not particularly interested in any of the shows, as I scroll through my phone and emails to make sure everything is still arriving as scheduled. I only have until mid-week when staff come to the shop and have training on the new equipment.

I look over my shoulder at the boxes stacked

against the wall. A few weeks ago, I asked for a sample of the best-selling products and lingerie to give myself some ideas regarding the layout. Everything is top quality, and I'm sure the price tags will reflect that. I have every intention of giving the items back; I just needed them for inspiration, but they've provided inspiration for completely different reasons now as I think of Will.

I already have my next consultation booked back in Manchester for two weeks from now, but I'd be lying if I said I'm not going to miss it here, in this apartment, around these people. Especially Honey. And maybe because of a certain Mr. Blue Eyes who provides a little bit of fun on the side. Not that I'd ever admit that to him.

I haven't heard from Will aside from the videos he's sent me. I don't know why, but I find it mesmerizing watching us fuck. I'd never really been into porn, but *this* unlocked something different inside of me. Maybe it's because I can see the way he worships me. Or maybe it's because of him, in his own unruly way. The man is fucking hot and knows what he's doing. Again, something I'll never admit to him.

There's a knock on my door, and I look up midbite. I'm not expecting anyone. I walk to the door with toast in hand. When I look through the peephole,

I see a very well-dressed Will, who looks like he hasn't shaved since I last saw him. It suits him, though it's strange to see, considering how he usually presents himself.

"Who gave you my address?" I ask around a mouthful as I open the door.

He smirks, plucks the toast out of my hand and takes a bite.

"Hey!" I demand as he barges past me. "You can't just let yourself in."

"I don't need to be given addresses when I can find them myself, love," he says as he does a once over of the apartment and then whips his blue gaze back to me. He scans from my feet all the way up as he appreciates my silk PJs.

He finishes the rest of the toast. "I prefer you without those on," he says around a mouthful, just like I did earlier. I try not to smirk.

I fold my arms over my chest. "So, what, you think you can just rock up whenever you want? You think I'm a booty call?" I demand.

He grins as he steps toward me and corners me against the counter. "Aren't you?" He places his hands on either side of me. "There's only so many times I can jerk off to our videos until I need the real thing. I need to be inside of you."

Heat floods my core. Fuck this man and his beauty. His ability to take and take and take. I know I should resist him. It's a game, right? I shouldn't be so easy. But I'm lying to us both by saying I don't want it and somehow punishing him feels more like a punishment to myself.

It's the same as last time, though. He's exhausted, black bags under his eyes. Whatever he's been working on... it's taking from him.

And for once, without resistance, I'm willing for him to take from me if it returns the Will that I know fully to me. It's nice to know he has demons like me. That he's real and only human doesn't mean I want to see him haunted by them.

"What do I get out of it?" I ask as he nestles his face in the crook of my neck, and I arch into him.

"What's the bet?" he asks, kissing along my neck, and I'm already melting into him. My hands trail down his stomach over his shirt, and I'm surprised my sharp nails haven't shredded it.

My hands fall to his waist. "I bet I can make you come inside me within five minutes," I whisper as I undo his belt.

He growls. "I thought you told me not to time sexual acts." His hand slips beneath my top and grazes up to squeeze my tit. I push my chest out, and we just stare at one another, our hands doing the talking for us.

"I told you don't put a time limit on a woman. But as a man, I think you'll be easy."

He smirks, that dimple coming to life, as he curls his fingers in my hair and pulls back. "Those are fighting words. And if I win?"

I free his cock, and he hisses as I squeeze hard and stroke down to the base. Fuck, I've missed this cock. And that mouth. "If you win, I'll let you handcuff me to the bed. If I win, I handcuff you."

His expression tightens as I drop to my knees. He stares down at me, a tic jumping in his jaw, as I dart out my tongue for a taste. "Do we have a deal?" I ask sweetly.

His fingers are still fisted in my hair as he all but growls, "Deal."

I smirk.

I like this power, the knowledge that although he's going through something, I can offer him relief in the same way that he's offered it to me. But I'm also feeling rather sinister tonight.

I wrap my lips around his cock, my tongue pushing and sucking underneath his shaft. He moans as his fingers tighten on my hair, and I can sense his reluctance to force me farther down his shaft.

As a reward, I do it myself, taking him all the way in until his tip touches the back of my throat. "Jesus Christ," he grits out. "I don't know how I've managed a whole week without these fuckable lips."

My core floods with warmth at his praise and the enjoyment of pleasing him. But it's selfish because I want to swallow every drop of his cum. I want to be filled by his cock and cum tonight in every hole. It's turned into a depraved fixation. One I'm willing to fulfill until Will and I inevitably part ways.

I suck hard and graze my teeth along his length. He hisses, and his cock jerks in my mouth with a small release of pre-cum. I savor it on my tongue, pulling back enough for him to see it mixed with my saliva as he looks down at me.

"Fuck, you're so beautiful. Such a good girl, sucking my cock and tasting my cum, aren't you? Do you want more? You want me shooting into the back of your throat like the greedy little whore you are?"

My pussy pounds and I nod encouragingly. Yes, I want that. So badly.

I want to force this powerful man to break apart in front of me.

I go faster, driving his cock farther back into my throat. I can hardly breathe as I choke around him, but I love how it fills me. His firm grip on my hair tugs at my scalp, and I love the searing pain as I coax him toward the edge.

Fuck, I want him to fill my mouth. I graze him with my teeth again, and he hisses, his cock jerking at the pain. When I get back down to the base, I bite down and drag my teeth back up.

"Fuck," he growls, and his hand fists tighter in my hair as his hips begin to thrust. "Fuck," he says again as he rolls his hips back and forth into my mouth. I'm pinned there, doing all I can to accommodate him as he smashes into my mouth.

My tongue and teeth scrape along his cock as he turns into a wild man. Tears stream down my cheeks and spit begins to spill from the corners of my mouth. I want him. All of him.

"Fuck, love. This sweet mouth of yours. Are you ready for your fill?"

I moan my body a heated flush and wet mess already as I anticipate my reward. "Be a good girl and swallow every drop," he says.

I rake my sharp nails up his legs and grab his ass, letting them dig in and mark him.

"Fuck," he grits out, and I do something I haven't done before. But anything goes with Will. I feel like his depravations have no limits as I slip a finger between his ass cheeks and nudge it into his asshole.

His eyes burst open as he stares at me. This man, full of power and lean muscle, pumping into me as if daring me to press my finger in deeper. And so I do.

He arches but growls like an animal as I press into him. He pumps only twice more until his cock jerks in my mouth and I'm rewarded with shots of cum going down the back of my throat. The vein in his neck pulses as a heated flush spreads up his face.

So much cum, and I happily swallow all, as if it's hitting right in my center. I'm already a wet, soaking mess.

His eyes finally spring open again as I retract my finger from his asshole and he pulls out of me. He rubs the tip of his cock along my lips and I follow it, wanting every drop.

He grabs me by the throat and lifts me to my feet. I'm powerless against his strength and I fucking love it. "Fuck, I've missed you," he breathes just before he kisses me and presses me against the counter.

I don't even have time to comprehend why that alone erupts a different type of fluttering in my stomach, because he's on me, demanding and possessive.

He grabs under my thighs and lifts them to his shoulders, hooking my legs over his back as his mouth goes straight to my silk-covered pussy.

After a few quick swipes with his tongue, he raises

his head and adjusts me in his arms. I laugh as I realize he's still wearing shoes and a shirt as he storms toward my bedroom. "Looks like I get to tie you up."

He tosses me on the bed and follows me down. "You can wait until I'm done getting my fill first," he growls out as he lowers his head between my legs again and sucks against the silk of my PJs. "Already so wet for me, love." I lose my next breath as he coats his face in my juices, and I realize with absolute clarity that neither of us will be getting any sleep.

CHAPTER 35
Will

I've fucked this woman in every hole and position possible. We tried to shower twice and ended up fucking both times. She's lying in my arms now, exhausted, and I can't wipe the smile from my face. I've never had any particular addictions, but I imagine if I did, they wouldn't have a hold over me like this woman's pussy does.

"I haven't even handcuffed you yet," she says as she draws circles on my chest.

"Give me a few minutes to recharge and I'm sure I can grant that wish."

She chuckles and props herself on an elbow to look down at me. Her fingers trail gently under my eyes, and at first, I'm confused until I realize she's probably tracing the dark circles beneath them. I kiss the inside of her wrist.

"Do you have to go back?" she asks.

"Why? Miss me already?" I ask arrogantly. She smiles, and what I'd do to have that expression aimed at me every day. I was a selfish prick for even thinking that when I could barely offer her half a man, and as she said last time, she wants marriage. I don't.

"No, you just seem tired. Do you want to talk about it?"

She's staring at me now with a sense of vulnerability. I don't understand how she can make me so easily slip from spouting humorous nonsense to tugging this part of me out that I don't share with others. Not even my sister.

"It's just a job." I avert my gaze.

"Is your job always this tiring?" she asks as she lays her head back on my chest.

I think about it. I've never really considered it before. Since Hayley's passing, it's the thing that I've buried myself in. If anything, Alina has been the first thing in a long time that's caught my attention and kept it for so long.

And doesn't that make me all the more of a prick, considering she was my previous target? She's never mentioned her past, and I don't particularly feel like prying. I already know everything there is to know about her. But getting to know her on paper and through photos is very different to being in the same room as her and actually talking.

"This task was a little more difficult because it was for a friend. He lost his daughter, and it brought back memories from days when I was a detective."

The circles on my chest momentarily stop, but then she continues. "How did he lose his daughter?"

"Bad people took her from him."

"Do you always help people like that?"

This time I shuffle onto my elbow and look at her. "You shouldn't fool yourself into thinking I'm a good man, Alina. I track people down and sometimes I kill them. Sometimes I don't even ask why. I just do it."

Her expression changes. I know I'm not the first dangerous person she's been around, but perhaps the last encounter was enough for her to understand she should stay away from people like me. Not that I'm willing to let her go anytime soon. Comparing myself to that shitbag of an ex doesn't do anything to simmer down the need I have to protect her. From men like him... and especially me.

"I get it. The whole self-preservation thing." She shrugs. "Don't start acting like you have a conscience now. It's not your job that makes you an asshole, it's your personality," she teases.

I chuckle and pull her back into me when she tries to sit up. "How about you sit on my face like a good girl so I stop talking?"

She raises an inquisitive eyebrow. "Or how about we honor the bet and you let me tie you up?" Her gaze drifts to the pair of handcuffs and length of rope. She'd pulled them out of a sample box that Dawson sent her. Of all the things in there, I was curious as to why this is what she wanted, but I was totally okay with playing out her fantasies as long as my cum will be running down her legs.

"A deal is a deal," I say, admiring her ass as she gets up. She starts with my right wrist and handcuffs it to the bedpost. "Have you ever tied a man up like this?" I ask curiously.

She begins tying the rope around my right ankle. It's so tight it bites into my skin. "No. But I've always been curious. You'll be like my own little sex doll that I can jump on whenever I want to get off."

I chuckle, tracking her as she circles the bed. This beautiful goddess of a woman is playing out all of my wildest fantasies, and I'm happy to do the same for her.

She starts on the left ankle. "This is new for me, giving up complete control," I admit.

"Oh, I imagine it is." She smiles slyly as she tightens the restraint on the second leg. I'm completely sprawled out, my cock hardening as she circles the bed. "I can't wait to get my fill."

She teases me as she snaps the next handcuff around my wrist. It clicks shut, and I'm completely bound now. Powerless against her, and yet extremely hard.

Watching her is a spectacle in itself. She shifts her long hair over one shoulder and makes a point to look back at the device I'd stuck on the wall. "You're certain it's recording?" she asks.

"It has been all night."

"Good," she purrs as she straddles me and lowers herself onto my cock. "Because I want you to remember this."

Her sweet pussy rolls up and down my length, and even as I tug on the restraints, I can't move. Watching her use me like this is fucking hot. The hottest thing I've ever seen in my life. Just when I think it can't get any better with this goddess, she shifts the gears on me.

She picks up her own pace, impaling herself on my cock. I can't look away as her tits bounce and she moans in pure pleasure. "Touch yourself," I beg.

The corner of her mouth kicks up, and I think she's going to deny me. But then her perfectly manicured finger trails down between her legs, and she begins to circle her swollen clit.

I lick my lips, wanting a taste. *Fuck me.* I try to jerk beneath her, to match her pace, but I can't. I'm unable to move.

"This feels so good," she moans. "You're going to fill me up good, aren't you?"

Jesus Christ. I'd been doing that all night. "You're so fucking perfect."

Her pace doesn't slow. If anything, my words only encourage her. "Those taut nipples. Your fucking waist, that thick ass. Everything about you, I just want to fuck the shit out of every day."

She keeps bouncing, moaning at my praise. "That mouth of yours looks best filled with my cock. And that sweet, sweet pussy…"

She continues circling her clit, her speed intensifying. Fuck, I don't know how much longer I can last when she looks like this. When she's using and abusing me like this. She's the only woman I would ever allow to tie me up.

"That sweet pussy wants me to fill it up again, doesn't it? Stuff you with my babies."

"Oh fuck," she cries, and something breaks apart in her. Her pussy's milking me, and when I realize how much that turns her on, it's the breaking of my own resistance. I blow into her, unable to look away as she rides me to her bliss.

Her eyes open as she slowly rocks back and forth. *Did I just say fill her with my babies? And did we both just get off on it?*

I smirk. This woman is just as depraved as me.

She continues riding me, not letting one drop go to waste as she asks, "Should we make another bet?"

"What's your bet, love?"

She smiles as she lifts off my cock and crawls over me. She wipes our combined cum over her folds, and I'm mesmerized.

"I bet you can't find me by the end of the weekend," she says, her eyes finally clear.

"What do you mean?" I ask with a half-smile, not following.

"Exactly that," she says, grabbing the towel and wiping herself down. She throws it over my semi-hard cock. She goes to her wardrobe, pulls out a loose-fitting dress and pulls it over her head. I tug against the restraints, but they still don't slacken. "Find me."

"How about you loosen these restraints first," I challenge. "And then I can play this little rabbit game you want to play all throughout the city."

She smiles and leans over the bed, pressing a kiss to my forehead. "No. I think I like you now as you are."

"Alina," I grit out as she slips on a pair of shoes and pulls out a prepacked carry-on bag. *What the fuck is happening right now?*

She glances over me with an appreciative sigh and then turns on her heels as she blows a kiss to the camera.

"Alina!" I yell. "You can't just leave me here."

She looks over her shoulder with a smirk. "Just think of it as foreplay, love," she coos before walking out of the room.

I hear the front door close behind her.

I tug at the restraints again, looking down at my towel-covered semi.

Fuck.

CHAPTER 36
Alina

My mother is currently making me soup for lunch. No one can cook like my mother. I'm sure most girls say the same thing about their mothers. But mine is extra special.

"So, do you want to tell me about him?" she finally asks.

"There isn't much to tell."

She looks over her shoulder to where I'm seated and raises a brow.

"Nothing to tell? Yet you've been constantly smiling as you sit there and stare at your phone." I glance away from my phone, annoyed with myself that she just made her point.

The truth is, I wonder if Will's still cuffed to my

bed. He's smart enough to get out of that situation, isn't he? But whether within enough time, who can say? I'm certain I should win this bet. Even when he does get free, he's most likely looking for me in New York. And even if his driver informs him I went to the airport, I could literally have flown anywhere.

I bite my bottom lip, wanting to have a glimpse at the photo I took of him sprawled out on my bed before I left. I mean, it's not the most romantic thing, but I know what that thing can do to me. And how he can actually back up his words. I've been with men who can't back up their words at all and were a complete letdown.

I'm very happy to announce Will is not a letdown.

"It's nothing. We both know what to expect from each other. Plus, our worlds don't really mix, and we're both super busy pursuing our... business ventures." Is that what he would describe it as? I don't need to explain to my mother what that means. But I know his world is dark, way darker than the bubble I live in. I don't want to be guided back into that world, because it already affected me once.

I'm happy to have acquaintances associated with that world. I like some of the people who come from there, like Honey and Rya and Anya, but I also know my boundaries. I adore Honey and Rya for accepting me wholeheartedly, and although I want to keep their friendship, I'm not sure if I want to get entangled in that world through a romantic relationship. Not again. And there is nothing romantic about me and Will. Just plain old hard fucking.

"Sometimes the most unexpected people surprise us. Like your father, for instance. I wouldn't usually have fallen for a man like him, yet I did. And I'm so glad I did, even if that meant I only got a short time with him, because he gave me you, and I had him for that time. Not many people get great loves, and I'm content to never have love again because none may match what I did have."

I sigh at her words.

Why would I settle for less when I know that type of love is out there? The type where you wouldn't go to any others. My father died when I was only ten. I don't remember everything, but I do remember how he used to love my mother.

I wonder if Will's wife was his greatest love and that's why he won't marry again.

Though I'm not sure I really want the answer to that question.

I was there to pick up the pieces after my father died. My mother worked so hard. She poured all of her love into me, and at times, I wondered if I was a burden. It's why I'm unsure if I want to have children. I couldn't do it on my own like my mother had. She's the strongest woman I know. Then again, maybe the thought of starting a family terrifies me. After all, nothing's guaranteed. It's so much easier for the man to up and leave. And it'll be me picking up the pieces again.

She's lived in the same house since I was a child. My parents bought this house before I was born, and my mother loves it here. It's a modest three-bedroom brick home. When my father passed away, she used most of his life insurance to pay off the house, keeping some for us to live off. She was able to afford things that she wouldn't, have living off one wage and raising a child. She had the same car all while I was growing up, and when I hit twenty, that's when she bought herself a new one.

She still has it.

I think it's why I crave change. I'm so used to my mother not wanting it.

"You know you could move on, Mom. You could open your heart to someone else, and it wouldn't diminish your love for Dad any less," I tell her.

I only have a few memories of my father, but I recall the way he would twirl her around every day when he got home from work, then he would dip her and kiss her. After he said hello to her, that's when I would get my hello.

He always said that she came first. She was the most important person in his life because she created his love, and me, but most of all, that love came from them. So why wouldn't he treasure the most important person in his life?

I never felt less than. I just loved my father, and I loved watching him love my mother.

When I was a child, I thought I'd be like some princess and one day I would have a love like that.

But the day my dad passed, and with everything that happened afterward, I learned that love can also break a woman and leave many pieces behind. I ended up seeking validation from men who didn't deserve me, and at the time, I was too naïve to realize it. For some reason, I was always attracted to the bad boys, until I snapped out of it and fled the last guy I'd been seeing.

I have kissed so many frogs that I'm unsure if I will ever get my prince. I don't even know if I believe in them anymore. Some people might think Will is prince-like, but he's anything but. He's an utter asshole. The only charming thing about him is his accent, and even then, when he speaks, he grates on my nerves. But that mouth can do so many other magical things.

"It's not that I haven't tried, Alina. I have gone on a few dates. But none compare to your father, so why even bother?" She shrugs and goes back to cooking her soup. "Tell me about Will."

I sigh, exasperated, knowing better than to try and change a topic with my mother. "There's not much to tell."

"There's always something to tell. Now, open up, missy, or you won't be getting any of this soup."

I roll my eyes because she knows I want that soup, and I haven't eaten since... Well, since I had two bites of my toast and Will ate the rest.

"He used to be a detective," I tell her. She looks over her shoulder at me.

"Used to be?"

"Yes. Apparently, he now gets paid a lot to track people down."

"Like a bounty hunter?" Her brows raise in surprise.

I smile wickedly, wishing he were here to hear it. "Exactly like a bounty hunter."

"What an unusual job. How do you know he gets paid a lot?"

"He told me. And if you ever saw him prim and

proper in his immaculate suits and expensive cologne, you would know the guy isn't any pennies short." I don't want to go into the fact that he's so loaded he can so easily bet away a plane and how my bank account is flush with cash right now, thanks to him.

I'm not complaining.

"I'm confused," she says. "He sounds like he has his life together. A businessman with ambition in his career is willing to meet your mother, dresses nicely, and has an accent. Where is he falling short?" Her mouth goes wide. "Oh. Is he... not well endowed?"

I throw my head back and laugh. He's the complete opposite, but I put on a serious face. "Yes, his penis is very small. Micro even. And he has a tendency to play video games and watches a lot of porn."

My mother rolls her eyes. "Not a gamer," she says sarcastically, and I laugh. I love my mother. She is, after all, from whom I got my dry sense of humor.

She scoops soup into two bowls. "Okay, well, let's eat. And tell me all about this job. I've been watching your videos on that app you showed me, and I love it," she gushes. "You are my favorite thing to watch, though you should show your face. You're so pretty and intelligent. You should be proud of your work."

I smile as she places the soup in front of me, and it reminds me of countless years living with her. It had always been just us two. Sitting here, even now, reminds me of that. Because I don't want her to be alone anymore, and part of me isn't sure if I want to be alone anymore, either.

That is a terrifying thought because I have no idea why all of a sudden I'm considering something outside of the bubble I've chosen to keep myself in for so long. Only recently have I realized I want marriage with the right person and potentially children. But that doesn't make it any less terrifying.

CHAPTER 37
Will

I'm shouting at Albert through the door. I don't know how long I've been here, but my shoulders are aching.

It suddenly goes eerily quiet, and then I hear a click, and River and Alek waltz in. River's eyes go wide as he looks at my sorry state, stretched out across the bed, and he throws his head back, laughing.

Alek, however, narrows his eyes. "Why the fuck did you put us down as an emergency contact with your driver? What are you, twelve?"

Albert stands behind them but averts his gaze.

I smirk. "You can't mock me for it, considering it's worked out in my favor right now."

River wipes tears from his eyes. "I have to admit, I didn't know she had it in her, but I'm impressed.

Anya's going to love this." He begins laughing all over again, which seems to only infuriate Alek. He turns and heads for the door.

"Wait!" I call out. "At least cut the rope at my legs."

"Where's the key?" River asks, not at all fazed by everything that's on display, because despite my situation, I'm hard by the little game my dangerous vixen has started.

"She took it with her," I tell them. "But I know you've picked harder locks than this."

River is still laughing as he walks around the bed and pulls out a thin pin. "Out of all the times I've had to save your sorry ass, this is my favorite."

I smirk, equally impressed. "She fucked me up good, didn't she?"

"You're not supposed to be so impressed by it." Alek scoffs, leaning against the doorframe.

"Don't worry about him," River says casually as he unlocks the cuffs. I finally feel blood flow to my shoulder again as it drops, and I shake it out. River goes around to the other side. "When he realized your driver was calling from the building Luca owns, he thought you got yourself in some trouble."

"Aww, Alek, were you willing to fight the Italian mafia for me?" I croon.

"Doubt it." Crue's voice creeps in from the entrance as he walks in.

"I was about to suggest he gets better security," Alek deadpans.

My other hand drops, and I rub at my wrists.

"I heard the screaming from upstairs," Crue says. "And you woke my son up from a midday nap. Which means he's going to be awake all night, kicking and screaming."

My driver pales and steps away from Crue's lethal edge.

"Sorry for ruining your chances of getting laid tonight, man. It won't happen again."

River laughs as he pulls out a knife and cuts the ropes from my ankles. I pick up the towel and cover myself—it fell off when I was struggling to get free. I suppose it's the least I can do now that I have an audience.

"I'm sorry it took me so long, sir," Albert says. "She had me drive her to the airport and told me you were sleeping. But when I couldn't get a hold of you, I began to worry."

"How long ago was that?" I ask, jumping out of bed and looking for my phone.

"Eight hours ago."

I whip my head in his direction, smiling like a

madman. If she went to the airport, that means she's most likely not in New York anymore. And if I were Alina Harper, where would I go for a weekend getaway?

I smirk knowingly.

"Sounds like it'd be handy to have a private jet about now," River jokes as the men begin to leave.

"Is that a camera?" Alek asks as he assesses the device stuck to the wall. I snatch it from the wall with a smile.

"You can leave now, boys. I have to hunt down a little rabbit who thought she caught me in her trap."

CHAPTER 38
Alina

After lunch, I spent the afternoon with my mother, shopping and buying her a lot of unnecessary stuff. But I feel like that's what I should do when I have all of this money. She's supported me my entire life, and it honestly feels nice to be able to spoil her like this. But she's still refusing most of the items I want to splurge on, so I realize we'll have to build up to it. After all, the money is just sitting in my account; it's not like it's going anywhere anytime soon. Well, not until I decide on where I'll be setting up an office. I don't know if I should base it in London or here in America. Maybe both? Should I look at bringing on a team?

It all seems like a lot to think about now, and so

I've decided to wait until after I finish with Dawson's shop.

These are the thoughts I'm having as I sit beside the toilet bowl with a tight stomach.

"I told you not to eat the pulled pork taco from the truck," my mother lectures as she hands me another bottle of water.

I groan. "But they're usually the best ones. I think I'm done now." I'd only vomited twice, and other than a tight stomach, I'm feeling a lot better now. If not, simply defeated.

The doorbell rings, and I realize with dread it's most likely the food we ordered. Which I have no interest in eating right now.

"I've already paid for the food, so you should be okay to just grab it," I call out after my mother as she walks down the stairs. I pull my sorry ass up and begin rinsing out my mouth. Much better now.

Note to self: Do not buying pulled pork from a truck for a while.

"Alina, can you come down here, please," my mother shouts from the door.

"I've already paid for it," I call back but still lazily make my way down the staircase anyway. When I reach the bottom of the stairs, she steps aside, and that's when I see him. *Will*. He's right in front of her, dressed in a tailored suit with a tie, and his hair done so nicely I wonder where he's going. He's wearing a shit-eating grin as I approach.

"What are you doing here?" I ask, rather clipped. I didn't expect him to find me. Especially not within a day. How did he even get out of his restraints?

"Sorry, I'm late. I was tied up with something else, but I'm here now."

"How did you even..." I don't even know why I was about to ask that question, knowing he can track anyone. "And what are you late for exactly?" I ask, crossing my arms over my chest. His crystal blue gaze moves to my mother.

"Oh, I'm Angela. It's so nice to meet you." My mother holds out her hand, and Will takes it and leans down to kiss her knuckles.

"Pleasure is all mine," he says, his voice heavy with his English accent. My mother blushes as he drops her hand. He then looks back at me. "There's an annual function on tonight. Actually, it's a charity fundraiser. Care to accompany me?"

"She's free," Mom chirps, which forces me to give her a major side-eye. I don't know how he got here so quickly or what he's up to. But there's only so much I can elaborate on without my mother realizing that I'd had him tied to the bed when I left at four in the morning.

"I didn't know you were so local," I say.

"We're still learning things about one another, love. I've frequented this area quite a few times now." He lifts his wrist, checks his watch, and smiles. "I don't want to pressure you with time, but the event starts in one hour. And I believe we made a deal. If I win, I can have whatever I want. And I'd like you to join me for an outing."

I try not to smile —this asshole.

"Unfortunately, I didn't bring anything to wear," I say, pretending to be sad over the fact.

"I figured as much, so I organized a local boutique to organize something." He steps back, and a lady walks up, holding a garment bag. This fucker is ridiculously efficient. "Take the bag, Alina. Everything should fit; I gave her the measurements myself," he adds with a charming grin. It goes without saying since his hands have been on every inch of my body, that he'd presume he knows my size. And he's most likely not wrong.

"He bought you a dress?" my mother leans in and whispers because she can't contain her excitement at what most likely appears to be a prince. I can hear the awe in her voice as she says it, and I don't have the heart to tell her he's nothing more than someone to pass the time with while I'm in New York.

She likes him.

Shit.

"I'll wait in the car while you get ready." He steps back outside, but my mother is quick to grab his wrist.

"No, come in. I'll make us a cup of coffee while Alina gets ready." He offers her one of his charming smiles, and she's absolutely besotted. It irritates me. My mother is my home, my safe place, the person I love the most and would do anything for. I don't like how easily he charms her.

"I had plans," I deadpan.

"You did not. You don't leave until tomorrow, and we've spent the whole day together. I'm tired anyway, so I can spare you for a night. Go and get ready." She grabs the bag from the woman, puts it into my hand, and pushes me toward the staircase.

I want to wipe the smug expression off Will's face but roll my eyes instead, giving in to the bet that I'd previously laid down. I don't know what he's doing in my hometown or how he knows about any particular event here, but I have no choice but to play into it. I really did this to myself.

When I'm in my room, I unzip the heavy garment bag and find a box at the bottom. In it is a pair of strappy black heels. How he knew my size, I have no idea. But I'm coming to discover that Will is a multi-layered man.

Pulling out the black dress, I see it's a wrap dress that can basically cater to any size. But it also goes around my neck, giving it an elegant look. Sliding off my sweats, I put on the dress and tie it around my waist so the bow is to the side. When I look in the mirror, I realize my panty line is visible. Since I only had a shower an hour ago, I slide them down and kick them off.

I admire myself in the mirror. It is a beautiful dress. I've never had anyone buy me a dress before, but I kind of like it. This is a dress I would buy myself. It's flattering but also unnerving to realize how much attention Will must pay to me to know my tastes, even down to the subtle jewelry.

When I walk to the bathroom, I can hear my mother laughing at something Will said, and I shake my head. He's an asshole, no doubt. But he's also charming and very clearly a man who is used to getting what he wants.

I didn't bring much makeup, so I use what I have, applying foundation and curling my lashes before I add mascara. Luckily, I always carry lip liner in my purse and I swipe it on before I fix my hair. I put it up in a high bun and brush back the flyaways. Considering the short notice, I think I look put together enough, and it only took me twenty minutes.

I call that a win. Heading out of my room with my black purse, I walk down the stairs and find Will leaning over the kitchen counter, his ass to me, as my mother tells him a story about my father.

It's strange to have a man fill the space in the kitchen again. Especially Will. And I don't know how I feel about hearing my mother sigh over memories of my father. It's a part of her heart that never entirely closed, and that terrifies me.

I clear my throat. "I'm ready."

Will straightens up and turns to face me. "That was fast," he says, his eyes roaming over me. I like how he's looking at me right now. Considering he's seen every nook and cranny of my body, he appreciates even the clothes I wear. And it's nice.

"Oh, honey, you look beautiful," my mother gushes. "Have the best night. And if you don't come home tonight, I'll see you in the morning." She kisses my cheek.

"That's a bit presumptuous. He doesn't need encouragement," I say to her.

"Well, at least he won't be playing his games and

playing with himself tonight, right?" she says, her dry humor making an appearance.

Will's jaw unhinges, and it's absolutely priceless. I laugh, and eventually so does Will.

"I don't know if I should ask what you've told your mother about me," he says, exasperated.

My mother turns to Will. "Only good things, of course. It was lovely to meet you, Will. Make sure you don't become a stranger." She presses a kiss to his cheek, and it shocks me at how welcoming my mother is. She has not one ounce of skepticism about him, yet for anyone I dated years ago, she was always cautious and worried. How do I tell her Will is the most dangerous of them all?

Will presses his hand to my lower back as we close the door behind us. My mother waving at me as if she's just sent me off to prom or something.

"I wonder if we have time for me to taste you before we get there," Will whispers in my ear. "After all, I had so many hours staring up at the ceiling imagining it." I chuckle and turn to look at him as we walk to the car.

"We shall see. Depends on how well you behave," I say, still shocked that he's actually here.

"Oh, darling, I can be the best boy. Please tell me you'll reward me if I'm a good boy." He presses me against the car before opening the door for me, and I can hear the lethal edge in his tone. Punishment for the little prank I played on him earlier.

"You'll be a good boy?" I ask, leaning in, and he nods, lowering his head to kiss the side of my neck.

"A very good boy," he purrs. "But before that, I believe you have to be punished for a certain little situation you created for me."

I chuckle as he presses kisses along my jaw.

"How did you get out of the restraints?"

"Let me have a taste first and then I'll tell you," he growls as he opens the door beside me.

I chuckle, now thoroughly entertained and curious. "Okay, I guess you can have a taste," I whisper as I slide into the passenger seat. He smirks as he closes the door behind me. And I'm certain it won't be long until his hands are on me.

CHAPTER 39
Will

She's laughing hard, her hand on her chest, as I explain the compromising position my driver Albert, River, Alek, and even Crue found me in. Not that I care about that; it's her laughter that makes me realize she needs to be punished just in case she plans on trying that stunt again any time soon.

We're in the back of the car, the driver's gaze discreetly fixed on the road, as I generously advised and paid him for.

"Did I tell you already how beautiful you look?" I ask, sliding a fraction closer to her. She smiles, those eyes darkening in pure fuckable desire. Everything about this woman oozes sex. I can't keep away from her.

"Thank you." She takes my hand and guides it

under her dress and between her legs. "Since you went through such an ordeal, it's only right that I reward you. Just a taste to appease you until you can prove what a good boy you can be." She winks, and, fuck, my cock goes rock hard, pressing uncomfortably against my pants. It was already hard when I first saw her tonight, and I had to think about dead dogs in order to not get a full-on boner in front of her mother.

"Oh, I'll be the best-behaved boy you've ever seen," I say, sliding my hand all the way up her dress to find her wearing no underwear.

Fuck. Me.

She's watching me carefully, and I lean in because I can't help myself around her. I kiss those fuckable lips that tease me without her even doing anything. I'm so wrapped up in her that I don't even know how I'm going to willingly let her return to London. I wanted her out of my system, but now I've had a taste, and cut off a job simply for her, I'm not sure when I'll be satisfied.

She tastes like peppermint and all the bad things I want to devour in this world.

Her being the main one.

Her lips part for my tongue, and her legs open wider to allow me whatever access I want as I touch her folds, sliding my fingers over her clit and rubbing it slowly.

She lets out a soft moan, and I can't help but slip my fingers straight into her while still rubbing her clit. She stops kissing me, but I can't stop kissing her. Even though I know she's concentrating on where my hand is, I still can't stop kissing her.

The car slows down, and I reluctantly remove my fingers. She moans at the loss of my touch and her eyes open again.

"I guess we'll have to finish this later, love," I say as the car comes to a complete stop.

She smirks as she adjusts herself. "How unlike you. I mean, we could just skip the event all together."

I kiss her one more time. "Not this one. You chose a hell of a weekend to visit your mother."

Her eyebrows furrow in confusion, and I don't blame her for not understanding. Hell, nobody from New York knows my connections to this town. I find it strange, as much it is coincidental, that this is the town she grew up in.

I walk around the back of the car to open the door for her, then hold out my hand expectantly, and she slips hers into mine. I don't know at what point it was that we fell into such an easiness around one another.

But I can't keep my eyes off her. I wonder if, in another life, had she come first... before my wife... if...

I cut that startling thought off, loathing that I even had the thought. I couldn't betray Hayley or our vows like that.

It's been seven years since she passed. I usually don't come to these things, but I had to visit when I saw the invite and knew it was close to where Alina was staying.

For Hayley.

For Alina.

For myself.

I've been having withdrawals from Alina, and although it doesn't dim the fire or loyalty I had to my wife, I notice the telltale signs of how my body and mind are wavering. I haven't touched or even looked at another woman since crossing paths with Alina.

It's like she has me under some spell.

One that I have to break free from soon because I won't be able to accept the repercussions if I don't.

I can't replace Hayley.

Never.

But neither can I look away from Alina.

CHAPTER 40
Alina

His hand finds my lower back as he guides me into the event. It's local to where I grew up and went to school, so I'm kind of hoping I don't see anyone I know. It's equally strange that Will has any type of association with my hometown. I really hope I don't run into anyone from my past. I haven't really kept in touch with anyone I went to school with, and the few friends I have are through my work.

The moment we step into the hospital, I quickly scan around to make sure I don't recognize anyone. I then notice Will watching me carefully.

It's not that I don't like anyone from here; it's just that when I moved to LA, I got caught up in the wrong crowd, and after that wanted an entirely different start.

It feels strange to return, especially with someone like Will on my arm. I don't really understand what's going on between us, but I also don't want to complicate things by asking. I don't want to feel like a silly woman seeing things that might not be there, but some of the stuff he says and does... This is more than just a booty call, right? I shove that thought down. If I don't ask, I don't have to know. And I think that's better for both of us.

That's probably not the most honest way to look at things, but it's the way I'm going to go, considering I leave for London in less than two weeks, and this—whatever *this* is—will be in the past. While Will is attractive, funny, and even rich, he's also had his great love. And while it's selfish, I don't ever want to be someone's second.

Maybe that's why I've never settled down.

Maybe it's a me issue.

And Will is not the safe guy to pour my heart and energy into. However, as I look at his side profile and see how he scans the room just like I had, I think if it were going to be easy with anyone, it would most likely be him.

"How long do we have to stay?" I ask.

"Already want to leave?" he replies, smugly pulling me into his side.

"Yes and no." I smile up at him. This beautiful fucking man can, unfortunately, be irresistible at times. The problem being, he fucking knows it.

"Will, how are you?" someone asks. He pulls away from me a bit but keeps his hand on my back as he turns to speak to the newcomer. I, however, take this as my time to look around and find the bar. I think I need a drink.

I place my hand on his chest. "Sorry to interrupt. Drink?"

"No, but I'll be here waiting for you." He lets me go, and I turn and head to the bar.

When I get there, I order a glass of wine and feel someone come up next to me.

"Alina?" I turn to see a tall man standing there. I'm confused at first because I think I might know him, but his name doesn't come to mind.

"Steven. We dated in high school," he clarifies, because obviously, my expression says it all. It suddenly clicks. Back then, Steven was a lot skinnier and lankier. This Steven is the same height but built out three times the width with a lot of muscles.

"Wow, I didn't even recognize you," I say, still

shocked, and step back a little. "You got bigger." I laugh.

"I did. Some things don't change, however. You look beautiful as always," he says, then turns to the bartender and orders himself a drink. I take my time to look at him, remembering him better now. His manners are the same, as are the smile and kind expression in his gaze. But his hair has grown out and his face has hardened. "What are you doing here? I haven't seen you around since you left for LA, like, what, ten years ago?"

"Yeah, I only come back to check in on Mom. I'm just here with someone."

He glances down at my hand, and when he doesn't see a ring, he says, "Not married?"

"Nope. I haven't found a victim yet," I joke. "You?"

"Nope. Work is, unfortunately, my wife." He chuckles.

"What do you do for work?"

"This." He waves his hand around to encompass the event. "I own the construction company that is raising funds to build another wing for the hospital. Can't say I do much of the building anymore; I'm more in the office, running everything now, but tonight's a fundraiser for the project, so I thought I should rock up in a suit for once. What about you?"

I try to figure out how Will fits into all of this. It's just a small local hospital; what could Will possibly have in common with this place?

"I have my own business as well. I design new concepts for businesses. I basically give them a rebrand and facelift."

"Oh, nice. Maybe I can hire you." He laughs. "It'd be nice to collaborate on something."

"If you think you can afford me, sure," I say back with a smile. Just then, I feel a hand slide around my waist, and then a kiss is laid on my shoulder.

"That depends on what services you're offering," Will interjects. "You were gone too long." But I realize Will isn't necessarily speaking to me because his gaze is fixed on Steven. And although Will has his dimpled smile on display, it doesn't reach his eyes.

"Will, it's been a while since you've been to one of these events," Steven says, not entirely friendly. "I wasn't expecting to see you here."

Will's mouth lifts from my neck as he looks at him. "I've been preoccupied. Work and things."

"Well, my sister was quite disappointed when you never called her back." I tense under Steven's harsh tone. If memory serves correctly, his sister was two years older than Steven and me and pretty as well, from what I remember.

"I'm sure she's moved on," Will says casually.

Steven looks as if he's going to say something to Will but doesn't. Instead, his gaze locks on me before he says, "It was good seeing you again, Alina. I'll reach out when I need your services." He doesn't so much as look at Will again before walking off. When he's gone, Will takes his spot and casually leans against the bar.

"You know Steven Chamber?" he asks.

"Yes, we dated in high school for like two months or something. How do you know him, other than dating his sister?" I say, raising a brow.

He smirks. "I've informed you I don't do relationships."

"Oh, my apologies. Other than fucking her." My face remains blank.

"Are you... jealous?" He leans in and goes to touch my lips, but I pull back before he can.

"The day I'm jealous over you will be the same day hell freezes over," I hiss, crossing my arms over my chest. Suddenly, I'm not really in the drinking mood and I haven't even taken a sip.

"Why are you really here? Like, really? You've told me you don't do relationships, that you've been married and don't plan on doing that again. So why are you here? Is my pussy that good that you can't stay away?"

He smirks, that single dimple forming, as he says, "Oh, yes, you have a magical pussy; I'm not denying that."

"So when you fuck other women, do you follow them all the way to their hometowns and put on a big display of sponsoring their local hospitals?" I place the wine glass on the bar. I'm not jealous. I'm just confused. Okay, maybe I'm a little jealous because of all these things he's doing... I can't make sense of them.

"Will." He ignores the soft voice of the woman behind him.

"No, I don't follow other women. But it's not just because of your magical pussy I'm here," he says matter-of-factly.

I roll my eyes, not buying it for a moment, as I turn my focus to the woman standing behind him, who is clearly after his attention. She's waiting for him to turn around, but he doesn't, as he's too focused on me.

"Will," she says again, and it's not until I give him an expectant look for him to address her that he sighs, closes his eyes, and then turns to her.

"Cheryl, how are you?" he says, grabbing me by the waist as I try to escape for fresh air. I'm pinned against him and awkwardly smile at the show he's making of us. She looks at me then, and that's when I realize she's Steven's sister.

"My brother said you were here with a date, but I didn't believe him. Not Will, who was adamant when he told me he only fucks and makes it very clear that's all he does." Her words are a slap in the face. "Do you know this about him, that he doesn't date, only fucks?" she asks me.

She's furious, and I don't know why, but that irritates me. I don't have anything to do with whatever happened between them, but I also don't like the spectacle she's trying to create. It's a little bratty.

So I put on a bright smile and bite back, "I do. We have great sex. Nothing more, nothing less. There's no dating or relationship, and that fits into my schedule perfectly."

If he's made it clear to her that's all it was, why is she standing here angrily confronting me about it? Or was he doing all the same things to her to make her confused in the same way I am? Shit, are we not that different after all?

"So, you agree to his outrageous terms, where he only uses you for your body? He'll just use you and spit you out like nothing." She eyes me as if she's making a powerful statement.

This woman is grating on me the wrong way.

"What makes you think it's not me who wants his body, and perhaps I'm using him? And I do very much enjoy his body," I say, sliding my hand across his chest.

Cheryl stares at me like she can't believe what I'm saying.

You and me both, lady.

But I won't stand here and let another person try to degrade me or question what I'm doing with my body and choice of man. If I were to follow him around like a lovesick puppy, a stranger telling me not to do so wouldn't affect me.

She blinks a few times and then looks back at Will.

"It was good to see you, Cheryl," he says, trying to end the conversation as he turns to me. "I need to make my donation and then we can leave."

"I'll wait here," I tell him. He raises a brow and glances at Cheryl, who obviously isn't done. But when he realizes I'm not changing my mind, he nods and walks off, not paying Cheryl any more attention.

"He's easy to fall for, isn't he?" she says, watching him go. And although I know he won't be gone for long, I don't understand why she hasn't left yet. I'm not particularly curious about the situationship they had either.

"I wouldn't know." I shrug.

Her gaze swings back to me. "How long have you

been seeing him? You know I'm not the only woman he's slept with in this town. As soon as he's fucked someone, poof, he's gone."

Interesting. So he's most likely been here more than once. But why?

"Do you want to know how many times we've slept together?" I smile at her sweetly, not giving anything away. "I would say he's made me come at least five times, or maybe I'm miscounting. Could be way more. And that's just today," I say casually. "What about you? Was he the best you had? Is that why you're so hung up on him?"

Her mouth opens, then closes before it reopens, and she speaks.

"We had one night together."

"One night. Wow. And you what? Feel like you had some right to interrupt *us*? Did he give you promises of a future I'm unaware of? Because if he did..." I step back. "Let me know, and I will gladly walk away." When she remains silent, I know he didn't. I couldn't see him doing that anyway, so it's just her who has false hope. I mean, I know how good in bed he is, but damn. Talk about cock whipped. Then again, aren't I right now? "I'm not going to pretend I know Will all that well, but what I do know is he is very straight with what he wants and doesn't want. Do you agree?"

"Yes," she admits, and I know it was hard for her to say that.

"Okay, good. Now we have an understanding. I'm going to stand here, wait for my date to return after generously donating, then probably fuck him in the car on the way home. So unless you want to watch, is there anything else I can help you with?"

Her jaw hangs open, and she looks absolutely appalled, which is ironic considering the shit she was trying to stir only minutes ago.

"You weren't like this in school," she states.

"No, I guess I wasn't. But I also cared too much what others thought of me back then." I shrug. "Now I'm just in it for a good time. Which I know Will can give me." Before she can say anything else, he returns, snaking his hand around my waist and not even paying Cheryl a lick of attention as he leans in.

"Ready?" he asks.

I nod and don't look back at her as he guides me out of the function.

CHAPTER 41
Will

"Alina." I turn as Steven approaches her, and not so much as gives me a second look. My hand is on Alina's back as we head to the entrance to leave. I eye him, waiting for him to say something. He's hated me since I fucked his sister. It was only once. It's not my fault she got hooked. I did warn her it was a one-off. Imagine if I fucked her more than once. Hell, she'd probably be planning our fucking wedding.

That's when Steven looks at me as if reading my mind. I can't help but smirk.

"Did you need something? We were just leaving," Alina says, glancing between us because the tension is palpable.

"Yes, I was hoping to grab your number before you leave. So we can catch up sometime."

My jaw tightens but I don't let it show.

I mean, what right do I have? She's not mine. We made it very clear. The voice of reason doesn't do much to control my possessive grip on her hip.

"Oh. Uhh..." She turns to me. I wait for a moment, not saying anything. That can be her decision. Something passes through her gaze, but I can't read it. Does she want me to step in? Does she want something from me? "Do you mind?" she whispers. Does she want me to stop her?

Because I won't. I don't have a right.

"Not at all." I nod, indicating she can do whatever she wants. I don't hold her back, and I have made no promises. We're just here for a good time. Or so I keep telling myself.

"Pass me your phone. I don't live here though. I'm based in London. I'm just here visiting my mother."

Steven smiles at that and hands her his phone, and I want to wipe the smug expression from the prick's face.

Maybe I'll hack his phone later and see what Steven has been up to lately.

Alina takes his phone, and the whole time, I'm drilling a hole into his head with my stare. I want to watch him squirm uncomfortably. Especially if it's unreasonable for me to hit him. And I don't even know why I want to hit him. She's not mine.

He's smiling, and his gaze flicks up to mine, not even watching as she puts her number in.

He thinks he won.

I lean in and kiss her bare shoulder, kissing my way up her neck to make a point. She doesn't push me away, but I do notice as she fumbles with her own number before she hands the phone back to Steven.

Fuck you, Steven.

"I'll be sure to call," he says. She nods, and before she can say anything else, I'm dragging her out. She laughs when we get outside, and it's like music to my ears.

That fucking laugh.

I love it.

And yet I grumble when I ask, "Why are you laughing?"

"At you being all 'I'm totally okay' but acting like a possessive boyfriend."

"I am not." My tone is curt, and she just laughs.

I don't even wait until we get to the car. The minute the cold air hits us, I spin her and slam my lips to hers. I don't care if we're at the entrance of an event.

She's mine, and this naughty little vixen needs to be reminded of that.

Mine.

I break away at the thought, and it's not missed by Alina, who clears her throat as someone walks in behind us. An older couple most likely discussing the spectacle they just witnessed.

Now she laughs as she throws her hands up in the air, but it lacks humor. "What are we doing, Will? Honestly."

My eyebrows furrow. "What do you mean? We're having fun, aren't we?"

"We're beyond that point now. And if it's been nothing but a bit of fun, maybe we should just leave it as that. I'll catch my own cab home." She goes to walk away but I grab her wrist.

"We're not done tonight," I say adamantly, never wanting to see that expression on her face again. She looks... tired of me.

And I never want there to be a world where this woman isn't drawn to me as much as I am her.

"Will, I leave soon. This has been fun but I don't even know what I'm getting myself involved with when it comes to you. Why are you really here in this town? How do you know the locals? How have you slept with half of them?"

I curve an arrogant smile. "Now who's acting like a jealous girlfriend?"

She throws her hand in the air and goes to walk away, forgetting that I still have a hold of her other wrist.

"I'm sorry," I blurt out. Her head whips in my direction because when, if ever, have I apologized to anyone for being a smartass? It's always been the easiest way to keep everyone at a distance, but I'm realizing now that maybe I want Alina a little closer. "Please let me explain."

She sighs and glances at the bridge a short distance away. "Let's go for a walk. I don't want to do it around here where another one of your fan club girls might corner us."

I sigh, grateful for her ability to put me at ease, though the conversation we're about to have will be anything but comfortable.

We walk over to the bridge and she stares down into the water. I notice immediately that the air is cold, so I take my jacket off and put it over her shoulders.

She smirks, almost disbelieving. "The problem is you're as much of a gentleman as you are an asshole. It could give any girl the wrong idea."

"I don't do this for other women. They've only

served a purpose for one night, and I've always been gone before dawn."

She sighs. "So why are you doing it for me? If it's because I'm friends with your sister, you don't have to."

"This has nothing to do with Maria."

"Then what?" she pushes.

I don't know why I can't keep Alina out of my thoughts. Why, no matter what part of the world I'm in, I'm only thinking of her and wanting to return to her. She's the first breath I've taken since Hayley died, and I can't make sense of any of these turbulent emotions stirring up. No matter how much I try to shove them back down, they perplex me in ways I don't want to deal with.

"I don't know."

She gazes across the water, and I can tell she's not entirely satisfied by that answer. "And the fan club you have here?"

I tangle my fingers together. Now to the heart of the truth. The uncomfortable conversation that I thought I'd never share with anyone.

"Hayley grew up in this town until she was ten years old. But she always spoke about it fondly. This was the place she wanted us to eventually settle down and start a family. Said this always felt like home." I confess the dreams of my deceased wife, whose memory seems to get further and further away. "When she passed, I frequented here for the first few years for... I don't know... to feel like I was honoring her, so that I could feel connected to her. I drowned my sorrows at local bars and buried myself in some women, trying to forget." I sigh.

Alina's staring at me now, almost in disbelief. "Small world, huh?"

I chuckle, trying to release this erratic energy around me. Considering she was raised in this very same town, I couldn't believe the slim chance myself. "Coincidental it would seem."

"Do you still think you'll settle down here?" she asks.

"No. But I think this will be a place I come back to often. I might just have to make sure I don't drink so much when I do."

She lets out a chuckle. "I guess I hit the list, then, didn't I?"

I give her a serious look. "No, you were never a one-night fling."

She goes to say something, as if to ask what she might be to me, but it falls dead on her lips. The tension around us changes as she removes my jacket and says with a beautiful smile, "Hayley was very lucky to have you for a husband."

"She dealt with a lot," I say with a nervous laugh, and she does the same as she places the jacket in my hand.

"I bet she did." Sad eyes meet mine. "I think we need to call it quits here, Will. I don't want to hate you, but I think we might both be in denial about what's happening here."

I fist the jacket, wanting to argue with her but can't find the words because I begrudgingly know she's right.

"I don't know what it's like to lose a partner like that, but I want to find someone who looks at me the same way you probably looked at her. And whatever we're doing now, I think we should end here as friends. Before it turns into something that both of us are too uncomfortable to address."

I try to smirk but fail, feeling defeated. I don't know why but talking about Hayley with Alina, and having Alina walk away is... uncomfortable. Like a part of me is trying to detach from Hayley and I'm trying my hardest to cling to it, to respect her and what we had. But the only way I can make space for Alina is if I let go. And I just can't.

I can't even laugh it off this time, and the truth of this situation is as shocking as it is a rude awakening.

Alina steps on her tippy-toes and presses a kiss to my cheek. "Thanks for the fun, Will, and I hope you find what you're looking for."

Ironic, considering I'm one of the best at finding things. And yet, as I watch Alina walk away, I can't help but wonder if I'm letting something important go.

But I'm frozen in place. I'm determined to honor my late wife and our marriage. Because if I don't... doesn't that lessen what we had?

CHAPTER 42
Alina

I jolt in the back seat of the cab, a heavy sigh escaping my lips. I don't know why, but I feel like I just broke up with him, even though we weren't anything serious. I had a lot of fun with Will, but the moment I realized even the town I grew up in was associated with his deceased wife in some way... I felt selfish. Greedy almost. And slightly jealous.

When Steven asked for my number, I looked at Will because I was confused. He said it was okay, but his hands were possessively screaming that I was his.

Maybe we're two fucked up people who no time soon would discover what love is. Well, certainly not Will, who already had his great love. But if anything, Will reminded me of something that feels like it's missing from my own life.

It was just sex, just fun, yet we've slowly been becoming attached to each other. Or maybe that was just me, and I'm romanticizing something that isn't there. I mean, Maria does it all the time, so why would it be so different for me?

I pinch the bridge of my nose. When did I get so sappy?

It was great sex. Nothing more. Nothing less. And yet the way he looked at me when I walked away was as if someone had stolen his puppy.

I harden my resolve, deciding to focus on what has always gotten me by. I was the only one I could depend on, and in less than two weeks, I'll be back in London —end of story.

I tip the Uber driver as I step out of the car, rubbing my shoulders at the chill in the air. The front porch light turns on, and I'm not surprised to find Mom still awake, watching one of her favorite dramas on TV.

"You're back earlier than I expected," she says as she mutes the TV. I bend over to undo my heels at the door. When I don't say anything, she comes over and leans against the wall. "Are you okay?"

"Yeah, the night just shifted quickly, is all," I reply, not wanting to elaborate. Once I kick the heels off, my phone dings in my purse. When I check it, I see a message from a number I don't recognize and see Steven's name at the end. "There were some people there I went to school with," I tell her. "Remember Steven, the guy I dated for like two months or something?"

"Oh, yes. You broke up with him because he had bad breath if I remember correctly." I laugh at that, then push off the door and kiss her cheek.

"And what about your actual date? Where did Will go?" she asks, crossing her arms over her chest.

I sigh. "He had a work thing."

"A bounty hunter, here of all places. Can you imagine?"

I laugh. "Don't let him catch you saying, bounty hunter. But I think we're over. We had a fun ride, but I'm off to London, and he's doing whatever he does best." I step around her, hoping that's enough to end the conversation.

"I liked him. I want that noted," she says.

"Okay, thanks for your input, Mother," I yell over my shoulder as I walk up the stairs.

"That won't be the last time you see that man. You can bet your bottom dollar it won't be. He was hooked."

I want to laugh at her words, because they couldn't be further from the truth.

And yet, it settles a cold and upsetting weight in my chest. And this is precisely why I had to break it off now. Because Will wormed into a part of myself that I didn't even know still existed.

And that's dangerous.

My phone dings and I expect to see Steven's name again, but instead it's an unknown number.

> You can't hide forever.

CHAPTER 43
Will

Alek is disassembling the man's gun in front of him. Not that the man in question can do anything with it, considering he's tied to a chair.

I go through the motions, not having yet picked up another job. It's only been three days since I last saw Alina, but it hasn't sat right with me—the moment she walked away from me on that bridge.

"I don't know anything, I swear!" the man screams before Alek gags him.

Of all the killers I know, Alek is the boldest. He adjusts his gloves as he decides which torture device he should use. It's midday, and for someone who's usually active in the evening, like a boogey monster, Alek has taken to torture during the day. Sure, it's an isolated space that no one will find, but he was changing, ever so slightly, to accommodate his wife's schedule so he can watch her performances at night.

I sigh. The guy's so fucking lovesick that it irritates me. I'm happy for him, but there's an almost begrudging feeling that I notice toward him for having it. For feeling like the one who I'd had was already gone.

"You being quiet is eerily creepy." Alek addresses my sorry ass where I stand in the corner of the room.

I smirk. "So you admit to missing my smartass comments?"

"No. I just don't know why you haven't taken up another job. Why do you keep attaching yourself to me?"

"That's what friends do, silly." I wink, and he's disgusted, most likely at the suggestion of calling us 'friends.' Good. That should keep him off my ass for a little bit.

A notification appears on my phone, and at first, I can't remember whose tracker number this is. For those I've decided to track or keep tabs on, I have an alert appear if they're within range of me.

My eyebrows furrow as I zoom in on the person in question, trying to remember who it is until realization snaps into place.

I shove off the wall. "I'm taking your car."

Alek's hunched over the man, ready to start cutting, as he looks up. His gaze narrows. "Like fuck you—"

I'm already moving, my legs working of their own accord.

I thought it was strange that Mr. Percy hadn't called me since I ended our dealings. But if he was in New York... I might be wrong, but there's only one person he'd come here for. There's no way he could know Alina is here, though.

But I'm not leaving anything to chance.

CHAPTER 44
Alina

The space is stunning. I might say this every time, but I think it might be my best work yet. I'm taking final photos and videos for my social media and portfolio. The bar space is my favorite part, with the greenery that pops beside the mural painted by the street artist.

Each lingerie section is themed with appropriate toys, and I especially appreciate the BDSM section, considering I had a taste of what the ropes and handcuffs can do and how much fun that element of control can be.

A nauseating swirl churns in my stomach as I immediately think of Will. We haven't spoken since the weekend, and a small part of me almost expects to see him popping up whenever he pleases. Surprisingly, he's kept his distance. I don't know why I'm surprised, though. It is what I requested.

I burp, and my hand presses to my stomach when I realize that it isn't just gas. I run to the freshly painted bathroom and vomit into the toilet bowl. *Are you kidding me?*

I groan as my head hangs over the toilet. I haven't felt well since being at my mother's, and I'm certain I got mild food poisoning from that pulled pork taco. Not that I'd admit it to my mother.

I'm just grateful it's not until tomorrow that the staff come in for training and the construction workers are done. It's just me here today, so I don't have to be humiliated by my run to the toilet.

I hear the door open and close, and groan as I rise to a standing position. When I step out onto the shop floor, a man in a flannel shirt is standing there with his back to me.

"We're not open yet, and the owner isn't in at the moment, if that's what—" My mouth snaps shut, and a shiver runs down my spine as he turns.

His smile stretches wide. "I finally found you," he all but purrs.

Memories come back of the man I'd stolen and ran away from. He's blocking my exit, but I could make a break for the back room.

"I wouldn't try that if I were you. I have a few friends with me, and you don't want to piss me off any more than you already have, do you?" Jack Percy asks.

"How did you find me?" I grit out. There's nowhere for me to run.

He laughs as he casually strides toward me, and that's when I notice two men standing outside the front door as if guarding it and blocking us in. Dawson's assistant might notice the security footage, but that doesn't mean they'll be here quickly enough if something happens. And there's a good chance something will happen if Jack's involved. Especially with the way he's staring at me with dilated pupils.

"It cost me a lot of money, actually. Some tracker ripped me off, telling me you were in London, even after he promised me he'd bring you back here."

A tracker? Surely not... Will, because wouldn't that mean... slow realization dawns on me. He was always around. From London to even now. No, it has to be a coincidence.

Jack continues. "But then I was lucky enough for one of my women to spot an interesting article about some big-shot designer with a big-shot name in New York. You weren't posing for the photo, but you were in the background, so I got to digging."

A shudder runs over me again as I recall the day the

journalist was here taking photos of Dawson. *Fuck*. I'd been reckless.

He's standing in front of me now and reaches out to touch a lock of my hair. I slap it away, and he grabs my throat. I grapple with him, panic pumping through me with adrenaline.

"I remember when you used to put up less of a fight."

I spit in his face, and he laughs like a madman. "You took something of mine."

"I don't have it." I wince under his grip. I'd always stolen things. This was now the only time there'd been a consequence of being caught. As if only now noticing, he releases me and pushes me into a stack of shelves. Boxes of toys go flying, and I barely catch myself on the shelf, cutting my arm.

He waves his finger back and forth. "Maybe then we have to come to some compromise, and you can give me its worth. Your company looks to be making a lot of money."

It was never the jewelry I'd stolen that he was attached to, but its value. At first, I thought I'd pawn it and deposit the money into my own bank account. But instead, I gave it to his younger sister to help her flee from the crowd he was surrounding them with.

"Does Tilly know you're here?" I ask. I'd been

attracted to his charisma once, the bad boy charm, until it wasn't just a charm, and his addictions and debt turned him into a monster. Now, it's had years to fester. He hasn't changed much at all, but at the same time, he has. He looks crueler. Scarier than the young man I'd been attracted to those many years ago.

"Tilly?" he asks, and there's a clipped edge to his tone. "She killed herself five years ago."

Everything comes to a stop, and my heart sinks. "She what?" My eyebrows furrow. I fought so hard to get her out of there. I thought the jewelry would help. I thought the money would get her out.

He snarls, "You always did take her under your wing, didn't you? You always thought you were better than me, huh? You tried to turn my own baby sister against me!" he snaps, and there's something that's switched in him. I immediately back up as I see the unhinged monster come to the surface.

The first time he hit me was when I left. But not before taking something precious. He's been fixated ever since. I thought he'd forget, but right now, it's not even me he's seeing.

"What do you want from me?" I shout back, praying that security has already been alerted, but I'm certain it's already too late.

"I don't know. Maybe I'll break that body of yours

first. Maybe I'll burn down this project you're so proud of. Or maybe I'll burn you alive inside of it." He walks over to my bag. "Of course, not until you deposit all of your money into my account," he says with a deranged expression.

Money. It's always been about money with this lunatic, and I'm about to pay the price for being young and reckless and stealing from him once. I'd hoped it'd give his sister a second chance. But instead, it'll be my ruin.

CHAPTER 45

Will

I'll definitely owe Alek a new car because I don't even think as I'm driving toward the building that's billowing with smoke and engulfed in flames. I accelerate toward the two men standing out front. The windshield smashes and blood splatters the glass. I'm out of the car before I even put it in park.

Cold terror grips me as I scan the outside of Dawson's shop. Through the front window, I can see smoke filling the space. I try the door, but it's locked and there are chains securing it. Sirens blare around me as Dawson arrives, but I don't look at him twice before I pull out my gun and shoot at the chains.

Fucking amateurs.

But they're enough to keep anyone inside. I crumble into a panic as the chains fall to the ground, and I shoulder the door open. Heat sears my forehead, and Dawson grips my shoulder, trying to pull me back.

"Get the fuck off me!" I fling him off and run into the smoke, using my shirt to cover my nose and mouth. I can't see anything, just smoke and red flames. "Alina!" I scream. It must have only been burning for a few minutes but was quick enough to catch everything alight. "Alina!" I continue screaming as I move through the smoke.

My heart is pounding, my nerves teetering on the edge as terror strikes me. I should've been here. I should've protected her. I should've killed him. I underestimated him. I should've—

"Help!" I hear someone call. I turn in the direction of the backroom. A low, hoarse coughing sound makes its way to me.

"Alina!" I take off at a run, then skid to a halt as a flaming piece of the roof lands in front of me. *Fuck!* I pull back my hand; certain a piece got my arm. I run around it and follow the sound of the coughing. "Alina!"

"Will!" she screams, and I use her voice as my beacon. I find her in the bathroom. It's filled with smoke, and she's trying her best to reach the small window; a small section of it is cracked where she's tried to break it. "Will?!" she cries, and her silhouette is a tangled mess.

"I've got you, baby." I scoop her into my arms, whipping my head back and forth, searching for an exit.

"Wi—" She breaks out in a coughing fit.

Fuck. I grit my teeth as I try my hardest to cocoon her and press her face to my shirt, trying to fight the smoke. I look back in the direction I came from, but I can't guarantee getting her out without being burned. I look back at the small window.

A shotgun goes off, and glass rains down on us from the outside. I cover her, shards slicing down my back, as I realize Dawson must've heard us from the outside and is breaking the window.

I don't even think as I look up and hear Dawson's voice. "Bring her through."

I stand, lifting her to the opening despite her best efforts to cling to me. Sweat beads down my face as I shove her through, and her weight slips through effortlessly.

"I've got her," Dawson calls.

I cough, choking on the smoke, and push through watery eyes as I grab the window pane and pull myself up. I drag myself out, dropping to the ground. I'm scampering toward her within seconds, pushing Dawson out of the way so I can check her over.

"Alina, baby, talk to me," I say desperately, my voice raspy. I'm not sure if it's from the smoke or the fear that's gripping me at the thought of losing her.

She coughs, then begins to cry, and I pull her into me, my heart pounding. "I'm so sorry," I sob. "I'm so sorry I wasn't here sooner."

She clings to me and tries to say something but can't. I kiss her cheek, her forehead, every piece of her I can reach, hoping I can take away the smoke that's filled her lungs, that I can scare away her monsters and the asshole who did this.

"Will," she cries, as if not entirely conscious. "You're bleeding." Her voice trembles as her hand reaches out for me.

For the first time since I arrived, I focus on something other than her. It's chaos as fire trucks and police cars arrive. Dawson is standing over us and is already on the phone with someone. I'm bleeding, and that's undoubtedly a burn on my arm that's aching, but I don't care about any of that.

I cup her face, staring at her in disbelief. My hellfire vixen is shaking, and I only have myself to blame for underestimating the fucker who did this to her.

"Was he here?" I growl.

Her eyes go wide, and she knows exactly who I'm talking about. With the knowledge alongside it that she's been my target all along. But she's so much more to me. She is everything. At this moment, she's the one person I can't possibly lose.

"We're going to have to check you two over for injuries and smoke inhalation," one of the firefighters says.

"Yes," I reply absently, my thoughts on only one thing—killing the man who did this to her. "Take her."

"Will, no," Alina sobs. "Let him go. He took everything. He has what he wants." She coughs.

My eye twitches at the reminder that all this man wants is money. He assumed she'd childishly clung to the jewels he thought would bring him a fortune. Instead, he made the mistake of robbing my woman and hurting her.

"No, Alina. He does not get to haunt you anymore."

"Please," she whispers. "I don't know what he's on right now, but I don't want you to get hurt."

My heart sinks, but a cruel smile curves my lips. Because she has no idea how dangerous the man she thought was just a fuck buddy is. I've never wanted to kill anyone more, not since I'd hunted down Hayley's killers. And make no mistake, this asshole is going to pay tenfold.

"I'll come back to you. I promise." I kiss her on the lips. "Watch over her!" I shoot the demand at Dawson.

"Where are you going?" I hear him shout, but from my expression alone I'm sure it doesn't take him long to figure it out.

I'm going to hunt the monster who thought he could touch my woman.

CHAPTER 46
Will

He hasn't gone far. In fact, he sits between two of his men at a bar, singing his praises. He's a fucking moron, and it was my mistake not to take his threats seriously. I should've tied him up like a loose end the moment I decided to protect Alina and not hand her over to him.

Not many people are in the bar, but they make way for me when they notice my expression. The room goes quiet, and a waitress scurries out of my way.

"I said give us another fucking drink!" the man yells to the bartender.

I step up behind them and loom over them like a deadly god. I'm not thinking clearly—only seeing the tears streaming down Alina's face—as I grab both of his men by the back of their heads and smash them forward into the bar.

The moment Jack Percy pulls out his gun, I smack it out of his hand and grab him by the collar.

"Whoa, man. Who the fuck are you?" he asks, putting his hands up. I drag him out of the bar by the collar into the back alleyway. I throw him into the dumpster as I pace, thinking of all the ways I'm going to dismantle this fucker. He trips over himself, trying to stand. He's high on something, but his eyes widen as his gaze darts over my bloody and soot-stained shirt.

"I-I didn't have anything to d-do with the fire," he stutters.

"Really? Or the woman you left in there to die?" I snap. *My woman! My Alina!*

His eyes widen as the realization hits. "The tracker? You're the fucking tracker I hired!" He's on his feet. "You fucking cheated me out of the last of my money!" He raises a hand covered with a bloody bandage. "I lost a fucking finger because of you!"

Because he couldn't pay back his debt in time, that has nothing to do with me.

He begins to laugh as if he's in some theatrical play. He pulls out a knife and lunges for me. I dodge him with ease, twisting his arm and taking the knife out of his hand.

Fucking loser.

And he almost... He almost hurt her.

He's too slow to react, and I'm already holding him by the shoulder as I plunge the knife into his stomach. He chokes, trying his best to laugh. I bet because of whatever he's on, he hasn't realized how fatal this wound will be.

I whisper into his ear, "You made a mistake thinking you could come after what's mine." He coughs, and the back door opens to reveal a set of blue eyes that take in the scene in a bored and unimpressed way.

Alek has his arms folded over his chest. "You're daring to kill a man in broad daylight."

I shove Jack out of the way, not in the slightest satisfied with the way he gurgles or his hands shake as he tries to pull the knife from his stomach. My arm is searing in pain from the burn, and I relish in the pain as if I deserve it because I wasn't there soon enough to protect *her*.

"What are you doing here?" I growl at Alek, who raises an eyebrow.

"I got a call from Dawson to ensure you don't do anything stupid. Your woman's been taken to the hospital."

I look back at the man who's now coughing blood.

His face blends in with the killers' of my deceased wife. And it does nothing to satisfy this bloodthirsty side of me, reawakened for another woman.

"Go to her. I'll clean up here," Alek offers, adjusting his gloves. "I must confess, I prefer you as a tracker. You're too messy of a killer."

"Be careful, Alek, it almost sounds like you care," I say, not moving from my spot until I watch this asshole gasp his final breath, hardly even satisfied by his death.

Too close. He'd been too close to taking her from me, and I want to watch him suffer and die alone. His greed had been his undoing, and I'll be the one to send him to hell.

He rasps his last breath, and I watch, still nowhere near satisfied.

This raging storm inside me hasn't been sated because I can't undo the past.

Had I been able to trade places with her, I would have.

Alek says nothing more as he quietly stands behind me, and for some reason, I feel the same rage and mourning that I did standing at my own wife's funeral. Everything begins to stir and come crashing in, and I realize no matter how hard I tried to push away the grief by busily working and acting aloof—it's caught up with me now.

But there's somewhere else I have to be. I need to rein it in and keep my shit together—for a woman I should've never tangled in this mess in the first place because she was hiding from her demon just fine until I got involved.

CHAPTER 47
Alina

Honey has been by my side since the moment I arrived at the hospital. Dawson phoned her immediately. Rya was only ten minutes behind her, and they both sit beside me expectantly.

The police have taken a report of my recollection of events, and I'm now resting after being examined and treated for smoke inhalation and some minor burns and cuts. I'm still pretty shaken up.

It's not from the way Jack slipped off the edge and turned into a monster that terrifies me. Or the way he had me transfer my entire life savings into his account.

It's the desperation and vacant look in Will's gaze, and when I saw that twist into something else, that terrified me the most. It was something ugly and predatory as he went after Jack, and that instilled that fear in me. I knew Will was a dangerous man, but this... it was something else.

He betrayed me, yet right now, he's the only person I want to be with, holding me and telling me it's going to be okay. And I want to give in to that weakness, but I know I can't forgive him for tracking me this entire time. And I won't know the whole story until I speak with Will, but I'm certain that's what his role was.

"I bet he's already dead," Honey says, crossing her arms over her chest angrily.

"Most likely," Rya adds thoughtfully. "Especially if Will saved you from the fire. I know any of our men would burn down cities to find the person who'd put us in danger."

"Will doesn't see me like that," I find myself quietly saying.

Honey and Rya worriedly look at one another. Honey rests her hand on mine. "I think you two have a bit to go through, but we can see how you look at each other."

I want to laugh at her, and tell her not to encourage the tiny bit of hope in my heart, but I know those aren't the facts.

"Did you two know he was tracking me from the start?" I whisper. *Had they been on it as well?*

Honey's eyebrows furrow. "What do you mean?"

Rya looks equally as confused.

I adjust myself in the bed, trying to get comfortable. I've always hated hospitals. The doctors have already run some tests, and want to keep me overnight just for observation. Just what I need, a big-ass bill after I just got robbed of all my money.

"The man who torched the place was the guy I was telling you about, who I stole from seven years ago." Tears well in my eyes as I say this. "I'm so sorry, Honey. I didn't know he'd find me at Dawson's shop and set it on fire. I thought he'd given up on finding me."

"Stop. We don't care about the shop, Alina. As long as you're okay, you're all we care about. I mean that. What does Will have to do with this? Do I have to kick his ass for something?"

I laugh and cry and then cough. My throat is sore, and I'm so tired. "I think Jack hired Will to track me down and bring me back to him. He thought I still had the jewelry I stole from him."

"How do you know Will was hired by him?" Honey asks.

"Apparently, the tracker had found me in London and was meant to bring me back to America but called off the job halfway through. I don't know. I just think back to how much Will was around from the start..." I thought it was because he was attracted to me. Because of the sexual tension, but now I realize it was all just a job. In my heart, I know that's the truth. I can convince myself it was another tracker, but I just know.

Honey goes a shade paler. "I don't think you're wrong, and no, we didn't know. Will paid for everything. For your flights and hotel. He was adamant that you were the best for the job after you worked for his sister in London. I just... I thought he'd taken a liking to you."

He what?

How did I not know this?

Is this why he was on the same plane and staying at the same hotel as me?

He organized it all.

Has he been buying me this whole time?

Is that what's been happening and I haven't even realized it?

Was the bet he made for my benefit or his?

Was it all just a game to him? I was in his trap before I'd even realized it. How had I been so blind to it all?

Rya mulls it over. "I do think he cares about you,

Alina. If he'd wanted to hand you over for a paycheck, he would've. Instead, he just ran into a burning building to save you. I think that counts for something. Sometimes actions speak louder than words."

There's a scuffle outside my room, then the door flings open, and there's Will, panting and looking disheveled. He still looks the same as I'd last seen him hours ago, right after the fire. When I see him, tears spring to my eyes. I'm relieved he's safe, furious that I care, and sad that everything between us was all a lie.

And fuck me, I let him in.

"Get out!" Honey snaps as she stands. "You don't get to speak to her right now!"

"Honey," Rya says, stopping her, and we're all taken back by her outburst. But part of me is also grateful. Protected. A true friend. "That's Alina's decision," Rya presses. Honey's eyes well with tears, and I know she's quick to get upset with the pregnancy.

"Please, I just want to talk," Will says, exhausted, and it's so different from his usual charismatic self. He looks like a broken man. But I don't know what to believe anymore. What I do know is he did run into a burning building to save me. A conversation is the very least we can have before I remove him from my life entirely.

"It's okay, Honey," I say quietly. Because even if I don't like the answers, this man and I have to lay something to rest. And I feel a small part of me break apart as I make my decision to push him away.

CHAPTER 48
Will

The Ricci sisters don't seem too impressed with me, so I'm assuming they've come to the realization that I had a hand to play in all of this. I don't care. As long as Alina is okay, even if she hates me for it. I wait until they've left the room and close the door behind them.

I made sure Alina had the best private room. Every need catered to, and constant attention. From what I'd been told, she hadn't taken in too much smoke, but I wanted her to stay overnight to make sure.

She's staring me down as I slowly approach the bed.

"You look like shit," she says, breaking the silence. I smirk but don't really find it humorous. I'm just grateful she's speaking to me at all. She shuffles to the side of the bed to make room for me to sit beside her. "Only for tonight. I can't be bothered fighting you tonight."

Tonight. And there's an edge to her tone that tells me this might very well be the last time I see her. I can't blame her. I'm a mess. But I'll take whatever little crumb she's willing to offer so I can steal even one more minute with her, especially before she finds a better man.

I slip in beside her, wrapping my arms around her shoulders. "I just need to make sure you're okay. You can hate me all you want," I begin. "I just need this. Please."

She sighs, as if defeated, and lets me scoop her into my arms, where she rests her head on my shoulder. "We're both really fucked up, huh?"

I want to laugh, but we're beyond that. Behind all the sharp wit are two individuals who struggle to show our true selves—the versions of ourselves we've been running from. Only for one night are we keeping it together to have a moment of reprieve, even though we can both sense it's breaking apart.

"Were you the tracker he hired to find me?" she asks, shifting so she can look into my eyes.

"Yes," I admit. No lies. No charm. No jokes. Only truth.

She nods slowly before resting her head against me again. "So this was all a game to you?"

"No." I adamantly force.

"Then what am I supposed to make of it?" she asks. "Were you meant to finish me?"

"No, I would've never done that." I sigh, defeated, and go on. "The only reason I took the job in the first place was because you were already working for my sister at the time, and I became curious. It wasn't difficult to recommend you return to New York to work for Dawson. They didn't know about it, by the way. I thought this way I could watch you closely while I waited for him to pay the remainder of my fees, but then I started to get to know you, taste you, be with you..." She was a blessing when she was only ever meant to be a paycheck.

"I'm so mad at you. And I don't even have the fight in me right now," she says, sounding defeated.

I sigh, exhausted, as I rest my chin on the top of her head. "Neither do I, love."

She's quiet for a moment, then says, "You know, when I left him, I thought I was doing the right thing. Their mother had just passed, and he planned on using all the inheritance and family jewels that were passed down to his younger sister. He'd already bled me dry of all my money, and I'd been stupid enough to let him.

His sister, Tilly, though..." She chokes on that. "She was only eighteen at the time. She didn't have any other family, and I thought if I stole the jewelry, I could get the money back that he took from me. But more importantly, I wanted her to get out of that environment. So I gave them to her so she could get a ticket anywhere and have enough money to set up a new life. I thought I was helping."

I'm rubbing her shoulder as she talks. I already know the end of this story, that the young woman she's talking about ended up involved in the wrong scene with drugs and ultimately committed suicide. Some paths are inevitable. Sometimes, you can offer a person the tools they need to escape, but if they don't have the courage to embrace a new environment, they'll go back to their old ways.

I can't help but smirk, thinking about how much that lesson applies to me.

"I'll replace everything he took from you tenfold," I tell her, with every intention of doing exactly that. Money means nothing to me. I have more than enough to set her free again. "No plane included this time, though."

I see the corner of her mouth tilt up. "I really hate you, you know that, right? I'm just too tired to cry or fight right now."

"I know."

"I never want to see you again after today." She looks up at me, and I'm forced to face the carnage of my own making. "Will, you might think you care about me, but I think today you saw more of your wife disappearing again than me."

Her words pierce straight into my chest. "That's not true," I say, but my voice breaks.

"Isn't it? We can try to make this look like a fantasized version, but the truth is you can't let go of Hayley, and I won't make you. I don't know if I can ever trust you after finding out that all of this was built on a lie."

"I never lied."

"But you did, Will—about so many things. I was a target. You orchestrated every part of my life over the last three months. You hide behind smiles and laughs, when, deep down, you're one of the most miserable people I know. And I want to be with someone who can move forward with me. I won't be compared to anyone else, and I don't think you're able to grow past that."

My grip tightens around her as I retreat into myself, taken in by the shackles that have kept me beside my wife's grave all these years.

"I was terrified to lose you today," I say honestly. "Not because of Hayley. Because of *you*."

She twists in my arms and puts her hand on my cheek. "I know, but it's not enough. And that's okay. Emotions are high because of what we've just experienced, but it doesn't change the fact that we should still be parting ways on that bridge."

I go to argue with her, but I can't. And I can't let go of her either.

My mind is a jumble of commotion, the thought of moving forward terrifying. But I know come tomorrow, with energy restored, she'll hate me. Her viper tongue will be back, and it'll lash at me for the secrets I kept from her. I know everything about her, and there are only small pockets of myself that I ever truly let her see.

She deserves better than me.

CHAPTER 49
Alina

When I wake up, Will is gone. I'm not surprised. And, in fact, I prefer it this way. The nurses check up on me, but all in all, I'm doing okay.

Everything about yesterday feels like a blur, and I'm still so in shock by the revelation of Jack hiring Will and re-entering my life, as well as the silent prayers I've made for Tilly. I'm sad to know she didn't get out.

I turn my nose up at the breakfast they offer. Although there doesn't appear to be anything wrong with it, my stomach churns with nausea. I haven't been able to keep anything down since the fire, and, who knows, maybe it'll take me a few days, but I've certainly been thirsty.

Honey arrives before I'm allowed to have visitors,

coming in with a bagel and coffee. "I figured you'd be hungry," she says with a smile, her pink, flowery, free-flowing dress swirling around her legs.

The moment the smell of the coffee hits my nose, bile rises in my throat, and I race to the bathroom to vomit into the sink.

"Are you okay?" she calls out.

I wipe at my mouth. I only vomited up liquid, but still, it's disgusting. "Better than ever," I lie, splashing cool water on my face. When I think I'm okay, I rejoin her, and she has the coffee on the other side of the room.

"I'm going to keep this as far away from you as possible," she jokes.

My bottom lip wobbles. "But I love coffee." So why am I not so much of a fan today?

"Maybe try to eat this. I'm sure your body is out of sorts from yesterday. How are you feeling?"

She offers me the bagel, and I take it, feeling rather famished, and this mountain of carbs looks just like what the doctor ordered.

"I'm fine. I'll be able to leave today," I tell her, then take a bite, savoring the cream cheese, grateful my stomach's not so sensitive to it.

"How did everything go with Will last night?" She takes the seat beside me.

I sigh, staring at the bagel. It was all just really messed-up. "We're done. It was only a fling, and besides, he lied to me about everything, you know? I think it's just best we leave it at that." I try to keep my tone as casual as possible.

"Is that really what you want?"

I sigh. It doesn't matter what I want. I can't change the mind of a man who is thinking of another woman —especially a woman he loved and who died. And I don't like how it makes me feel. At least I have him to thank for making me realize that perhaps opening my heart to the right person won't be so bad. Not that I ever thought the day would come.

"It is. Insurance should be able to help me get my money back after the robbery, and I have a consultation in Manchester for which I might go back. Maybe rest up in London for a bit. If you'll have me again, I'd love to work on the next project."

"Yes!" She claps her hands together, hopefully. "We're letting insurance do its thing, but in a few months, we'd like to have you back. Well, if you're willing to come back."

"Of course." I smile. "I'm very grateful to you and Rya, Honey. You've really welcomed me, and I appreciate everyone here. So thank you."

Tears spring in her eyes. "Don't make me cry; you

know I'm hormonal." She laughs through her tears. "Oh, this is from me and Rya. We were going to give it to you when the store opened, but, well, close enough." She hands me a light blue bag from Tiffany's. "Just a thank you for all your work, your friendship, and everything you've done."

"You didn't have to get me anything," I say, touched.

"Of course I did."

I open the gift to find a custom Tiffany necklace inside. I love it.

"It's so perfect. I'm never going to take it off," I gush, leaning in and giving her a hug. It's nice, and also bittersweet, to know I'll be going soon. It's been a while since I've felt so at home somewhere. That I've actually allowed myself this comfort. Besides with Maria, of course. Who I'm excited to see again. Preferably without her knowing about me and her brother. Maybe I'll wait a week or so before I tell her I'm back in town when I return to London.

"I was going to ask if you wanted to come to my baby shower, but I don't want to intrude or make you feel like you have to since I know you're flying back to London." Her hand goes to her stomach.

"When is it?" I ask, admiring the beautiful necklace.

"In a month."

"I may be able to make it work. I may have to change a few plans around, but I would love to if you would have me." Another swirl of nausea hits me, and I all but throw the necklace at her as I race back to the toilet and throw up the two bites of bagel I ate.

"Are you sure you're okay after the fire?" she asks, coming to my side and patting me on the back. I'm dry heaving, trying to hide my face. She hands me a towel and I use it to wipe my mouth.

"Thank you." My voice is hoarse. My throat feels like hell from the fire, and add to it the vomiting; it's definitely not my idea of a fun time. When I look at her, she's staring at me warily. I wipe my face again. *Do I have vomit on my face? How embarrassing.*

She crouches, then gently asks, "Alina, you're not pregnant, are you?"

I scoff. "That's not possible. I have an IUD, and I got my period like two wee—"

The words die off. Wait, did I get my period? I'd been so busy with the shop and distracted by Will that I can't remember when my last period was. I laugh. "No. I... No."

No?

No.

CHAPTER 50
Will

"You fumbled that one," Anya lectures in her Russian accent when I walk into her and Rivers' home after visiting Alina in the hospital. I wanted to make sure Alek cleaned up Jack Percy's body as promised. And as much as I enjoy pushing his buttons, barging into his apartment was never an option, so I did the next best thing. I barged into his sisters instead.

"What?" I ask, confused, as their two dogs race up to greet me.

"Alina. She's returning to London," she says matter-of-factly.

"I already know that. And since when do you care about my personal affairs?" Anya hates me, and rightly so, because her husband loves me more.

"I don't. But I don't like it when you get messy because my husband seems rather fond of you. Getting messy makes you a liability." She raises a brow at me, then adds, "Alek disposed of the body."

"You can't tell me you wouldn't have done the same," I retort.

"Well, of course." She waves a hand in the air as River enters from the kitchen.

"Is she okay?" River asks, approaching in a loose pair of pants. He kisses Anya on the cheek, then focuses back on me. "Are you okay?"

Anya snorts. "Does he look okay? He looks like a lovestruck puppy."

I sigh, exhausted.

"My beautiful wife, you're as subtle as a rhino," River jokes half-heartedly. I just don't have the fight in me today. "You're going to let her return to London just like that?" River asks more gently.

"I'm sure you'd have no trouble tracking her," Anya declares as if that's the problem.

"If you go after her again, that would be considered serious," River says, eyeing me. He's right. If I did, it would be.

So why do I want to go after her right now before she's even gone? Why does a part of me want to turn around and find exactly where she went and follow her there?

Fuck.

"She deserves someone better than me." And it goes unsaid the reasons why I can't follow her. Because if I do, it'll mean admitting that I've found someone else to love. It's not the thought of rejection that hurts the most but the idea of being unfaithful and misguidedly straying from my marital vows to Hayley.

"I'm just going to shower here and then be out of your hair," I say, making my way to their bathroom.

"Don't you have your own shower?" Anya calls out after me, but I hear River cooing at her to give me a break, just this once.

Because River is the only one who knows the ghosts that keep my feet dragging.

This is best for both Alina and me. So why do I feel like I'm breaking into pieces and missing out on something really important?

CHAPTER 51
Alina

I've been back in London for two weeks, and it feels so nice to be back in my quaint, little apartment. It's so different from the rowdiness of New York, though a small part of me misses the others, especially Honey and Rya.

I successfully acquired the contract in Manchester but don't start for another couple of weeks, so decided to use this time to figure out the perfect location for my shop. All my money was reimbursed, and I find myself sitting on a massive nest egg. However, it has done nothing to put me in a decisive mood about what to do with this... pregnancy.

I've been a sophisticated mess, continuing the day-to-day of my life until I'm back home alone. Some days, I think maybe I should keep the baby. I mean,

I'm not getting any younger, but I'm terrified at the thought of doing it on my own. I always thought I'd have a husband if I were to decide to take this step. It terrifies me to think I'll be the same as my mom. I love her, and she did so many incredible things for me growing up, but I remember picking up the pieces.

There's always the option of... not having the baby. But I don't like that either. I'm terrified of both options. I don't particularly know what to do for the first time in a long time. Honey suggested I speak to Will about it, but I don't want to make matters worse. I think we should leave things where they ended. And besides, he's not able to move on from his past, so how could I possibly ask him to consider this journey or future? It's better if he doesn't know. This is for me to deal with alone.

I haven't seen or heard from Will since the night we spent in the hospital. I know I pushed for it, and I still can't wholly whip my head around the notion that I'd been his original target. But I've been lying to myself that he isn't the person I miss the most. And that makes me all the more foolish for falling for his charm.

In a less fucked up world, I don't know what I might've done had he pursued me. Even when sitting in my apartment alone with a cup of tea, my mind drifts to him, and I'm embarrassed by the fact that I let him in. I hate him. But I want him. And it's not fair. Especially when I'm doing everything I can to put what happened between us in the past.

When I caught up with Maria last week, she asked questions about New York. She'd heard about the assault and fire, which made headlines in certain magazines, but past that, she never asked about what transpired between me and Will. For that, I was grateful. I hadn't brought up the pregnancy either. Honey is the only person who knows, and because I'm eight weeks along, I feel like I have to make a decision soon. But it's strange to know there's something growing inside of me. I have all the means to support a child, but I'm not sure if I'm brave enough to do it on my own. Ultimately, no matter how independent I've always thought I am, it turns out I'm still a coward at heart.

A knock sounds on my apartment door, and I stand up expectantly. I stayed in touch with Steven, and when I mentioned I was looking for a storefront in London, he let me know he'd done some work here previously and knew a few real estate agents who could help me.

Apparently, he also has a cousin here he was due to visit, but I don't know how true that is or if he was just trying to sound less eager to help me. The last thing on my mind right now is dating.

When I open the door, Steven is standing there with a smile. I forget how shiny his positive demeanor is. It's refreshing, to say the least, especially during a drizzly week.

He looks good, dressed in a cream suit and a dark overcoat, as the weather is starting to get colder now. His eyes light up, and he immediately leans in to kiss me, and I give him my cheek.

"It's so good to see you," he says, his hand still holding my arm.

"And you. I just have to get my bag and we're good to go." I turn and grab my bag from the small table by the door, and when I step into the hallway, I find him waiting for me patiently.

"Coffee first?" he asks.

"Sounds good." I live relatively close to a lot of shops and cafés, so we decide to walk.

"How have you been? I know we message, but it's good to see you again. When I saw you last month, it was a bit awkward. I felt like we couldn't really talk. Are you still seeing Will?" He hasn't actually asked me about Will in the last month that we've been messaging, and I'm glad he didn't because it would have been awkward. I needed time to work out my feelings for

Will, process the fire, and transition back to my life in London. Not to mention the other big thing I have to make a heavy decision about soon.

"Nope. Just a casual fling, like I told you. I haven't spoken to Will since I left New York."

"Okay, good. I didn't want to get in between anything you two may have had going on." I don't like the implication that he thinks he's getting involved with anything. I side-eye him. I mean, someone like Steven is a great example of an ideal partner. So why can't I fall for someone like him instead of some Xbox-playing bounty hunter?

"Nothing going on," I reiterate, trying to restrain the bitterness in my voice. Why do I always go for the guy who isn't right for me? Steven and I have plenty in common, and he's intelligent and physically attractive. Shouldn't I be after someone like him? Wouldn't my mother approve if I brought someone like Steven home?

"I'm glad to hear it," he says, trying to hide a hopeful smile. A small part of me likes it. After everything that happened, it's nice to be wanted, even though I don't look at Steven in that way. I'm wondering if I ever can.

We walk into a café and each order a coffee. He pays as I take a seat at a table and wait. A few minutes later, he hands me mine and sits opposite me. "It's good to see you, Alina. Really good."

"Thanks." I smile. The way he said it makes me feel like he's complimenting something else.

"I don't get it. I don't understand how you're still not married. You were the girl everyone wanted back in school."

I try not to snort my coffee out my nose. "That's news to me."

He smiles when he looks at his coffee. "Surely, you knew. Then again, you shot down most of the boys as quickly as they showed an interest in you."

"I didn't shoot you down," I point out, though I can't entirely remember how we started dating in the first place. He wasn't my first boyfriend or my last, and I was young and naive to the notion of love and dating. Years later, I'm just jaded from it now.

"Have you been close to marriage?" he asks curiously. The question catches me off guard. Okay, so we're going down this rabbit hole. And it's probably my least favorite conversation to partake in, considering I'm in the midst of re-evaluating everything in my life.

I wrap my hands around the coffee cup.

"No, no marriage. Just work and discovering who I am." I pause. "What about you? Ever get close to getting married?" Because how do I explain the enigma of my past? I almost think it's easier that Will studied up on me and knew most things in finer detail, so I didn't have to explain it all. It felt like a cheat code, one I was surprisingly okay with.

I try to return to the conversation with Steven instead of my mind wandering to the one man I vowed I'd stop thinking about.

"I was engaged once. But she ended up leaving me for a friend. Said I was too married to my work," he says with a hint of bittersweetness. "I think it was for the best, though, since apparently, she was having an affair with my friend for like a year, and I had no idea."

"Ouch. Not a friend anymore, I'm assuming?" I feel for the guy. That's rough.

"No, not a friend anymore. You can imagine their shock when I didn't accept their wedding invitation." He laughs when he sees my expression.

"Ooof. That's brutal. What about your sister?" I ask, and the question is out there before I think better of it. Was that tactless to ask, considering the exchange we had at the party?

"She's good. She's actually married."

"Really?" I ask, surprised. Then why is she pining over Will? I hadn't even checked to see if she was wearing a ring. "Wow, I didn't think she was married with the way she acted toward Will."

"Oh no, she got married last week. She's on her honeymoon now. And not that I'm advocating for her, but Will is a touchy subject for her. It took her months to move on from him."

He says it like that makes it right. It actually makes it worse that she was sad about another man while she was about to marry another. I hope one day when I get married, I'll never be like that. I want the man to be just as obsessed with me as I would be with him. Especially if I chose to marry them. My thoughts of marriage seem to dwindle more and more in my future.

"Nice," is all I can say.

"Yep. Will has that effect. He fucks them, leaves them, and they end up married. So maybe, in a weird way, he's a good luck charm."

I laugh at that. A good luck charm? Will? Please. "You know of others to prove this theory?" I ask.

"Yep, one of my assistants as well. She's married now, too." I bite the inside of my cheek, imagining the way his head would inflate if he heard this. "You may be lucky next." And the way he says it makes me believe he's hoping to be that lucky person. I don't see it as good luck as Steven does. I see it as Will telling them how it was going to be, and that's it. Good for them, they got married later.

"Steven, I don't know if I'm exactly dating material, let alone marriage material," I say, trying to subtly let him down.

"You don't know until you try," he says optimistically. His phone begins to buzz in his pocket. When he fishes it out, his smile widens. "That's the first real estate agent, Luke. He's a good friend of mine. Are you ready to meet him?"

I smile appreciatively, not entirely comfortable with how he boycotted my subtle way of letting him down. But I'm equally excited to find the perfect shop space. Not working on a project is spiraling me into a version of myself with which I'm not entirely comfortable.

CHAPTER 52
Will

I hit the cue ball and sink two solid-colored balls. I then sink another. And another.

River sighs. "You might as well be playing pool on your own at this point if you're not going to even let me have a turn."

I sink the eight ball. End of game. Another win.

I flash an arrogant smile that doesn't hold any humor. Nothing does since Alina screamed at me over two weeks ago. I know she's safe after the fire, but how can I face her after she knows the ugliness of my truth? Besides, for just a second, I thought... I wondered what it might be like to have a life with her instead of the one I'd imagined with Hayley.

It felt like my path was correcting its own course

with the way everything happened. Making sure I wasn't being misguided away from my vows to Hayley.

Nobody in the rundown bar has approached us since we walked in. I wanted somewhere quiet, unseen and not memorable as I drank away my sorrows.

So if I feel like this with Alina, why do I feel like I'm mourning for my wife all over again? I don't get it. For the first time in a long time, I've sat in my misery for the past two weeks. I've mainly tried to drown out my sorrows with liquor.

River licks his lips anxiously. "I can't do this anymore. You can't stay like this, man. You either run after her or throw yourself back into work, but you can't keep dragging me out every night so you can drink yourself into oblivion."

I throw back the whiskey just to make a point of his previous comment.

"It's better this way," I say.

He sighs as he leans against the bar stool. "For who? So you originally found her because of a job, but you chose her over the money. So why should her finding out about it be any different?"

"That's not the problem here, and you know it," I grit out through my teeth. The ghost of my wife stands between us. Neither of us can see her, but it's always the presence felt when he brings up any mention of a future with Alina.

His shoulders sag as I go to the bar and order another drink. As I'm waiting, I turn to where I left River. He's racking up the balls for another game.

The bartender offers me a tentative smile and passes me the whiskey, but I'm not interested. How could I be when I'd been with the most beautiful woman only weeks earlier?

When I rejoin River, he leans against the pool table and studies me. "This is about Hayley?" he daringly asks.

I glare at him. River and Alina are the only two who know about her.

River sighs, defeated. "I'm not going to tell you how to live your life. But it's been seven years. I imagine Hayley would want you to be happy instead of living for a ghost."

"How can you say that? If someone took Anya away from you, do you think you could so easily replace her?" I snap back.

River's jaw tics and I'm apologetic at throwing that situation out there, but there's no way he can offer advice when he hasn't felt pain like mine. Hasn't known what it's like to lose the woman you love and honestly know whether you're allowed to continue having happiness. Those types of vows and loyalty don't just dissolve because she died.

My shoulders sag because I'm a fucking mess, a jumble of mixed feelings and grief I know I never truly dealt with, and right now, I don't know the way out from under its weight.

"You're not replacing Hayley. But you've been happy with Alina around. It's the first time I've seen the real you come out. I didn't know Hayley, but I sure as hell know that you deserve to be that person. To have that joy, even if it is irritating to everyone else." I can't even smirk or find humor in his jab.

"There you are!" a woman yells out across the bar. River's and my head both swivel as a very pissed-off Honey storms in with Dawson only a few steps behind her.

"Fuck," I murmur under my breath, knowing I'm about to get an earful.

"I didn't know Jack was going to find her. I'll pay whatever you need for the shop and—"

Slap. I'm stunned as the heat of her palm spreads across my cheek. But I surprisingly welcome its sting.

I adjust my jaw as I look at her in a new light. To be perfectly frank, I didn't think she had it in her.

"We don't want your money," Honey growls.

"Why are you still here in New York? Why haven't you gone after her?"

I shoot a glance at Dawson, who is staring at me. We might be friendly enough, but I imagine if I disrespect his woman, I'll have my head spiked even if she is running on crazy pregnancy hormones. That is what this is, right?

"She doesn't want me around," I say as I circle the table and chalk my cue stick again. When I line up the shot, her hand shoves the stick down. I grudgingly look at her as she demands my full attention. She has one hand on her hip.

"For someone who's wearing a very pretty yellow dress today, you're don't seem very sunshiny," I comment.

"Do you want me to slap you again?" She purses her lips. "Do you have any idea what she's going through on her own right now? You should be there."

I'm confused. "Why would she want me to chase after her when she basically told me that if she saw me again, she'd set me on fire."

"I didn't think you were such a coward," Honey hisses.

My jaw clenches, and I look at Dawson again, who now has his arms folded over his chest. Right, I'm definitely going to get a lecture tonight, whether I like it or not.

"You love her, don't you?" Honey demands.

"No."

"You're a liar." She points her finger in my face.

How dare she when she doesn't even know...

"I see the way you two look at each other," she says defiantly, and that takes away my irritation. "The way you laugh with one another and gravitate to each other. And I don't know who the bigger idiot between the two of you is for denying what you actually have together. But no matter what, right now, you need to be with her before she makes a decision she'll regret."

That snaps me to attention. "Is she okay? What's happened?"

Honey steps back, surprised by my immediate change in attitude. She then seems to realize what she said because she steps back into Dawson's chest and she carefully considers her words. "I'm just saying, as a friend, you need to be with her now," she grits.

"Honey, what do you know?" I demand. Is she going to hurt herself? Is she not okay from the fire? What happened?

Honey's eyes begin to water, and her hands cover her stomach. It's not Honey, I see, but Alina. The hand on her stomach...

My eyebrows furrow as something springs to mind. It couldn't be....

"Is she—" I choke on the word.

Honey seems to have realized where she placed her hands because she removes them, and tears spill from her eyes. "No." Her voice jumps. "Fucking hormones," she quips herself.

I go to grab her out of desperation for information, but Dawson's arm wraps protectively around her shoulders, and he stares me down. Touching his wife is completely off-limits.

My mind is running at a million miles an hour. "Honey, is Alina...?"

I can't even say it out loud.

Is she carrying my child?

Is that even possible?

I never thought... never knew... never thought of the possibility.

"You need to find her, Will. She's not in a good place right now."

My world feels like it's tearing apart as if I've made the biggest mistake of my life, and my feet are moving of their own accord as I rush out of the bar and toward the woman I should've never let go.

Something in me shifts. No matter the turmoil. No matter the pain. No matter how uncomfortable it all is. There's something new. A new life. A new need for me. A new opportunity for me to be a better man. A new path and future I had never even considered. I can't put it into words, but it removes any restrictions I've put on myself. For the first time in years, I feel like I'm running toward something.

But first I have to catch the girl.

A private jet would've been a fucking bonus right now.

CHAPTER 53
Alina

Steven's friend showed me a storefront with office space yesterday. It was really nice. In fact, its location is almost perfect, and I have the room to potentially add a team of four. But something feels off. I don't know if it's me or if I'm still unsure as to whether I should be setting up in London or New York. I know I can eventually have an office in both cities, but I'm so undecided, and I think it mostly has a lot to do with everything else going on.

I told Steven I'd meet him for dinner tonight. When he asked me out for dinner after meeting with his friend, a small part of me expected that I'd say no, that I don't feel anything for him other than friendship. But another part asked, *what if it grows into something more?* The matter of the pregnancy might complicate things, but it's nice to be seen and to be desired.

He isn't using me for sex. He hasn't even made a move to kiss me. He's been respectful the whole time, and I feel guilty he flew all this way, even if he does have a cousin he's visiting.

When I walk into the restaurant, I give the reservation name and am taken to the back and seated at a table. Getting my phone out, I check the time. I'm ten minutes late, but Steven hasn't messaged me, and I realize he's not here yet, either.

The waitress comes over and asks me what I want to drink.

"She'll have water," I hear someone say as they take the seat across from me. My heart rate picks up, and I clutch my hands beneath the table as they immediately start to feel clammy. I freeze, staring at the man dressed in a sharp blue suit who sits opposite me like it's his God-given right.

With one hand, he undoes the button to his suit jacket. I'm lost for words at the sight of Will's tight lips, which are usually a dazzling smile. I never thought I'd see those blue eyes again.

"Hello, love," he says.

"Love?" I cough, shaking my head. "You've given

up on *milady*?" I spit back at him. "And you aren't welcome here. That is someone else's seat."

"Oh, I know. Steven. You can do better." When he notices the waitress isn't sure what to do, he adds arrogantly, "Make that two sparkling waters, please."

She nods and scurries away. I cross my arms over my chest.

"I can, can I?"

"Yes, of course you can. With your skills and beauty, a woman like you can do better."

"Oh, and are you better?" I question. He offers a smile, but it doesn't reach his gaze. His eyes are rimmed with black circles, most likely more sleepless nights. It's satisfying to know I'm not the only one.

"I would be a great start, but no."

"Why the fuck are you here, Will? Can't you just leave me alone?"

"No," he abruptly says, and the tone in his voice catches me off guard. My hands naturally gravitate toward my stomach protectively. The moment I realize I'm doing it, I stop. I don't understand any of it.

"Last time we spoke, we promised to go our separate ways," I remind him.

"Yes, and you told me that you hate me."

"I still do," I bite back. "The only reason I'm not

losing my shit and flipping this table right now is because I quite like this restaurant."

He smirks. "That's never stopped you before."

The waitress brings over water and leaves as quickly as she came. "Why the fuck are you here, Will? Are you actually trying to break me?"

His gaze lifts to mine, and he licks his lips, but he seems temporarily lost for words for once. I laugh and roll my eyes. Great, more head fuckery. It's certainly starting to make Steven look like a fucking treat.

A cruel smile tilts my lips. "Have you heard that all the women you fuck end up married after you?" I ask, thinking back on Steven's words. "Maybe Steven and I will get married. Maybe he can offer me what I want, leaving no room for someone like you to be here."

He only considers this for a moment before his quick wit takes over. "What a boring marriage that would be. I don't think he could fuck you the way you like it," he states blatantly.

"And what, you're an expert on that?"

"Of course I am. I'm well acquainted with all things Alina and her body."

I lean back, one eye twitching. "I'm sick of these games, Will. I'm not your toy. I do have a heart somewhere beneath all of this."

"I know," he replies solemnly, and it's the first time

I've seen him so quiet and reserved. The energy around us shifts as if momentarily both of our guards are down. *What the fuck is happening right now?* "How did you even find me? And what did you do with my date?"

"I don't want to talk about Steven right now. I want to talk about us."

I stumble over my next words. "Th-there is no us, Will. We made that crystal clear before I left New York. You need a new plaything to distract you, and I need..."

"What do you need?" he asks, leaning in as if everything hinges on my following words.

"Will, this is ridiculous. I'm supposed to be having dinner with another man right now. You don't do relationships, remember?!" The older couple beside me flinch at how loud my voice is, and I reprimand myself.

"Fuck that guy!" Will has no issue with matching my tone. "What if I... What if I wanted to try to have a...relationship."

I laugh in disbelief, and when I realize he's serious, I laugh harder. "Will, you can't be serious. No. We're done. There was nothing more than just some fun between us."

"But there is more, and you and I both know it."

There's a lethal edge to his tone, and it snaps me out of my hysterics because I wonder... Does he know?

An unsaid tension runs between us, and I'm snapped out of it as Steven walks in, flustered. I immediately avert my gaze from Will, not entirely sure what just transpired between us. He can't be serious. Will Walker wants a relationship? No. Surely, I heard him wrong.

"Will?" Steven says, shocked. Great. This is just fucking great. If looks could kill, Will would be six feet under. Will, on the other hand, just offers him one of his dazzling smiles.

"You're in my seat," Steven says adamantly.

"Oh, it seems I am. Sorry. Just saw Alina sitting all by herself, as her date was late, and figured I could steal her time." Will stands and steps over to me. He grabs one of my hands, lifts it, and kisses the top of it, his eyes on me the whole time. I hate the effect his touch and imposing presence have on me. I hate this guy. I try to remind myself of that, but I'm not an exception to his charm. "You and I are not done," he says intensely before turning and leaving.

I don't know what to do or say. I still can't believe he's here and spouting nonsense about trying... trying what? A relationship between me and Will? It sounds like a disaster waiting to happen.

Steven looks pissed as he stands beside his chair territorially as if Will might take it from him again.

"I didn't realize I was late," Steven says, eyeing me. "I got your email today about the change of time."

My email?

I stare at the back of Will as he walks away.

That son of a bitch hacked my email.

I'm slightly impressed but pissed at the same time.

"Sorry. I made it in earlier than I originally thought I could. I'm glad you're here now. That was awkward," I say, trying my best to defuse the tension forming between us.

Steven doesn't seem convinced as he sits across from me, and he does nothing to fill the space of the man who was there only a minute ago. He's dressed in a gray suit today. And while he looks good, he doesn't look as good as Will, nor does my body gravitate toward his like it does Will's. And I fucking hate acknowledging that.

Will has this air about him that he knows he's the best in any room. And while I think that may be true in some aspects, to others it might just come off as him being an arrogant asshole.

Which he may also be considered to be as well.

But deep in my heart, I know a part of Will that they don't get to see, and it's that which clouds my judgment. That is reserved for a woman who no longer exists except only in memories.

But that has nothing to do with the head fuckery I experience with Will. I respected his wishes and his deceased wife, and yet he feels like he can just come storming into my life whenever he pleases. For what? A quick shag? Whatever his definition of a relationship is?

"Alina, I want you to know that I like you," Steven states, and it's so abrupt that I'm pulled out of my spiraling thoughts. "And while I don't like Will, I am willing to help you through this phase."

Phase? What the fuck does that even mean?

I sit, confused, and wait for him to clarify his statement. Surely, I didn't hear him right. But when he speaks, I wish he didn't.

"Will is bad news. Not only does he deal with criminals, he himself is one. And I believe you know better than to associate with those kinds of people, considering you're trying to build up your business. How would your customers feel knowing you're associated with men like him? Would they feel comfortable with that? All I'm saying is, I would cut all ties as fast as possible before you get in any deeper."

I'm sure he thinks what he's saying is helpful. But the way he says it, and the way he speaks of Will, is low, even for him. I sit back and say nothing while he calls the waitress over and orders us each a glass of red wine. I stare at the untouched glasses of water, realizing that ordinarily, Will would've ordered us a bottle of champagne or wine. But this time, he ordered water.

I still at the thought with the dreaded realization that I think he knows.

On top of that, I'm not feeling overly friendly toward Steven for condemning "people like Will." He's not wrong and is entitled to his opinion, but I have friends who are associated with the criminal world, and they have been the closest thing to sisters I've found in a long time. They've uplifted me and supported me, offering me further opportunities. Maria, Honey, and Rya. Would Steven look down on them the moment he realizes they're a bit morally gray?

Most likely. And in my heart of hearts, I know I'm not entirely a good person either. I steal things for a kick. And where Will found it entertaining, I realize this man—an average man—would not look upon that fondly.

We're just too mismatched, even if I do think a man like Steven is better for me.

I hardly speak through the meal, and to be honest, I don't even know if he notices. Or cares. He talks about himself a lot. And besides a few words of encouragement on my end, my head's spinning, and I feel like my decisions are crowding in on me.

It's as easy as that for Will to simply walk back into my life and cause an avalanche and ripple effect. Because again he's all I can think about, and I hate this power he has over me. I don't understand it or the intense pull I have to follow after him. And I hate that.

When Steven asks for the bill, the waitress informs him it was paid for. By Will. This makes Steven's face go red as he stands.

I silently follow him out as he begins bad-mouthing Will again and tries to flag us down a cab. I remain near the entrance until he finally looks back at me as if actually seeing the real me for the first time. I realize, as sweet and attentive as I thought he was this last week, he's not looking at *me* but simply someone who can fill the fantasy of what he has for a partner or wife.

"Thank you for everything, Steven, but I don't think this is going to work," I tell him. "I like you as a friend. But I don't think it will go any further," I say honestly. At first, he stands there, confused, then he steps up to me.

"Look, I know I can come on strong sometimes, but it will work, I'm sure of it," he says matter-of-factly. "We both love the same things, and it could be so easy for us." It goes without saying that I've never done anything easy in my life. "We just need you to remove yourself from him. He's toxic." Steven shakes his head, still fuming about Will. And I get it. Will has a certain knack for pissing people off.

Maybe some of my confusion has to do with Will, but I'm confident I know what I want for myself. Well, at least I know it doesn't involve Steven.

"It's not Will, Steven. I just don't see you that way." Before I can tell him anything else, he kisses me. I freeze at how quickly it happens.

I didn't ask him to kiss me, and I don't want his kiss. I shove him back, and when he realizes I'm not smiling, his smile drops, and his brows pinch together.

"Really? Nothing?"

"Nothing. And the only reason I'm not kicking you in the balls right now is because I know you thought that was a good move to make. It wasn't. Don't ever do that to a woman again." I wipe at my lips, feeling disgusted, not having the heart to tell him that his breath still smells.

"I'm going to catch my own cab," I say. "Thank you for everything, but I think we're done here." I walk away, holding my jacket tightly.

"He won't ever love you. You know it's a waste of

time, right?" Steven shouts out behind me. I say nothing back. I didn't mention Will, he did. So, I'm not playing into that game at all.

When I round the corner, I throw my hands in the air, furious. "For fuck's sake."

"I bet he tasted foul," Will says, leaning against the wall, watching me. "Would you like me to change the taste in your mouth?"

I ignore him and continue walking. He kicks off the wall and follows behind me. "Your apartment is the other way," he says, and I hate that he knows that. He knows everything about me, and yet I still can't figure out what that brilliant mind of his is thinking. I gave up on trying to figure it out weeks ago.

"You can't just hack my emails," I yell, knowing he can hear me. He's smart enough to at least keep some distance between us as I weave through people.

"Yes, well I wanted to spend quality time with you, is that a crime?" he says behind me.

"It is. Move on like you were supposed to. Stop dragging this out," I furiously say without turning to look over my shoulder at him.

"I'd like to drag something, but not you, maybe *through* you..." I gasp in shock, and come to a stop to face him, embarrassed if others heard. He seems smug with himself as if knowing that would get me to stop hastily walking and get me to bite.

"Come on, love, just stop and let me drive you, home." He sounds desperate.

"Just leave me alone, Will! I can't keep doing this dumb shit. We're not teenagers. There is no us! You can't leave the past and I won't make you!" I snap. People walk around us, curious about the spectacle.

"I'm trying, but it's not easy for me. But you didn't tell me about the future we could have. You kept that from me," he scolds. I wince at the lethal edge in his tone. The vulnerability and hurt. He knows about the pregnancy. He has to.

I grind my molars. And like a coward, I flip him off and keep walking. I can't talk to him about this. It has nothing to do with him. It's my decision whether I keep and raise the baby on my own. And the decision won't be dependent on this man.

I shouldn't have worn my heels today. That was a stupid mistake. One I'm now paying for.

I cross my arms over my chest and try to walk faster, but I can still sense that he's following me, so I try my hardest to lose him in the crowd. I'm unsure why he's here, and to be honest, it's messing with my head. We aren't teenagers, and I feel like we laid everything out perfectly before I left New York, so seeing him again makes my heart beat faster and my hands sweatier, and I hate that he can get this reaction from me. No other man gives me heart palpitations like he does, even if he is hacking my emails.

Fucking asshole.

Before I can turn the corner, arms wrap around me from behind, and my legs are flipped out from beneath me as Will carries me bridal style, knocking the air out of my lungs. He turns me around and starts walking back the way we came.

"What are you doing? Put me down!" I demand as I thrash in his hold, equally embarrassed at the people watching us. I purposefully push at his face, which he spectacularly ignores.

"No, you're cold and not thinking right. You're angry and irrational. You can hit me when we're in the car or you can wait until we get to your place. But we're discussing this."

This.

Us.

The enormity of what hasn't yet been said out loud.

I kick back and forth, trying to escape his ironclad hold, furious that he knows. Wild that he can't just let me go, to let me have enough breath from him to think straight. I keep hitting because I should hate this man. I do hate this man. But a tiny part of me clings to the fact that he followed me. A small part of me breaking, realizing that I can't keep doing this.

"A little harder, love. I may like it." I stop hitting him, and even when I try to wiggle free from his grasp, he doesn't let me go. He just strides on, and the busy crowd parts for him like he's some kind of God.

He finally stops and puts me down when I see an all-black car. He opens the door, but I refuse to get in.

"No, Will! Enough. I won't be some consolation prize!" Now, I don't even care who can hear me.

"You're not!" he says desperately. "I'm losing my mind and I don't know what to do. But, Alina, I know it all keeps coming back to you. I *need* you."

"I need someone who can love me unconditionally, Will. Someone who won't have me comparing myself with their past. Someone who makes me feel secure!" I adamantly say.

"You want me to drop down to one knee? I will," he replies breathlessly.

My mouth opens and then snaps shut. Tears water my eyes, and a hot rage fills me. "How fucking dare you! Do you think I'm going to be appeased because you want to shut me up with a ring?"

"No, but I'm willing to give you whatever you want. I will take vows to chain myself to you, Alina, if that's the start to make you feel secure."

I scoff. "Is that what I am to you, a ball and chain?"

"You're so much more and you know that," he insists. "It's not just the fun we have, Alina. You are a piece of me I didn't realize that's missing. That I never thought I could have again."

It's a cruel, twisted joke as I try to laugh between sobs. "And what about Hayley?" The ghost in the room, my unsaid competition. And I hate that I even think of her that way because I've never felt this way about someone who is so attached to his ghosts.

"I'm learning to let go," he says quietly, and tears begin to well in his eyes. "Please, Alina, I'm trying. I want a future with you. I want a future where we can grow and build a family."

I scoff at that last part, but I can't even see him through the tears that fill my eyes.

"You never told me you were pregnant," he adds, and I can feel my heart breaking.

"You don't get a say in this!"

"Of course I get a say in this!" he screams back. Right now, despite the public display, it only feels like us.

"This might be a moment for you, a chivalrous responsibility you're feeling, but this is *my* life. *My* responsibility. When you decide to come and go, *I* will be raising this child."

"It's not just you!"

"How is it not? How can you expect me to believe that you can go from 'we're just having a fling' to 'I want to put a ring on your finger and raise this child together'?"

"I ran into a burning building for you! I don't know how else I can show you other than with actions as to how much I love you! I was in so much fucking fear that day that I thought I'd lose you!" More tears well in my eyes at his confession.

"I've tried so hard to keep you away because I thought it was best for you, but I'm too fucking selfish for that." He takes a step forward. "I can't... I just can't imagine you in a world that doesn't allow me in it. Yes, you started off as a job. But, Alina, you turned into a beacon I didn't even realize I needed." He's a mess as he reaches for my hand. "Please, Alina. I will prove to you that I can be a better man. I will do anything that you ask of me."

"And if I ask you to leave me alone?" I squeak out because this is ridiculous. It brings me too much pain and turmoil. It hurts and splits me in two, and I can't handle the hold he has over me.

"I can't do that," he admits as he takes another step and encroaches further into my space. "I won't let any other man have you. Steven's lucky I didn't fucking shoot him. I can't do this without you, Alina. I'm fucking miserable."

Tears stream down my cheeks as I look into his blue eyes that are also leaking tears, and I think this isn't only me he's mourning but perhaps what he's forced to relinquish as he makes this confession. The wife of his past and the future with me he's imagining for himself now.

"I fucking hate you so much," I confess through a shaky breath. He should've stayed away and made it easier for the both of us. But I'm so tired of fighting him. Of fighting this connection.

"I know, love." He dips his forehead to mine. "But I will find you no matter what part of the world you're in. I just can't stay away from you. Please let me stay," he says quietly, and the vulnerability breaks me in two.

"It's so complicated, Will. You can't just decide to be with me because I'm pregnant. It's not fair to either of us."

He laughs, and it dispels the heaviness of the situation as I look up at him through wet lashes, surprised and uncertain. "If anything, it was the catalyst for me to get my sorry ass moving sooner. I want this with you, Alina, more than I've wanted anything else. I want to move forward with you. So I'd call it a blessing."

I'm shocked, and the honest words slip from my mouth. "I'm scared. I've never done this before."

He lets out a nervous breath, and his hand comes to rest on my cheek. "Neither have I, love. But with how much I filled you with my cum, I can't say I'm all that surprised. And maybe I was a selfish prick for hoping it'd happen."

I'm a mix of fury and disbelief. Don't get me wrong, I understand we both got off on it, but I never actually thought it'd eventuate to this... Before I can feel any other type of way he confesses.

"I'm not a good man, but I'm yours if you'll have me."

I sigh with exhaustion and a spark of hope.

But there's also the need to preserve myself, to want to shield myself from this vulnerability since I'd already been hurt by it before. The thought of hope and fear mix, trying to outweigh one another.

"This is wild, Will." I try to envision what we might look like in the future.

"This is us, Alina. Wild, explosive, and hopefully a lot of hate fucking."

I laugh at that, hating that he can make me laugh even under the circumstances. He wraps his arms around my waist, his gaze never leaving mine.

"When I tell you I love you, Alina, I mean it. I've

been fixated on you from the moment I met you. No games, no ulterior motive. I just want us to move forward together."

"What if you hate me for it?" I ask quietly. "What if you feel like you're being trapped into this? Or you can't let go of the past, or I don't compare. Or…"

"You are your own experience and love, Alina. You're not to be compared, and you trapped me inevitably the moment you first called me an asshole, and I tasted you for the first time on that flight."

My heart is pounding because it all feels too real, too magical. It's a gamble and a bet but with the highest stake–my heart.

"Here I thought I dodged a bullet with you," I say, with the realization as to why I care so much about him hitting me at that moment. Because as much as we denied this thing between us, I've learned so much about myself with Will, and I wasn't willing to admit that when I was in that fire. Besides my mother, he is the person I thought of most. And when he broke through those flames, I knew then, without a doubt, that I loved him. But I was always too scared to admit it. Because it was easier to push him away than risk the chances of my heart being broken.

He sighs, almost sounding defeated. "You and me both, love."

"I love you, Will, but I still hate you."

"I wouldn't have it any other way, milady," he says before kissing me. It feels like the first breath I've taken since leaving New York. Like the piece I was missing has finally returned to me. And I realize now why it'd been so hard for me to settle on a location for my office. It was never about the place but the person I wanted to call home.

CHAPTER 54

Will

"Are you sure about this?" Alina asks quietly. I hold her hand. I'm nervous, sad, and unsure, but not about Alina being back here in America with me or the fact that we're walking to the gravesite of my deceased wife. I'm sure I want Alina with me, but I'm unsure as to how I can truly say goodbye to Hayley and let go now.

"I don't have to come with you, Will," she says nervously.

"I want you here with me, love. I just need to say goodbye one last time," I confess. It might be selfish to bring her here, and I don't know why I had the urgency for them to "meet" in some kind of way, but it feels as if while closing one door, I'm showing Alina the truth to my words—that I'm willing to pry the door open to our future.

The flowers I had delivered only two weeks ago have begun to wilt on Hayley's tombstone. I sigh as I pick them up and put the new bunch of flowers down. My hand is tight around Alina's. It's been some time since I've returned here.

But as I stare down, I'm frightfully aware that it's something I should've done sooner, or perhaps it would've never happened until I met Alina, who pushed me to live again. I'd forgotten my hopes and dreams when Hayley died. But more than anything, I couldn't wait to be a father and a loving husband who devoted myself to his wife like my dad to my mom in my own childhood.

I thought when Hayley died, I couldn't have any of that. That I was betraying her if I ever sought it out elsewhere. But when Alina almost perished in that fire... I was reliving the panic all over again, and a rude awakening snapped me into action.

Alina's been patient with me, even when I didn't deserve it. I don't deserve her, but I'd give everything, including my life, to have her by my side.

I realize now it doesn't take away the love I had for Hayley and that there was a reason I didn't die with her. I look at Alina, who's staring down at Hayley's grave, and I brush my thumb over hers.

From the past to the future, no matter what it brings. Most likely a spitfire of a child who's as much of an asshole as they are fiercely independent. A small smile curves my lips as I look at the woman who's beautiful in every way and soon to be the mother of my child. It's early days, but without a doubt, I know I'll live the rest of my life by her side.

"What is it?" Alina asks quietly.

"I was just thinking about how lucky I am to have you."

A small smile flicks up the corner of her mouth as she leans over and presses a kiss to my cheek in reply, and we both look down at the grave.

Thank you, Hayley, for loving me. Thank you for letting me go.

CHAPTER 55
Alina

"We're not having a shotgun wedding," I say adamantly to Will as I do up his shirt buttons. We'd just had another fucking marathon, and had I not already been pregnant; I'd most likely be pregnant from the acts we just performed in his new penthouse.

"But you said you loved the ring I bought you," he says arrogantly because he does have good taste. It's been sitting on the tableside ever since he showed it to me.

"It's beautiful, Will, but right now, there's a lot happening, and we need to focus on those things first. I'm opening a storefront here in New York and in London. We're here for Honey and Dawson's baby shower, and I'm starting on a new project in Manchester. Engagement and weddings can wait."

He pulls me in by the waist. "I thought you wanted marriage."

"I do. But it doesn't have to be today. And besides, I'd hate to take away from your sister's enjoyment of turning into a bridezilla on my behalf."

He chuckles as he squats down and straps my heels on for me. His hand grazes up my calf, and I slap him away. "Will, we're already late. We're not fucking again," I grit out. He looks depressed as he sighs and stands. He takes my hand and leads me outside.

When we're in the car, I flick through emails and contracts. Because we didn't know where we wanted to live yet, Will bought an apartment in New York, and I bought a bigger one in London. We now also own a private plane, which is rather handy despite how grand it feels. I've only used it when traveling with Will, but he insists anything that's his is now mine.

Turns out, among all the push and pull, he's a lovesick puppy and a fool at that. It feels like I'm the only one resistant to how quickly everything is changing, yet I'm so happy. Genuinely happy. Because no matter how much I fought it and called it sexual attraction, Will has been the only man I've been utterly captivated by, as much as I hate his arrogant male pride.

But I also love him because of it.

Maria was surprised to hear we were officially dating and almost passed out when we told her about the pregnancy. I was nervous it would tarnish our friendship, but she broke down into tears, celebrating that she'd finally get a sister.

I felt that so deeply.

The same goes for my newly found family here in New York.

We arrive at Honey and Dawson's lavish mansion, where only a few cars are parked. A house attendant greets us as we walk in, and Honey squeals in excitement when she sees me.

"I was wondering what was taking you so long," she says as she stares daggers at Will accusingly, and he puts his hands up in defense.

My eyes bulge at the massive, wrapped present in the hallway. "What on earth is that?" I ask.

Honey laughs as she tugs me toward it and whispers, "I'm too scared to open it in front of everyone. It's a present from Anya and River. She said she would never attend such an occasion but sent a present anyway. I'm scared as to what Anya might interpret as baby-friendly."

"It looks like a fortress." Will whistles beside me, inspecting its size.

"That's what we thought," Rya says as she comes up and gives me a big hug. "It's good to see you couldn't stay away from us for too long."

Will's face lights up as he sees Alek and his wife, Lena. I haven't officially met her, but know it's her from the way Alek is glued to her side. He looks uncomfortable with the children running around. Will flitters off in his direction, and I watch Alek's expression slacken.

I chuckle as Honey drags me toward an attractive couple who look to be in their fifties. "These are my parents. Mom. Dad. I want you to meet Alina."

I freeze momentarily as I greet them because I remember the Ricci sisters describing their father. As I look around, I notice how many security guards are standing around the place. Definitely not a normal baby shower.

"Come back," I hear Crue grumble behind me as a toddler does his best to escape.

Honey laughs as she catches the boy. "Eli's recently learned how fast he is. Haven't you?" she says, settling him on her hip. Eli's bright blue eyes scan the room from the new height, and I suddenly understand why

Rya's concerned. This kid is definitely going to be a handful.

"If you're happy to take him for the time being, I'm going to corner my wife for a few moments," Crue says. It's not so much of a question but a demand as he goes to seek Rya out.

It's chaos as everyone flutters around us. I'm terrified by the idea of having a child. But I realize that even without Will, I would've had all of this around me. Part of me is excited that I get to experience this with the Ricci sisters. And that makes it slightly less scary.

Honey's already started giving me advice, and it's... nice.

Eli reaches out to me expectantly, and Honey passes him over. It's awkward initially because I've never had much to do with children, but he seems interested in my hair as he tugs on the fringe part.

A hand snakes around my waist from behind, and Will leans over my shoulder. "We've got a problem if the child comes out with stark black hair," he whispers as he kisses me on the cheek.

I laugh. "Well, we were just a fling. You didn't think you were the only one, did you?" I joke, and his grip tightens around my waist.

"I know every person you've been in contact with and anyone who ever entered your room in the past six months, Alina. Don't try to play this game, or you will be punished."

The promise of being punished runs a thrill through me. I sigh and lean against him, comforted by his strength. It feels strange right now to be holding a toddler when we don't even know where we're going to end up permanently. Maybe we'll go back and forth between New York and London for years.

But it all feels right. Right now. For us.

A wild, chaotic mess.

Being brought together by an unexpected pregnancy.

And a soon-to-be marriage, apparently.

I smirk at the thought. Of course, I want to marry him, and of course, I love the ring, but there's something rather exciting about fucking with him a little.

"What are you smiling at?" he asks, pressing another kiss against my shoulder.

"Just thinking about all the fun we're going to have," I admit, but not the fact that it will be at his expense.

"I look forward to each day, love. Out of curiosity, when were you going to return the gold-plated card you stole from my back pocket when we walked in?" he asks, and I shoot him a smile as I look up at him from the corner of my eye. I didn't think he noticed that time.

"I'm going to go on a shopping spree after this. Do you have a problem with that?" I arch a challenging eyebrow. It's turned into a game to see how long his things would go missing before he realized. Unfortunately for me, my fiancé is very attentive when my hands are on him.

"What's mine is yours," he says with a grin. "I love you, Alina."

And it fills me with warmth. Every day, he reminds me. And I never take it for granted.

"I love you too, even though you're an asshole."

I immediately freeze as Eli stares at me in bewilderment. And I pray that the curse word I just used isn't the first word he learns.

Also by T.L. Smith

Black (Black #1)

Red (Black #2)

White (Black #3)

Green (Black #4)

Kandiland

Pure Punishment (Standalone)

Antagonize Me (Standalone)

Degrade (Flawed #1)

Twisted (Flawed #2)

Distrust (Smirnov Bratva #1) FREE

Disbelief (Smirnov Bratva #2)

Defiance (Smirnov Bratva #3)

Dismissed (Smirnov Bratva #4)

Lovesick (Standalone)

Lotus (Standalone)

Savage Collision (A Savage Love Duet book 1)

Savage Reckoning (A Savage Love Duet book 2)

Buried in Lies

Distorted Love (Dark Intentions Duet 1)

Sinister Love (Dark Intentions Duet 2)

Cavalier (Crimson Elite #1)

Anguished (Crimson Elite #2)

Conceited (Crimson Elite #3)

Insolent (Crimson Elite #4)

Playette

Love Drunk

Hate Sober

Heartbreak Me (Duet #1)

Heartbreak You (Duet #2)

My Beautiful Poison

My Wicked Heart

My Cruel Lover

Chained Hands

Locked Hearts

Sinful Hands

Shackled Hearts

Reckless Hands

Arranged Hearts

Unlikely Queen

A Villain's Kiss

[A Villain's Lies](#)

[Moments of Malevolence](#)

[Moments of Madness](#)

[Moments of Mayhem](#)

Connect with T.L Smith by tlsmithauthor.com

Also by Kia Carrington Russell

Insidious Obsession

Mine for the Night, New York Nights Book 1

Us for the Night, New York Nights Book 2

Stranded for the Night, New York Nights Book 3

Token Huntress, Token Huntress Book 1

Token Vampire, Token Huntress Book 2

Token Wolf, Token Huntress Book 3

Token Phantom, Token Huntress Book 4

Token Darkness, Token Huntress Book 5

Token Kingdom, Token Huntress Book 6

The Shadow Minds Journal

T.L. Smith

USA Today Best Selling Author T.L. Smith loves to write her characters with flaws so beautiful and dark you can't turn away. Her books have been translated into several languages. If you don't catch up with her in her home state of Queensland, Australia you can usually find her travelling the world, either sitting on a beach in Bali or exploring Alcatraz in San Francisco or walking the streets of New York.

Connect with me tlsmithauthor.com

Kia Carrington-Russell

Australian Author, Kia Carrington-Russell is known for her recognizable style of kick a$$ heroines, fast-paced action, enemies to lovers and romance that dances from light to dark in multiple genres including Fantasy, Dark and Contemporary Romance.

Obsessed with all things coffee, food and travel, Kia is always seeking out her next adventure internationally. Now back in her home country of Australia, she takes her Cavoodle, Sia along morning walks on beautiful coastline beaches, building worlds in the sea breezes and contemplating which deliciously haunting story to write next.

Made in United States
Troutdale, OR
06/08/2025